Cultural Attaché

A Novel

G.A. Chamberlin

Titles by

G.A. Chamberlin

The Handmaiden Legacy

Cultural Attaché

Rare Earth Element

Outbound

Somma

Unintended Consequence

The Particle

The Kneeling Woman

At Auction

—

Kathleen The War Years

Cultural Attache

Printed in the United States
ISBN 978-0-9904027-1-8

Crown Eagle Publishing

Book Distribution Ingram

Cover Graphics Jennifer Chamberlin

Rare Earth Element

climate, culture, commerce...Too important to ignore, too well written to overlook. And too technically suspenseful not to wonder about...

* * *

The Handmaiden Legacy

The Handmaiden Legacy is a contemporary thriller full of corporate interests, beautiful seas and ancient legacies...

---*G.A. Chamberlin is an International Thriller Writer!*

"International Thriller Writers ...that will surprise "
--Agent, Thriller Fest, New York City

* * *

Cultural Attache

"...Amanda Wells is lecturing on the historical integrity of medieval works at the University when she is informed that the original manuscript of a major work...has been stolen from the vault.

This is a work of fiction. Names, characters places, and incidents either are the product of the author's imagination or are used fictitiously, and any resemblance to actual persons, living or dead, business establishments events or locales is entirely coincidental. The publisher does not have any control over and does not assume any responsibility for author or third party websites or their content. Nor does the author assume any responsibility for activities that might have been published as source material for fiction. Cultural courtesy is the professional standard.

Cultural Attaché

...An international thriller

Amanda Wells is lecturing on the historical integrity of medieval works at University when she is informed that the original manuscript of a major work...has been stolen from the vault.
...But when the death of a student and a political trial about the ownership of a sunken treasure threatens to unravel the financial credibility of a government...she must run from the truth and dive into the past to survive.

* * *

*

Cultural Attaché

A Novel

G.A.Chamberlin

One

England 1601

"My name is ....*Ahrrrrgheuwy!*" he started, clutching his throat.

"Spit" yelled a voice from the audience.

"No. Not Spit. You Idiot!"

Growling, throat clearings.

"My name is Rheum-to-Spit then!"

Laughter.

"No! Not Rheum. But Plume. My Nome-de-..."

"*Dieu*?" shrilled a youth

"No. I be not God, you fool"

Laughter.

"Nom-de-Plume is William. Though my mother did call me by another ..."

"...*Bastard*?"

"I be not *that* Sir! For that be worse than God..."

"Where you *there* then?"

Laughter.

It was a riotous start to the play thought Sir Henry, smiling into the red beard that rimmed his jawbone. Shakespeare handed him the script, assuring his patron of his commitment to memory the lines with a tap to his heart, then stepped forward.

Sir Henry left Blackfrier's from the rear passageway. He rolled the script hastily into his pouch, and took from the young stable hand the reins to his waiting Grey mount. Without a word he broke into a full gallop along the ridged highway where two horsemen joined him, his cloak in full voile.

The mists of England closed easily behind them.

Sir Robert Devereux, Thomas West and Charles Blount were in attendance to Sir Henry Neville. They had considered the affairs of the state; theirs was a righteous cause. They were, all of them, Lords of the realm.

Still, the loose-leafed folio trampled in the mud was picked up by the stable boy. A beginning page, he deduced, with a Nom and two columns that looked like Roman pillars to him, lettering that he could not read. No matter. He would wait for the Play. And then he would understand. Such was the world of dissemination to the common man. And he ran to tell his friends.

* *

Two

Nestled between two vaulted medieval arches of darkly polished architecture, the image fairly glowed on a large overhead screen. For now at least, with the houselights dimmed, the past would illuminate the minds of all who studied here in high definition.

American-born visiting lecturer Amanda Wells felt less like a digital technologist than a sorcerer's apprentice culling magic. Yet her audience was captive.

"...In this image, notice the border lines that display fluidity of the penmanship..."

She flipped to the next screen.

"...under magnification, you can see how oxidization in the ink shows remarkable fluidity, indicating a highly refined carbon grinding in its composition. Whereas here, you see greater granules and a deeper impression on the manuscript, suggesting that while the same hand wrote both, these words were not written in the same place or with the same care. Indeed, most forensic scientists agree that this is both authentic and same-authored..."

Amanda looked up at her class, all waiting. "Why the mystery over the author's identity, we ask?"

A dinner gong aroused them from a reverie. "Remember to register your sources with citations when you browse your articles at the library, please...everyone!" she called after them. And it wasn't until the last student had left that Amanda realized how fatigued she was.

The night walk down Munster Street in a January twenty-knot blow made the light switch to Amanda's apartment an apparatus of sunlight over an oasis.

"Jack!" she called, leaving a trail of bag, shoes, coat and laptop all the way to the kitchen

"Here Jack!"

The orange cat was perched on the fridge, watching with detached curiosity as if he too could disappear at will. She poured Friskies into his bowl with a rattling that brought him down in two leaps.

"Did you miss me?" she asked, washing her hands and lacing on a chef's apron labeled *Dean and DeLucca*.

"Bet you did! And I...am... starving!" she bantered, opening the fridge door. She extracted a steak covered in wax paper, well marinated. "So here I go..." she said, facing the gas stove with some fear.

She twisted the knob of the burners and heard an anticipatory roar, but no fire.

She paused, checked the pilot then tried again. Nothing. Out came the matches. Flame in hand, a muted bang lit up the gas broiler at full throttle, scattering Jack from the kitchen with a howl, and Amanda to checking if her bangs were singed.

Jesus!

It was almost midnight when she gathered the papers on her bed. She leaned over from her nest of pillows to stow a book under the bed when she saw the silent images on TV.

Trevor MacDonnell was on the news. He was standing on the steps at Westminster Palace wearing a dark coat, scarf and briefcase in hand. By the time Amanda retrieved the TV Remote Controller from beneath Jack and increased the volume she heard "...Thank you" Then watched him cut away for the commentator. "So there you have it Ladies and Gentlemen. According to one Member of Parliament, the event can be described as 'A storm in a tea cup'. This is Thera Morris-Williams reporting for CNS News"

Amanda smiled.

He looked good, his boyish features now mature and distinguished by business clothing; closely cropped hair, and as always, his height. The last time she saw him he was being carried on a stretcher into a plane heading for Germany. She had bargained for his life.

Centuries ago.

She turned off the Power and lay there, Jack curled at the base of the bed, her thoughts a mess.

Finally the cat stood up, stretched, and jumped off. A peaceful night's sleep, evidently, wasn't happening.

* *

Three

London, 1601.

The trumpet blew. "Hear Yea. Hear Yea!"
"Now listen to the Lord, men..."
A crowd had gathered at the Globe Theater.
..."On the next occasion of the players, you shall hear the Play *Richard II*
..."Then you shall see that we'll have the rightful monarch at our head, with the right men at his side!"
"Aye!" They cheered.
..."For England! Not a bloody Spaniard!"
"Aye!"
..."Nor a monarch with councilors of evil advice to the ear!"
"Aye!"
"Yea. Aye!... Or *Ale*?"
He cocked his ear to listen.
"Ale. Ale. Ale ye say?" he scolded.
They roared at his pun.
..."Then, *that* as well... if you'll be so kind!... A play shall here be performed on February 7th Thusly. Mind ye - men and women, all welcome!"

They cheered.

"It shall be paid and brought with the gift and color and gayness of his Lordship, Ye Second Earl of Essex..."

The Town Crier was hard pushed to subdue the press of the crowd, now fully excited.

Behind the stage both Neville and Devereux listened. What they heard pleased them.

The Crier's trumpet blew again.

"And on the morrow...Ahoy...And on the morrow, after you partake of the Festive Play, shall ye take to the Streets of London. Thus it is. I say, Ale it is!...For all who shall bear arms. I say again, Ale it is!"

"Aye!"

"Aye!"

Neville and Devereux looked at each other with deep and troubled eyes. These were most somber times. Yet choose they did. And act they would. For there was no other way.

They parted. God be with them, they said.

Robert Devereux, Second Earl of Essex, had been at the Queen' s side for countless occasions, producing as a result numerous notes of poetic gratitude, love and devotion to her. Indeed Essex, as he was called, became the envy of others for his proximity to the throne and for his colonial ventures. Especially for his wealth from the carry trades, all patronized by the Crown and funded by London merchants.

That is, until he returned from Ireland.

Essex was a distant cousin to the Queen and himself in the lineage of Royal succession to the throne – a matter increasingly at hand as Elizabeth approached the end of her reign without issue. Rule of the land was at stake.

Elizabeth's advisers were powerful men. Thomas Cecil and his son Robert, titled The Lords Burghley, were two men also deeply vested in the carry trades. Administrators at the Court, they served as Treasurer and witnessed all state affairs. They had sustained Elizabeth through her long reign, even if at some hazard to themselves. Now in her old age, she trusted them. Or rather, they ruled her.

The Cecil's did not trust Essex. Queen Elizabeth, as they reminded her, had paid dearly to be on the throne as Protestant heir of Henry VIII, her father. Many had tried to take that throne from her. Indeed many, if history were just, had even greater claim than she to be on that throne.

One was a young red-haired man with a goatee that lined the sharp features of his face. Sir Henry Neville was a direct descendant of John of Gaunt in the historical lineage of the monarchy. He and Essex had been schooled together.

Sir Neville had just returned from France as Ambassador to reconcile the marriage of Henry IV, King of France. Where the affairs of Court could easily lead to affairs of State, Sir Neville was the ideal emissary from England.

Educated, travelled and a linguist, the young Sir Henry Neville lived in a culture that prized ornate oratory and eloquence, such that poets and playwrights were richly rewarded for their words and power of influence. Using such skills to assuage political misdirection in the manner of seventeenth century entertainment, he authored for the French Court a comedy, its desired effect to solicit domestic felicity. It was called *Love's Labor Lost*.

On his return to England, he wrote another play for his friend Essex, who was in trouble.

The play was called Richard II. As was the custom of Lords to keep Players and Troupes in their households for entertainment for their community, this play was to be disseminated and sponsored in London by Essex. It had a public message.

Essex had been sent to Ireland to subdue colonists there in rebellion under Hugh O'Neil, Earl of Tyrone, a Catholic stronghold. However, the Earl of Tyrone would not be subdued with arms.

Moreover, Essex was less interested in the conquest of Tyrone than in subduing the influence of the Cecils over the Queen. He petitioned to return to Court.

His answer came quickly from the English Court. Charles Blount, Lord Moutjoy, was sent to replace Essex in Ireland. With him was an Army to subdue colonists!

Essex was considered a failure. He and Thomas West, Lord De la Warr, returned to England whereupon Essex was immediately placed under house arrest by the Cecils for almost a year and deprived of his offices, including his own ancient Earldom rights to the patent of sweet wines producing £50,000 in annual revenue, forfeit and redirected to the Lords Cecils.

Essex, when freed, understood where he stood. He made plans to exercise his hereditary rights to ascend to the throne of England, and he called upon Charles Blount in Ireland to bring back the Army to support his *coup d'état*.

In reality, it was neither a *coup d'etat*, nor an insurrection. Rather, it was an assertion to ascend to the throne upon the death of Queen Elizabeth, the natural right to succeed as the next ranking male heir of seniority.

The Lords Burghley, Cecil and his son Robert, had aspirations of their own. And, for the present, they held sway at Elizabeth's Court, even as she lay on her deathbed.

Essex and his friend Sir Henry Neville agreed to meet in London in January 1601.

They had both seen injustice at Court. They understood the potential of individual trade and mercantilism emerging now. This was a time of flourishing prospect for England.

Rivalries and contention ruled the Court of an ageing monarch and agrarian absolutism, greatly enriching the Cecils.

Essex was outraged. He claimed he was in the company of some of the brightest minds of the century. In sponsoring the play Richard II at the Globe Theater on February 7th, he was making a public protest.

The Queen heard about the upcoming Play. It would show the tragic history of a monarch who would lose his throne because he listened to evil advisers. The

Cecils condemned the play as "seditious". The Queen, it was claimed, was to suppress the play.

On the morning of February 8th 1601, the Crown sent a mounted party comprising of Edward Somerset, Earl of Worcester; the Lord Keep Egerton; the Lord Chief Justice Sir John Popham and Sir William Knollys to Essex House to consult with Essex himself.

In the cold, they beat on the door.

The Earl of Essex himself met them at the entrance. Outside, a menacing crowd had gathered, suspicious and angry at the visitors.

"Kill them! Kill them!" they chanted.

"To the Library!" blurted Essex, slamming the door and leading the way.

The crowd pressed in, rebellious, and started beating on the front door

"Kill them! Kill them!"

"Gentlemen. You will be safe here, I assure you. I shall post at guard at your door here!" said Essex. He locked the Library door. "Francis!" he yelled "Stand firm for armed defense of the door, and bring two more men for you aide!"

The Cecils heard what happened.

Later in the day of February 8th the city of London was in turmoil.

"Traitor! Traitor!" proclaimed a Herald from his horse. The street gathering was suddenly alarmed. A horseman, Chief Guardian William Parker approached them and attempted to disband the horde.

Behind him, Thomas Cecil arrived with a larger contingent of mounted men. Moving through the city in full armored livery, pikes, swords unsheathed, they would deliver a remonstrance. A Proclamation, they yelled. From the Queen. *Essex was a Traitor!*

Chief Parker tried to disperse the crowd before the proclamation was read out loud, but chaos and shrieking filled the streets, unnerving city dwellers. Parker felt he had restored the peace.

Without warning, a horse charge and the disruption to his own ranks threw him from his horse. He fell into the river, his armor weighing him down to drown. He was pulled from the water, and a search with a warrant was issued.

Essex was found. Not barricaded in his home, but kneeling in prayer at St. Paul's Cross where the sermon had just been delivered. Robert Devereaux calmly mounted his horse, put on the Livery of his official House, and with 300 men of noble birth and royal lineage, marched to London at Ludgate shouting *"Murder, murder, God save the Queen!"*

It was a pre-emptive move to aggregate his own defense.

Later, in the records that survived, William Parker would write of the account. *"My conscience tells me that I am in no way guilty of these Imputations and that merely the blindness of ignorance led me into these infamous errors"*

He addressed the letter to Sir Robert Cecil, son of Lord Burghley. And he was released.

The others were not. It was recorded in the Record as *The Essex Rebellion.*

* *

Four

Amanda was excited.

Today she and Bill would be putting some sketches together to plan an Exhibit for a national tour of museums. The theme was to capture the essence of the mid 18th century.

London could be a city of surprises that belied its function as a capital. Amanda turned off Thames Road, crossed the River at Richmond and spotted Kew from the bridge.

Gift to the world from Joseph Banks, she mused. Not because of his wealth or voyage to the Pacific. Nor even the Commission to create Kew given by a British monarch who had just lost the American colonies, but rather, for the wonder of exploration. That was his gift, she decided.

She turned left on Defoe Avenue and entered the National Archives on Bessant Drive. From a distance, the Archives appeared lowly steeped, but as she approached, the deeply pitched brown roofing revealed a rich design of structure along Kew Riverside Park.

She parked her Morris and opened the door to release her seat buckle, then leaning forward, collected her briefcase and Coach Leather tote tossed to the floor, all contents strewn.

She emerged with as much dignity as her gear would allow, one shoulder holding up a strap, both arms full, and her cellphone buzzing. Amanda Wells approached the security desk assuring Bill that she was in the building and on her way up.

Bill met her outside the Conference room. He took her cotton trench coat to the hangers mouthing a few incoherent and apologetic sentences about the exhibit. Then flung open the Conference double doors.

"Gentlemen, may I present Ms Amanda Wells..."

She stood there, her hair a tossed cascade of auburn waves, breathing hard from the dash and her briefcase still on the floor.

"Sorry to surprise you Amanda. But we wanted to deal with this as quickly as possible..."

If startled she did not show it. She acknowledged introductions with a steady smile, innately grateful that she had chosen well for appearances today. It was the men who took in the rich brown Stella McCartney linen jacket and tailored pants. Neither was the pale silk tie, if loosely hung from a Drape shirt, a detail lost on the assembly.

That's what you pay the bucks for, she heard her American mother saying...

Nothing prepared her however, for the last man rising slowly to his full height.

"Hello Amanda" he said extending his hand.

"You two have met before I believe..." Bill was saying.

"Yes" she said evenly. "How nice to see you again!"

She felt him squeeze her hand sharply, and if nothing else, she sensed warning. Trevor MacDonnell was never an alarmist.

"Please be seated Amanda" said Bill holding out her chair at the head of the table "I do apologize most sincerely...for taking you by surprise. This is all my arrangement. I knew we had a scheduled meeting here between us this morning."

Amanda felt her bag vibrate from her cell phone. "Thank you" she smiled up, taking her seat.

"We were wondering Ms Wells, if you could inform us as to the integrity of a provenance..." began a young man at the far end.

"Yes. Yes!" Bill jumped in "You see...we have a bit of problem with some recently discovered Finds that might be of interest to ...err.." he look up briefly at the array of faces 'the government.' Mr. Delaney of the Ministry of the Interior is concerned with matters of sovereign entitlements when it comes to historical artifacts..."

The phone purred again within her bag. "I see" Amanda said, interestedly.

"And naturally the Foreign Office, and its many legacies all over the world, are interested to cover any cultural aspects ... you understand, represented here by Lord Valentine" continued Bill by way of explaining.

"So we wondered Amanda, knowing of your particular provenance studies and identification valuations, how we might base our premise with regards to Findings of err...*international* locations that clearly originated from the British Isles..."

"Um" she said, waiting for Bill to take it to a more specific level.

 "Well in terms of insurance" he added, nodding to a Mr. Schmidt from Lloyds.

Now was her queue. Again the cell vibrated.

"Well it depends largely on the integrity of the collection. Forensic questions would be many. Do we have... consistency, implying divided issues that might have several sides to tell. Or, is it a whole representation, such as the entirety of a mission, telling its function and intent."

She noticed Trevor shift his position.

 "It depends on review of course, including the items themselves. Individually for valuation purposes, and then in terms of historical significance and their attendant value."

"How...do we...err... Ms. Wells, can we establish... ownership?" said the young man who started the ball rolling at the top of the table.

"Well, from a legal point of view, for example, it's not always a clear case of proprietary supremacy. Location, function and intent often define ownership... Other issues can have equal bearing, like cause of loss, liabilities, ageing. That is, in addition to the body of evidence that informs the provenance..." She paused. "There may be questions of geography, or maritime laws of the sea..."

"You mean...where it is territorially *found*?" he interrupted.

"I think" said Trevor in a definitive tone "what Ms Wells means is that it needs careful study before any of us can arrive at any conclusions."

Amanda knew that tone of voice when she heard it. It was both conclusion and cover to make a run for it.

"Absolutely!" she agreed.

Bill's eyes roll upward in frustration.

"I would be more than willing to give it my full attention..." said Amanda, "if Bill... *that is, if I don't kill him first* - would be kind enough to let me view the file in question. I can assure you that we at the University would give it careful review."

"Could we count on your *discretion*, Ms. Wells?" shot a middle aged gentleman to her right.

"Absolutely Sir! I shall keep the matter confidential, and sequester any material within our vault. We have excellent security and restricted access." He seemed satisfied and leaned back into his seat.

The cell in her bag was at it again, and Amanda wished she had left it in the car where the damned thing belonged. But then again, she hadn't expected Bill to set her up for a public hearing.

It was all over within 20 minutes. Trevor whispering the words "I'll give you a call..." and the others shaking her hand and handing over their business cards. Trevor had handed her his card.

"I am uploading a working website for our investigation. I'd be pleased to hear from you as you develop your conclusions..." he said "It's a secure access code for my Eyes only."

It was all very businesslike.

Bill, whom she could easily slay with one look, hung back shuffling chairs and office furniture.

"Bill..?"

"...I'm sorry Amanda. Look. I had little choice. I had you coming, and they wanted to ...."

She turned, walked out and was almost at her car when she finally read her text message.

It was Emily at her office who had called four times and texted twice.

"WHERE R Y?" and "COME IN! V. IMPORTANT. ASAP. PLEASE!"

Amanda perched her items in the rear, and stood up in her fleece-lined raincoat, drenched from an icy downpour.

 She drove and she was muttering.

Bill, Trevor, Lloyds... Who was the "we" he referred to? Let's see. There was the Department of Interior. The Foreign Office. The Insurance Officer. The Exchequer's Offices...

That leaves Trevor playing for Scotland then?

"We are... if you will," had said one of them "assembling as a sort of 'Protectorate'"

Jesus!

Five

1598, England

She was plucked from the group by the wrist. *Oh, that hand!*

Bess looked desperately at her companion in line, Lady Maryanna, an elder woman from the Queen Mary's reign, who noticed nothing, giggling with those walking before her in the train of the Queen, all of them holding their morning skirts just off the stone floors of Hampton Court.

"Sweetest" came the word hotly in her ear.

The pillar concealed him. And out she peeped again to see if she were missed from the procession of Ladies in Waiting. He pulled her back into concealment.

"How... I do *long* for thee" he nudged at her neck.

"Sir!" she said, in apprehension

"Sir me not..." he breathed across her face "But *Sire* me do!"

"Oh dear Father of Heaven" she uttered.

"Ah Bess! My Love Bess! How lovely art thou...golden and perfumed and a plum of sweet desire!"

"Pray, plead with me *not!*" she managed, his hands groping her breasts.

She had spent almost an hour preparing herself for service to the Queen. Only once had the Queen looked her way and made a remark. "She wears my father's jewels today!"

The Ladies giggled at the comment in less than subtle ways.

Bess had gathered the Queens robe and toweling after the bathing was done. Once the chamber was vacant, she had cleaned and piled high the food; ladies' effects, pets; and toys...all of it. Then opening the windows and drapes for air, presented the waiting flower girls and musicians with toast and sweets left over. All this preparation for the moment of the procession into the Throne Room.

"They wait in attendance to her Majesty, the Lords... Go, I must!"

"Am I not a Lord?"

She curtsied by gesture only. "Aye My Lord"

His hands were inside her clothing, his breath strong and vibrant in her ear. She held her breath, afraid to respond.

But respond she did.

"Bess! Bess! Hold me quick lest I burst my soul with desire for you!"

Her hand, still holding a gilded sack of ladies herbs, went to his groin, and together they leaned against the stone, he throbbing at the throat and she wanting to receive him.

On May the 30th 1591 with the tulips of Hampton Court full grown by Dutch gardeners and the trees offering shade after a long wintering slumber, the Queen let out a scream that would reverberate down the centuries. Elizabeth "Bess" Throckmorton was with child.

Even secretly wed! Without her permission... And to her first courtier, Sir Walter Raleigh. Eleven years her elder.

The meeting between the two women was a desperate one. It could change England, said the Queen. So justice was quick.

Bess was to see the child to full term, and immediately upon delivery, the babe would be given to a wet nurse at Durham House. Thereafter, Bess was to see the child no more.

Sir Walter Raleigh was to be closed in the Tower of London, and considered dead. Only there could Bess she be united with her husband, and only there could they consider their family in their ancestral home, said the Writ.

The disgrace was deep, enduring and public. Not only was this incident considered a breach of trust by her Lady in waiting, but a hint treasonous.

Queen Elizabeth I of England was childless. Her father, Henry VIII, after eight wives and a tortured life, had failed to produce a long–term surviving male heir to the Throne.

Without an heir, England as a power , was impotent.

 Bess, her father long ago executed for High Treason, was the daughter of Nicholas Throckmorton, cousin to Henry's VIII sixth wife, Katherine Parr.

Moreover Bess, it was speculated, might have even been conceived at that time, making her the Queen's illegitimate sister since her mother Elizabeth Carew had been the mistress of Henry VIII, receiving gifts from him when she later married and produced a son with her husband, Nicholas Carew, friend of the King. The gifts in fact, were jewels...Jewels that the Queen should have inherited in proper fashion from her father.

Yet at this moment, the real jewel holding the future crown of England rested gently in the womb of Bess Throckmorton, wedded to Sir Walter Raleigh, a man trusted with wealth from new world riches, and himself of some Royal lineage...

The infant born was named Damerei. And it was reported later, that the infant died within six months.

Neither Sir Walter Raleigh nor Bess Throckmorton sued to become reconciled with the Queen. Rather, in their devotion and quiet world within the Tower, they conceived again. First Walter was born, then a second son Carew.

It was five years before Sir Walter Raleigh was released from the Tower of London. But only to divide the spoils from the captured Spanish ship *Madre de Dios,* it was noted by the Spanish Ambassador Count Gondomar, a man who hated the very sight of Sir Walter Raleigh. For the spoils of these and other Spanish ships captured by Elizabeth for England had filled the coffers of the Treasury, locked in the Keep of the Tower. There watched by her most trusted men of the sea.

The Tower then, was Treasury.

Six

Jeanette Bevan, Director of Physical Anthropology opened the door to a hallway of waiting staff and students. She was in parting with Inspector Brown from New Scotland Yard.

"I promise to call you..." she was saying. "We truly regret the disturbance this might have caused"

With the door firmly closed behind her and the crowd disbursing, she spoke with a calmness aimed at diffusing any alarm.

Jeannette gestured to Amanda who was still standing in her raincoat and bags.

They both took their seats, Jeannette at her desk, Amanda on a hard folding chair designed for students in jeans.

"What did you do with the manuscript after your lecture last night?" asked Jeannette, her dark eyes protruding.

"What manuscript?"

"The one you checked out of the vault yesterday morning to put up on the screens for the afternoon series?" her voice was tinged with sarcasm and impatience.

"I didn't!" said Amanda.

"Oh Yes you did."

"No. Actually. I imaged the manuscript with the Nikon inside the vault. I made a digital record to load into the computer. It never left the vault with me. Mr. Hendrickson was in there while I did it..."

Jeannette sat there, her face pale and angry.

"Why?" asked Amanda politely.

"Because the Vault has been breached!" Jeannette stood up and poured coffee from her thermos. "Someone stole several objects...." She took a long drink.

"Are you sure..." she said, peering at Amanda. "You didn't take anything at all?"

"Umm. Hendrickson signed me in and signed out, sans cargo, with a complete inspection of my belongings...I'm in the Vault Logbook" added Amanda seeing the grey in Jeanette's eyes.

"That bloody idiot Hendrickson. Can't do his job worth a damn!" Jeannette Bevan was weighing the damage to her department's reputation...to her credibility and perhaps, as Amanda thought, her popularity.

"Did you file a police report?"

"Of course we did. We had to! But we still don't have a full inventory of what went missing....Oh God!"

Jeannette's phone and cell were both humming, as was Amanda's.

"Call me!" she said to Amanda by way of dismissal. "And keep *la bouche firmee*, will you?"

Yes Sir! thought Amanda with an almost salute.

Amanda settled into her own office and checked her mail. The thoughts in her head went racing back to the meeting with Bill.

> *Absolutely Sir! I shall keep the matter confidential, and sequester any material...our vault where we have absolute security and limited access"*

Amanda Wells returned a few calls, spotted Emily who came in with her hair dyed, holes in her jeans.

"Hey...How-ya-doing?" said Emily softly, placing the contents of Amanda's Inbox on her desk. They had been collected from the Department Central office, and Emily arranged them in a neat pile.

"Hia sweetie" answered Amanda without looking up "Let's just say it's already been a long day..."

"Yeah.. I can tell. Sorry about all those calls...It was like kind of wild around here for a bit...So, What's with the big-heavy?" she asked, nodding to Jeannette's office.

Amanda looked up.

Emily stepped closer and lowered her voice to talk over the desk. "There was Police everywhere. A Superintendent from New Scotland Yard and a Rookie Adam Smith or something...sounds like a name from Economics or Mathematics of something...and all them prodding and picking things up to *inspect*. They asked for *phone* records. *Correspondence. Email* addresses the *lot*..!"

For a shy student, Emily could be quite articulate. Especially when it came to places in her heart for those to whom she felt loyalty. Otherwise, for Emily, everything was just "Shit!"

"How's your Final Paper coming along?" asked Amanda evenly.

"Ugh!" said Emily, turning on her heels and leaving the room.

But Emily was not offended, Amanda knew. She was the only professor who cared to see the girl graduate. And everything, evidently, was under control.

The day was passing quickly. Amanda finished her email responses, made her appointments, and headed for the cafeteria at about 3 pm.

Her work was far from over. She was giving a class tonight, and would go to the Fine Arts Department to create a carousel of slides.

The subject of her lecture in the Fine Arts was on the topic of identifications and Signatures on Oil Paintings. She would focus on English and Dutch paintings - for which she had already invested some time over the weekend from her own online sources. But what worried her was the collection itself from which she was to draw examples: How up to upload those images? Had they been imaged *without* advanced lens, at higher digital resolutions? Or where they still using old photographs at the University?

 "Budgets!" is what Jeannette had said, to excuse poor stewardship. Perhaps this time, she would be surprised.

But there was one call she needed to make.

"Hello Roger!" she said into the cell phone. "How are you doing..?"

Roger Hendrickson picked up. He was at home. Summarily 'suspended' by Jeannette Bevan and under instructions 'not to leave the country' from the

Inspector, he explained. This, after "thirty years of loyal service as security guard" he said.

"Roger. Don't panic. It'll be explained and sorted out eventually. So Relax. Take a little time off to enjoy things. You have family in Wales? You're almost there for Spring Break, right? So don't worry!"

* *

Emily finished her Work-study duties early. The library was closed. It was a damp day, and she had exhausted her quota of little gray brain-cells, as Edward called it. Time for some R & R at the local pub since the sun wasn't out and the ramps down to the River too wet to skate board on...There, she would meet the girls, at least. The University Rowing Teams were out on the water and not in the boathouse working on crew hulls. Edward was on the Rowing Team. He would doubtless return her call later.

She plugged into her ear phones, tuned her IPod, and started nodding to the beat as she walked.

She made her way to the parking lot across the University city. Edward's car had a place there. She'd take a look. Just as she had yesterday.

God, was there anything more annoying than calling people without a response, thought Emily. She looked down at her cell. Five calls to Amanda. Eight calls to Edward. "Shit!"

She pulled the plug from her ear. He always answered. Playing games on his phone Apps was a source of entertainment, much to her ennui, and he frequently plugged into to his car recharger when he drove.

She spotted the car at the far end of the lot. Yes. Edward's car was just sitting there. Dirty, loaded with debris on the dash, but new. A fresh year's Model of Cooper. Silver and black.

She peered inside, at least he had locked it! The disorganized mess of shirt, food wrappings and note books from his class were strewn on the passenger side. Even her own Undies still in the back. Nothing to show he'd been back. She looked at her cell, and pressed for another call to him.

She was stepping away from the car when she heard the ring. The jingle to his cell was an odd tone of dark greeting. It wasn't that common. And yet she heard it ringing. She turned. The cell phone was in her hand when she realized she was still "On." It was ringing. Inside the car.

* *

The young lieutenant was visibly shaken.

"It was on him alright" he said to his Superintendent, producing an Evidence bag containing a cell phone.

"She never saw the body. She heard his cell phone ringing from *inside* the car..."

The Superintendent led the lieutenant a few yards away from the car.

"I'm sorry Tim... It's a grim scene. Let's call it a day. I'll see you in the morning."

"Yes Sir."

* *

Seven

The flowers arrived Tuesday morning by special delivery. Ostensibly, they signified a Thank You for Amanda's participation in the meeting at the National Archives. Significantly, they were a message. She had a commission to complete. She knew who sent them.

Amanda lifted the card from the bouquet, picked up the vase and walked into the students' central office. She placed the Spring blossoms on Emily's desk.

They were grieving. Emily's loss affected the whole class of students and faculty. Edward was her boyfriend. Everybody felt distressed.

Amanda was determined to remain around, to stay for anyone who wanted to talk.

"Roger?" she asked.

"Suspended" answered one of the students.

Jeanette, it was said, was fielding a police investigation, everywhere, there was quiet gloom.

Emily had discovered the body and Amanda made several calls to her cell phone.

Technically, the incident occurred off the premises, so the College took no official position. But Amanda was worried.

She had come in a few times. Then she was passed from friend to friend so as not to be left alone.

In the Department, the police had been relentless in their questions. Notes, recordings, repetitions. They shifted their focus from student to student with suggestion and insinuation, probing for answers... It rattled the students, most of whom did not know Edward personally.

Jeannette was a disgrace, behaving more like a diva on stage than a department director showing leadership. The quietness needed on the scene came only from Amanda who kept her door open. Many came through it in tears. Jeanette stormed through on several occasions. Others just left the university.

Amanda stayed calm, checking frequently for any response from Emily.

Certainly there was plenty to do. She was presenting a paper in Paris next week, and she managed to keep eyes on her desk.

Jeannette wanted a full report written up on the Vault situation. Roger, she announced, would not be returning to his job unless this was resolved. She wanted a scapegoat.

On Amanda's desk was a pile of papers. Two classes had just taken a test, she had to grade them all with remarks.

A special delivery package arrived. Sent by Bill to her directly at the University, it nevertheless had to pass inspection by a detective.

Perhaps Bill could shed light on just what it was that tribunal-of-officials had been wanting when she faced them at the National Archives.

Bill's file read more like a motor-manual than a narrative. It was diagram of charts, maps, dates, connections and historical voyages.

Another pages was a list of case files, legal contestations, depositions and judicial findings.

One thing was clear though. Trevor was waiting for a presentation on her credentials to fulfil her tasks - That, plus an explanation on the integrity of security on the premises of the University!

As the day wore on, more information was emerging. A statement here, another there, and the detectives lingered.

Amanda resisted the urge to interfere.

Emily. *Where was she?*

Had she gone home? Why was she not answering her calls?

Amanda worried.

* * *

Eight

Amanda got a message. The Chair of the College wanted an interview with her today - before Amanda gave her evening class. This, she managed to postpone to the end of the week.

The phone at her desk rang. The Foreign Office representative, Edwin Smithson asked if she could do some work for one of his councilors who needed a full report on the duties of a Purser aboard ship over the last two centuries. This, she promised before the end of the month.

It was dark outside before everyone left the department. On campus it was quiet, and she felt exhausted. She was about to leave when she got an email.

It made her smile. A request which she had initiated came back with a reply. The Antiquities Department of Israel responded to a review of a document made at the University of Haifa.

Thank God for some diligence somewhere...

By the time she walked home, Amanda discovered that Emily was staying – of all places – at Jeannette's!

She felt relieved, and she entered her apartment with a sigh of relief.

"Oh my God!"

The place looked like a neglected rat's nest. Long hours at work and not enough cat molly-codling was clearly the punishment for her neglect. Jack wanted nothing to do with her.

She sank to her bed half dressed. Whatever laundry, dishes, dry-cleaning pickups and provisioning *especially fresh bags of kitty litter and cat food -* would have to be done tomorrow, she decided.

Jack slinked in and curled at her feet.

The next day saw Emily standing at the doorway of the Central office and everybody rushed at her. Jeanette had brought her in.

She looked pale, nervous and unkempt. She grinned, if painfully, and she came in to Amanda.

One night at Jeannette's, evidently, was like being held in a police station answering questions. Before that she had spent two nights at the boathouse -since she couldn't return to her place with Edward's belongings still there...

That left her without a fresh change of clothes, she said weakly.

"Come" said Amanda, gathering her from the door jamb and leading her down the hall.

Amanda took Emily to the cafeteria. They found a quiet enclave behind pillars with comfortable seating and warm rays of sunlight.

Amanda found Emily dozing with her eyes closed when she returned with a tray of food. "Here."

The plate of lasagna, salad, rolls, cake, coffee and a carton of chocolate milk revived Emily.

Then came tears.

It too some time. She was shocked. Terrified.

"The police...they said that I..." began Emily.

Amanda took her hand and held it softly.

Emily looked up. She seemed lost, her eyes flashing with scenes of horror, fear, a throat slit.

"Here. Look at me...Emily!"

Emily nodded weakly, her body slumping.

"I'll be with you..Ok?"

They left together, Amanda propping her up with one arm about her shoulder. "Will my place do for a bit?" she asked.

Emily nodded.

"Oh, and there's Jack..." added Amanda.

Emily cracked a small smile, and she breathed.

* * *

It was all Amanda could do to pull herself together. She reached for the anthracite Lanvin vest and pants for her appointment with the Chairman of the College. Presentable, but only just.

Emily had wept all over her cream silk blouse; the folds now draped were hiding mascara, and her hair had gone unwashed and kinky. She applied hair-spray to keep the waves off her face.

Less a fatherly interview than a check list, the Chairman's concern was to limit liability to the reputation of the College. This he made abundantly clear. He had heard that Emily was with Amanda, and he asked several probing questions. He wanted to be the first to know, he told her, of any new developments.

Finally, as she stood to gathered her portfolio for the night class, he seemed satisfied - first with a firm handshake at the door, then a general pat on the back for a job well done. Even a salutary remark about her serving on the Faculty Adviser Board so admirably...

Amanda left his office searching for fresh air.

Especially after Trevor's name had come up. Clearly, there were spheres of influence where his good name mattered.

It had been a long day.

Emily had served as her TA on occasion.

Emily was normally gregarious, especially when she sat through the entire class to keep the slide show going. There was always lively discussion in Amanda's class.   But not so tonight. Amanda was prompting Emily all evening to turn to the next slide. Now she was standing outside, all out weeping.

They ate. Emily did not feel like talking much.

Jack had greeted them both, and he crouched beside Emily when she stretched out on the sofa and slept.

Amanda drew up a cover and observed her face. She seemed calm, relaxed.

It had been a week, and Emily was barely functioning. Still, for tonight Amanda was glad for the quietness in her apartment, even with company.

Amanda was about to recharge her cell phone when she checked the last few messages. Trevor had called several days ago. Dinner. Tomorrow, he had asked in a text message.

"Sorry. Swamped!" she had replied.

Within minutes, a message had flashed back "Next weekend. Rugby?"

"Paris..." she texted.

"Paris then!" he replied. "We leave Monday"

The message was sent less than two hours ago.

* *

Nine

At Claridges Hotel in London, Trevor waited in the Foyer for his mother.

He sat beneath the work of Basil Ionides by the Lalique door panel, reading the morning paper. Then he heard the commotion and smiled. He got up and strode across the glossy parterres to greet his mother.

She was shorter than he, but clearly the Scottish resemblance was seen in her ice-blue eyes and generous face. Wavy white hair shone from beneath a hat that matched her coat, and pearls adorned her neck. She smiled brightly and filled the room with quiet glamour.

The doorman stood by her and there was a lot of luggage being unloaded.

"Mother!" said Trevor.

"Hello Darling!" she said, raising her white gloved arms to receive a hug. "How wonderful to see you!"

At her age, she was still able to command attention.

"My God mother, you look stunning!"

Trevor recognized the brooch which had been in the family for generations.

"Thank you my dear..." she said simply.

"I see you've been at it again..." he said, lifting the Harrods packages at her feet.

A bellboy was beckoned from the Hotel Front Desk. He gave the young man a set of keys, a tip, and instructions to deliver the bundle of bags to his car.

"Yes Sir. Thank you Sir!

"How often is it... " his mother was saying "that *I* come to London?"

"For a bit of glamour ...is it?" he laughed.

"My dear, the *Works!*"

They followed the Maître D' into the Regency Afternoon Tea Room.

They sat a table of damask white cloth, laid out with silver, cut crystal and tall flower arrangements.

"No" she giggled, leaning forward. "It's not a matter of needing London's fashion designers *because* we're Scottish" she said in a brogue. "It's the *New Total Treatment Spa* I'm after! "

Trevor laughed.

An array of finger sandwiches, sweet pastries and freshly baked raisin scones arrived. Beside them, a tea service tray held china for Marco Polo jelly and Cornish clotted cream.

"Bottle of champagne, if you would, please..." ordered Trevor.

"*Acht* my dear..please make it two Scotches, do! *After* the tea please!" said his mother.

"Of course!" smiled Trevor

"The works..." explained his mother in conspiratorial tones "consists of a Spa treatment, a make-over with exercises,   a   massage,   sauna   and   hair treatment...Upstairs tomorrow!" she giggled.

"You're incorrigible!"

They picked their sandwiches.

"*Anchovies?*" she asked, watching him.

"Umm" he swallowed. "Terrific on a pizza too!"

They laughed.

"So, I'm delighted you've come to London, and I know how you love to come here where you and father stayed during the war years... But I do hope you'll be at the house tomorrow evening for the party!"

"Goodness, yes! But you know..." she added, looking up around. "I did *so* enjoy this place when it rang out with Gershwin, jazz and dancing. It was turned over to the American Delegations and various exiled sovereigns during the war, as you know. "

"Tell me, did you know the Neville family?"

"But of course! Pass the cream, please?.." She poured. "You see, our relationship with the Neville's springs from quite an event..."

"Oh?"

"Sir Henry Neville was a friend of your father during WWII. He was the Earl from a long line of Neville descendants, you know."

Trevor knew his father was involved in the war effort as a Senior Advisor for strategic defense at the War office. There, and certainly after the war during his long political career, he had engaged with many people.

It surprised Trevor little. He looked up and found his mother smiling.

"Funny," she said "it was in this very building where once we danced, that we were gathered for conferences and meetings about the war...imagine!"

"It's hard to find any place untouched by that war. Most estates were used for billeting of active or returning soldiers. " remarked Trevor.

"Indeed. And right here, dealing with Sovereign Leaders of countries displaced by a world gone crazy, thinking they could rebuild Europe... even as bombs fell about them!"

"Yet if you think about it, they *did* rebuild the establishment of Europe, even as bombs fell about them, as you say. Difficult as it must have been for them all..."

"How astute you are dear! No wonder you make such a wonderful Member of the House...I am so very proud of you. As would be your father, I am sure!"

Trevor allowed a smile. But inside, he glowed. What a privilege it was to have a parent alive as you tackle life. As if their simplest compliments made no difference to your soul, what a shame that England had developed a sanitized proclivity to dispense with the elderly. He looked at his mother sitting before him wearing her beautiful ensemble; white hair and pearls. His mother was an exceptional woman, even at her age. Joy would never leave her eyes.

He cleared his throat. "Now back to business mother... You were saying about the Neville affair...?"

"Oh yes. Where was I?...It happened just as the war ended, I believe. Sir Neville came upon a dreadful accident, he and his two young children. They were on their way to visit his wife who was recovering from food poisoning at a convalescent home. He had decided to take the two children, aged 3 and 5..."

She looked at Trevor "*Victory Day* brought hubris to us all - even though we all knew there was much still to do... But Neville must have rolled out his old jalopy, pulled the convertible top down and popped the two children in the open trundle back seat..." She wiped the corners of her mouth with a white linen serviette.

Trevor could guess what was next.

"They found the car the next morning. .." she demurred. "Those damned cars were so unstable that it killed him instantly when it overturned on the road. The son had been tossed into a hedge and survived. Your father was named Executor of the Will. Also, a Trust of his was passed to the keeping of your father until the boy came of age..."

"What about the girl?"

"Well that's the mystery. You see, the girl disappeared from the scene! They never found her, though they did discover her pink colored coat..."

"Oh?.."

"They explained it, but it was rather hush-hush you know. With so many war-dead, and so much distress to reconcile, here was a man of privilege killed while jaunting about in his convertible sportsmobile...The papers agreed to keep it quiet. After all, he had made a contribution to the war and was a man of some renown, you understand. It wouldn't sit well in the public perception..."

"I see" said Trevor.

"Well. We all had our suspicions, of course. But it was politely declared that the poor girl had been tossed from the car in the jolt and hurled down the ravine – you know those parts. Perhaps she fell victim to a wild animal in the countryside where agricultural husbandry had left fencing unattended during the war years. Her body was never recovered."

"But you had your suspicions...?"

"Well. Yes. I though the whole thing odd. I mean, why was the pink colored-coat not worn by a child in an open car? ... " She paused. "Evidently, the boy was considered dead at the scene. He survived! But the girl...Well, I don't know of course." She munched.

Trevor waited.

"There was evidence, your father told me, of another car in the proximity. Also, gasoline igniting the car with fire came *not* from the gas tank, you know, those primitive gas holding-bladders in those three-wheel Morgan's but from seeping through the upholstery of the car. As if someone had played foul. But it was never known."

"I'm sorry. That must have been awful."

She sighed. "It was..." Her voice trailed, and she lapsed into a stillness. "But we were all inured by the war years. Even here! So, a dignified burial and public display of grief was appropriately given to the Neville tragedy, rather than a sensational story in the newspapers, avoiding scandal. But a loss, none the less..." she paused, her voice tapering, and her hands folded on her lap.

Trevor reached over. "Come along mother. That's ancient history! You're to have your spa treatment, then to come down for a party this evening at the house. I'll send the car!"

She beamed. "Will Sir John be there?" Her eyes held a teasing sparkle..

"But of course! He's been an admirer of yours since you were 23. He'd kill me if he knew you were in town and no invitation for him to see you!"

She laughed. "The nice thing about being my age is that I can say what I want!"

"True. But you never do."

One thing that resonated with Trevor was the lack of an official report. He made a mental note to discover more. *Why had his father kept the Trust of Neville's mandate so quiet?*

"By the way" said his mother "The Trust was kept on the premises of their title estate, your father insisted on it. Under the keeping of the family solicitor Sir Nigel Combersby. You might want to talk to him, or his estate. And of course your father's responsibility was properly executed. He recorded the Trust at the Bank of England"

"Thank you! That's very helpful to know mother" he said, pecking her on the forehead. "Now I must go!"

"Yes of course. But do tell when you aim to marry...?"

He rolled his eyes. *Of course, the seasonal question* "I will..." he laughed.

Sharp as a pin, as always!

* * *

Nine

Amanda did not like the way the Investigation was going. Plus she was an outsider. She needed to get to the bottom of this, she decided.

She asked Emily to provide her with the details of what was considered stolen from the Vault.

Aside from her own materials used in class.

Emily had not cooperated. The clue, it seemed, came from Jeannette herself.

She overheard her belligerent voice emanating from a conversation with New Scotland Yard.

"What the hell has early Shakespeare manuscripts got to do with our vault...Lieutenant?"

So wrapped by the silence of the night, she got she sat at her computer and emailed a trusted colleague in Washington who might have some answers.

"Is there anything unique about findings on early Shakespeare manuscripts? Who would want to change the record of a poet?"

<SEND>

* *

The next day brought a pall on the entire Department. The police Investigation evidently, was being relayed to the upper tiers of the University as requiring a full fledged investigation. Once Amanda got home she opened her email. Amanda printed up the Attachments and decided she would read them later.

* *

Jack was delighted with his house guest. This he made clear by leaping up to nap whenever Emily collapsed on the sofa.

The weekend had gone remarkably well. Together they had accomplished their chores, including cleaning up and shopping for food, which was just as well since Emily was eating her way through the supply of provisions in short order.

More than anything else, Amanda appreciated that all necessary laundry, suits and shoes had found their way to the dry cleaners, and back, on hangers, or tagged, boxed and bagged - something Emily advanced with grace knowing how busy Amanda's week could be. All that remained was the big event: To accompany Emily back to her place.

It began with a breakfast at the local café and the Sunday newspaper. Emily found the obituaries.

"Damn the Royalty..." Emily burst, eyes ablaze "You'd think he was a commodity or something to package, trade and advertise!"

She wiped her eyes. "Look at this. All about the family name. Not a word about his personal life, his....his...dreams ..his fun and the things he liked to do!"

"Emily. It's a closing of the ranks to uphold his reputation.." began Amanda

"Well they didn't ask anyone... did they?" she snapped.

"I'm sorry...Yes. A personal touch was needed."

She read the words again, her face betraying a growing sense of frustration. "He was so accepting and ...always encouraging others...."

Amanda reached out to touch her elbow.

Emily looked up, uttering words that had held her thoughts for days. "Why would anyone want to hurt him?"

Amanda sat back in her seat. "*Hurt* him?"

"Oh yeah" Emily blew her nose into the paper towel that served as table napkin. "Someone killed him. I saw the body. That was no bloody accident...That was no *accident* of his own doing, as they imply."

She struggled for composure.

"He loved ... his crewing. And I've got news for them...."

She leaned in for privacy, her lips quivering with emotion "He Never shot drugs!"

"Oh Emily..."

"No! I mean it" she flared. "Never! He was clean..." she rose to her feet and was heading for the door. "Emily! Slow down" Amanda caught up with her outside by the car.

She turned, her face now dark with anger. "They're full of it...those cops. He smoked, sure. But Roger was clean...Someone killed him!"

Emily's apartment demonstrated that he had all but moved in with Emily. His clothes, books, cigarettes, movies and games were strewn all over her place. This, over a layer of Emily's own predilections of gothic collectables.

But as Amanda helped gather, clean up and bag his belongings, she noticed a tenderness between them that was touching "For the girl of the castle" she found on a card under a crystal dragon.

"He-Man of my life" Emily has written on a picture of Roger in his crew hull at the boathouse.

"The gang" was clearly the subject of a collage showing them all together raising boats, drinking, bare-chesting for the photographer.

Nowhere was there more evidence of his presence than the bedroom and bathroom where his T shirts, jeans, cigarettes and socks intermingled with Emily's own mess.

"Sorry…" she pleaded, owning the mess before Amanda waved away any further need for comment.

After removing all his evidence with as much rearranging as Amanda could manage, she left Emily in a fresh apartment with food in the fridge; the TV on, and a pile of material to sort, look over and edit for work by morning.

Emily thanked her with a wordless hug. She could take it from here.

When Amanda returned to her apartment, she found Jack waiting with dignified patience. When she took out the trash, Jack retreated.

* *

Ten

She settled down to open her Email Attachments. They drew a picture she could never have imagined.

> *"The authenticity of the authorship of the plays are now coming under increasing debate. Embarrassing for some scholars who dedicated their life work to the author. But not really, if it is the beauty of the works themselves that draws the scholarship, and not the ego of the scholar.*
>
> *As for insurers, museums, and investor interests, then the stakes could not be higher...Integrity of Authenticity of high priced arts and collections is serious business in the world of Finance and Investment.   Much depends on the evaluations given them, let alone the rights of ownership!"*

She replied.

"Too bad they marginalize historians these days!"

"Or kill for..." came the quick reply.

Amanda stared at the screen.

Re. Your query.
"It seems that there are several candidates for the location of original Shakespeare manuscripts. The main items lie with the great families of England who have personal collections. It was their stewardship to hold on to such rich treasures of the realm. Hence private collections offering much to view at Museum Gift/Loans. Or Universities for scholarship, and also for general exhibition tours. If authenticity, authorship is in question, then there is a material value to be validated.

Amanda read carefully. While grateful for the communication from her trusted colleague, she felt certain that she had missed something.

She read on, informal as he was in his email.

Like, if one goes missing - even if acquisitioned, or taken as a conquest of war by invading forces - it's theft of a national treasure, the stealing from national identity. Icons are symbols of a culture in which society invests heavily to give it meaning; recognition, codes of conduct.

Finally, such questions shake up the art world; the black markets and insurers who underwrite these things. So, yes, it is big business. Big fincance. And big costs in liabilities, let alone public reputations.

So tread carefully!"

For example, one collection of the manuscripts had been with the family of Sir Henry Neville, lying dormant in his estate. It is now possible there is a reason. One ancestor could well have been the writer!

New scholarship finds that the Sir Henry Neville of the 17th century could be the author, not only of plays, but of a reform movement that changed the course of history and give us today the modern world we live in.

Some assert that Shakespeare, a country school boy from Stratford on Avon was a Catholic of the Spanish Holy Roman Empire influence who sub-vented his faiths for a new world. (See Harvard University, a Jesuit institution, work of Greenblatt.) Today, such thinking is ascribed to political liberals who prefer socialism over free market capitalism. This implicates government policy, foreign affairs, immigration and finance! Others, British scholars (James & Rubenstein of Universities of Portsmouth and Aberystwith) examine Neville as the author, chiefly because of his personal connections with the world events described, and, as Shakespeare's patron, writing those words of protest and reform through public plays in London - a city of restless rebels and competing interests for opportunities in the new world. (Writing Incognito may well have been the indictment for ruffling political feathers.)

However, see for yourself.

Read carefully below, his account of what happened, who he was, and why his authorship is being examined. .

Remember, Protestant Huguenots were held to be wealthy merchants and former Crusaders – much to the envy of the Holy Roman Papal Church, who persecuted them.

Amanda put on her reading glasses, fetched a cup of tea, and settled in for some reading. It wasn't often the narrative of a past informed a present day windstorm.

"Henry Neville was travelling as Ambassador to France in 1600, during the last fretful years of Queen Elizabeth's reign. And before her successor was found in James I, from Scotland.

"His pens, ink and letters of importance were held by his Secretary Ralph Winwood. He was after all, not unknown, being a direct descendent of Chaucer, whose tales and poetry had fashionably tied the nuptial bonds of marriage of European Royal Courts- chiefly words committed to paper for peasants to follow, and princes to rule.

"With that legacy, Sir Henry Neville was sent to the Court of Henry IV. Especially to save that royal marriage, and the kingdom from dividing. His refined entertainment might have the desired effect on the 16th century audience of that court. Or so it was hoped by the English. Because the alternative was becoming diplomatically clear.

"As a playwright, and poet, a play performance was a gift of love. Or so he made it in a tenuous world where divertissements - efforts at distraction or assuagement over painful realities - were considered acts of selfless giving.

"Sir Henry Neville knew that on a world stage, serious matters of state could be diffused with laughter, puns, and love. In the hands of a skilled wordsmith, even justice and God could be debated by mortals!

"His works were well known in England where he and his family held a notable stage and touring players. There was the Midsummer Night's Dream; the Merchant of Venice amongst others. Plays already describing the strangeness of Europe and the change from sovereign dominion to mercantilist domestic consumption. Modern ideas, written by a modern, literate and well-travelled nobleman engaged in commerce himself. And far from the reach of the Holy Roman Empire who had to compete with ancient Norman laws rooted in feudal principalities and princes for territories, licensed trades; land proprietorship and commerce.

* *

It was all Amanda could do to absorb the enormity of what she was reading. The implications were beyond all that she had studied academically. How does one turn from a literary icon and view it differently? Or are the works too enduring, she wondered.

She walked about the room, thinking. Then she was pacing.

Was she about to turn the prevailing wisdom on its head?

No. She had to consider the case carefully.

Amanda sat back to imagine the circumstances. She wrote notes. They might help. And she thought it.

The only known contemporaneous document of that time would be the event of the translation into English from Latin of the *King James Bible*. Commissioned by King James IV in 1610, the Bible was unreadable to most English people. The reason was simple.

In the long history of the medieval, people were largely illiterate. They trusted the rule of their lives to the Latin words of the Bible offered by priests - intermediaries, the Catholic Church said – for Jesus Christ himself! They dispensed justice, mercy, forgiveness, punishment, distribution of treasure and picked who should be monarchs and whom they should marry, for inherited continuity of their Administrations.

This Amanda knew.

But the Bible translation was hardly original work. It comprised of the Holy Scriptures; the Old Testament followed by the New Testament. Nor were Printing Press a common things.

Thus, through plays was the voice of Protest to against Catholics heard.

Especially once Henry VIII, father of Queen Elizabeth, purged the Catholics from England.

But was without an heir.

Her age, her health, her successor.... Without an heir, your dynasty did not continue?

Trade changed everything.

It was the struggle for the realm; the appeal to the hearts and minds of the people; the philosophy and faith of a sovereignty yet able to divide state from church. The plays became the crucible for change with ships, manufacture, trade items, opportunity, expansion and overseas wealth!

Society was changing from the medieval world to the early modern world.

Since the license to trade was given by the Royal court, much depended on their authority.

Amanda researched the matter, and after dinner, she returned to her reading. There was more to discover about the author of the Shakespeare manuscripts.

"In France, a similar situation was fashioned by the King of France, Henry IV and his wife Marguerite of Valois. But unlike England, they were still under Catholic dominion.

"The King of France was known to Neville. He was in his mid- forties, and still without heirs to the throne. The king preferred mistresses, lovers, secret liaisons, and his infidelity liaisons confounded the conventional courts' contracts given in patronage, including standing liberties and rights of license and monopolies to trade...

"Sir Neville knew that if he failed to reconcile the deteriorating condition between King and Queen of France, wars of royal succession would follow. That was bad for England, its neighbor and trade partner.
"As a diplomat and a poet, Neville had to convey to the French the necessity to stay united. Neville had work to do. He had a mission to accomplish. A diplomatic mission of great impact to the English. The play then, became a foreign affairs tool, if not a threat of war.

"But there was more to this mission: The royal bloodlines of Europe had long intermingled, over the centuries. The French Queen, Marguerite of Navarre seated to view the play, was related to Neville. They both descended from Joanna of Navarre... second wife to Henry IV of England in 1368.
"Much has been made of this play. I ask that you read the fundamentals from my notes, and come to your own conclusions.
"So, laying out his quill and parchment, he made his decisions as to how to write his play for presentation in Court before the French couple and their court.
It was to be comedy "Love' Labors Lost."
Coded in the story of the play was messaging, as it deployed for entertainment. It went as follows.

> *Ferdinand would the King of Navarre. Berowne, Longaville and Dumaine would be the attending Lords. Dull, the Constable, and Costard, the Clown.*
>
> *To write the plot for the nuptials in a delicate way, the King and his nobles would take an oath of chastity while studying -- Even if the Princess*

and her ladies were coming to the kingdom town. If the ladies made their camp out of town, insisted the King, there would be no temptation! However, Love' Labors Lost would show that even the Spanish swordsman would fail to win his country wench because she fell for Costard - the country idiot.

For frivolity and entertainment, the "Lords" would set up a boy's Latin play production, a play within a play, which they themselves would critique. Hence a production about themselves! ...And their ladies, of course - all trying to be true and celibate - including the Ladies manservant "Boyet".

Then, like a judgment day, word comes that the Princess' father dies, and that the Princess must take her place on the throne! Fidelity must be proven, said the ladies, by one year and one day of celibacy....."

That's the impulse behind the play. Politically, the royal marriage was crumbling, fault lines already taking shape with armies in the wings to defend territorial liaisons made between the royals.

"Neville's diplomatic mission, it was perceived, had failed to achieve its objective. And failure was failure. Especially in light of what happened next.

It would be said, by some, that the play had been written with an intellectual content more suited to the Inns of Court in England, where barristers and Lords would adjudicate. As if in his defense.

Neville was punished.

By Neville's own admission, if the marriage of Henry IV had been reconciled, he would write another play, *Love Labor's Won.*

Instead, the play was handed down as written by William Shakespeare, actor.

* *

Eleven

Hyde Park, New York. 1942

They decided to gather, all of them together, on the grounds of the President's Home in the Fall of 1942. The situation had worsened since June, and now it was dire.

The Royalty of England, and other first families of Great Britain, were still seared from the social movements that had swept through Europe after the First world war, overturning traditional hierarchy with vengeful acts of socialist reform. The monarchs of Europe, as Churchill put it, had been replaced by dictators.

King George V of England however, appeased a restive population stricken by unemployed with acts of charity and kindness rather than repression and obstinacy. Unlike other stiff monarchs of Europe, he engaged with his people in sympathy and appealed to his Parliament for generosity. Further, King George dropped the audacious name of Saxe-Goethe from the English Royal family name, a title brought in by Prince Albert when he married Queen Victoria. The Royals would now be known by the simple name of Windsor.

Still, with World War II raging, German bombs fell upon London. Nothing was safe for the English in this war. Not their homes, not their possessions, neither their factories nor their ports. The RAF fought off thousands of enemy aircraft crossing the Channel to invade. And so far, England – an Island - had not succumbed to the enemy as the rest of Europe had fallen. But still their lives were in danger. Already, children had been evacuated away. Valuables, and all English treasure was shipped to safer quarters rather than fall to plunder by invaders, even as the Americans were starting to enter the war as an Allied force.

While bombs destroyed physical landmarks like the great cathedrals and houses of medieval architecture, they could be repaired. But there was something more that they valued. The icons of their culture. Their beliefs and values. National treasures that would represent not only commercial worth, but the moral values of a people. All that they believed in, fought and had died for. Their traditions, their Faith, democracy and intellectual works, moral, civil principles of society. All of it potentially plundered under enemy attack as spoils of war.

The great families of England had endured through the ages with their titles and responsibility of stewardship, often trustees of great treasure and items of value. It was code of societal obligation to keep them safe for posterity, for England.

But what of now?

It was agreed. They would be saved. But first, they had to be gathered and readied for transport. Where were they kept?

Today, they would make their plans. They would sign over these valuables for safekeeping to America and Canada. o save them for England, they agreed.

Hyde Park, a place of beauty on the banks of the Hudson River, was home to many whose success came from the fruits of the Industrial Revolution, finance and technological advances like the train, the automobile, the telegraph and the factory conveyors. Here, it was the home of President Roosevelt.

The President's Secretary of Works would make the logistical arrangements of transport and safe passage. Others would follow and confirm their itemized *Lists of Assets* with British Embassy officials in Washington DC.

Roosevelt was conferring with Congress, his task incomplete with Liberal Democrats unhappy about the war. Even as Churchill dogged him for desperate aid. For England, the war was not going well.

Today was particularly brutal day in terms of loss and defeat. The House Secretary was courteous when she approached them. But she was firm. The President was out of reach.

They understood, knowing that every factory in America had been building ships, rivets and guns for three years already.

Still, it weighed heavily amongst them, coming with hat in hand to seek protection of their prized possessions from the United Kingdom. A declaration by America to enter the war was still without definitive clarity as to its scope. And it disquieted them. Plus the newspapers faced them everywhere.

All of Europe had been conquered. The German Army was on the move in Russia, even proceeding through North Africa to threaten Europe's colonial wealth in gold, silver, diamond, copper mines and Persian oil fields. The world seemed to be collapsing.

Further, Japan was on the march in Asia. Unstopped in the Pacific, neither in South East Asia nor China, Japan had invaded the Aleutian Islands in June. Now they were establishing a substantial military base.

Worse, if Roosevelt's plan to deploy the Lend Lease program were underway, Japan just put the entire Pacific supply lines and sea traffic in jeopardy!

Convoys delivering gold and platinum across the Atlantic as payments for Lend Lease troops, arms and provisions for Great Britain had taken a terrible beating in Murmansk and Archangel.

The losses of cargo at sea were severe. Communications traffic clearly had been compromised. Only *three* convoys of supplies were sailed during April through August 1942, the rest were sunk by German U Boats and surface torpedoes. Two of the convoys that made it were from Reykjavik Iceland, one from Oban. With a need so desperate, and ocean shipping the only method of transport, it was eventful when American supplies arrived at British docks to provision the English, now in shortages.

But it was dangerous, and deadly. The world seemed to be collapsing.

If public spirit and courage were the provenience of the people, intelligence was the provenience of the Admiralty in Great Britain.

The enemy seemed to be everywhere! Only high-speed Naval vessels traversing from Russia to Great Britain at the time were known to have avoided submarines and detection in transit. Well known were the losses of the famous *HMS Edinburgh* and *HMS Trinidad*, sunk by German actions.

What was most disheartening to the Allies however, was that the enemy had spies amongst them everywhere, spies left over from by the social revolutions of the First world war. Theirs was not a cause that fostered icons of great beauty; treasure or decorative art, let alone intellectual notions of elitism. Meanwhile, France was handing its entire national arsenal to Britain and America, for all the good them. Paris fell. Clearly, they could not withstand the German invasion oncoming. With the world falling victim to a German machine of WWII, the national treasures of England were now at risk of plunder. Only Roosevelt could save the world, of that they felt certain. For those gathered together now at Hyde Park, the imperative was clear. All items of value should be removed from Great Britain and given shelter in America.

Sir Neville, Eleventh Earl of the family title in a long line of descendants, had a meeting with the President's senior official.

The meeting occurred just before leaving, and it was to discuss arrangements for Lend Lease, an elaborate diplomatic exchange by which America was to join the Allied forces.

One of Roosevelt's most trusted Advisors lived across the Hudson river from Hyde Park and he was at home with his family preparing to leave for London himself. He requested to see Sir Neville. They had, after all, ties that went back centuries.

In a long and strange way, many Americans had roots that entwined them with European backgrounds. Many, greener in American history than early settlers, had migrated to the new world as recourse from an old world bogged down by tortuous progress through modernism.

Still, the Advisor knew of the legacy that the Neville family held. And it was he who informed Sir Henry, over a casual dinner of barbeque steak and American ham, of the strategy and plans laid out for Europe by the Americans. None other in the assembly from Britain was privy to such advance information but Sir Neville.

Further, said the Adviser, there was a bigger picture at hand for the delivery of treasure from England. Only the President and Prime Minister knew of it. If security were compromised, it would be devastating to the Allies, but this, Sir Henry must know.

Arrangements for the national bank's sovereign supply of gold bullion, silver and platinum was to be shipped to America. Diamonds and other items of value should be taken to Canada mainly as diversion from American ports. Enemy spies and sabotage were everywhere planted. Especially at the docks where socialists groups gathered. *No one should be trusted!*

Moreover, valuable Fine Art was to be packaged and flown over Iceland and into Toronto. As were original and ancient works of literary composition, like hallmark manuscripts; sacred writings and historical documents of the British Empire. Including those held in the Neville family...

If an invasion of Britain were to happen, or a social revolution to take hold as it had in other monarchies across Europe, then Britain's valued assets must be removed from English soil... It was his own family in Europe, after all, that had engaged in the art of the first writings of medieval scholarly thinkers!

What Sir Henry should do is sent *his* precious cargo by separate shipping. On the same vessels as the Sovereign gold. Even if they were stacked as great bound books, for safety. The packing crates could be arranged. They would be bound with metal straps; skins and loaded like the rest of the cargo, gold.

Sir Henry kept this information to himself. Or so he thought.

Yes. The world seemed to be collapsing.

* *

Twelve

England. 1688

The legacy of the Protestant Tudors was enduring. James IV of Scotland ascended the throne of England and the King James Bible was translated from Catholic Latin to the English language. Shakespeare completed his plays, and a new era of mercantilism flourished. In seafaring trade, the English colony of Virginia was settled, and the spirit of Martin Luther's individualist agency, as theology, prevailed.

But it did not last. Regicide followed a disastrous English civil war and a penitent new heir to the throne betrayed his realm. Parliament languished, the era of Restoration perished and England was drawn into war. Finally, eighty six years after Elizabeth I died, Parliament settled for a new monarchy.

It was called the Glorious Revolution. William III was invited to ascend to the throne of England.

The wetness of that autumn day was nowhere more visible than in the muddy streets and wooden houses of Brixham. Every public house, private estate, barnyard and tavern was garrisoned with foot soldiers.

By the time the ship Brill approached the dock, a large ceremonial canvas and pavilion had been erected for the great disembarkment.

William III, in full battle regalia, came ashore declaring "the liberties of England and the Protestant Religion I will maintain."

He eyed his Aide, who nodded. He had pronounced the words correctly. William could not speak English.

Offshore stood a fleet of 100 warships, 400 Transports carrying 11,000 infantry and 4,000 horses. He came with an invasion army.

It rained.

In the surrounding fields and pastures, soldiers made camp and quartered their horses, sending long roads of supply running to and from Brixham in endless motion. The provisioning alone, according to the ledgers, fairly depleted the English Board of Victualling Storehouses.

More soldiers filled boggy fields. Billeted in make-shift tents, they were hungry, belligerent, fully uniformed and crowded. They had made a harrowing crossing of the Channel in tall ships and shallops.

Supplied with Arms, and standing on English soil with their own William of Orange from Amsterdam, none could speak English.

Less than 10 weeks later, William III summoned a Convention Parliament at Westminster Palace to discuss the terms of his kingship in England. His Aide was his translator.

Mary, his wife, was glad to be home again. But she had doubtless begged William to spare the life of her father King James II now fleeing to France, and vacating the English throne.

Parliament objected to William's reign as sole monarch, even with his own lines of succession of royal blood of Europe allowing for his English ascendancy.

"If it is possible to imagine, His Highness, with the Queen Mary II at his side..." began one Minister to the Impresario as they walked the lengths of Westminster Hall.

"Impossible!" said William's Dutch interpreter.

"He alone should be sovereign of the land!"

"Of course. That we understand" persisted the Minister, his long and heavy robes bringing a full redness to his face with heat and perspiration.

"But it is the Queen Mary, his wife, who has superiority to rule in the line of succession!"

The negotiations were going nowhere.

"He must reign in his own right. He shall refuse to be Monarch as Consort-only to the English Queen"

"Then he must rule as an invading force Sir!" replied the Minister hotly.

"...might I suggest" said another of the English delegation "that there be a rule of duality, to ensure his continued kingship at her death...?"

The Dutch moved away, and together they consulted for a few moments.

When they returned, it was the English who preempted their reply.

"In any case, Gentlemen, we in Parliament, without consent of a dual Monarch of the British Isles, shall continue to debate in Parliament at the Vacancy of the Throne still unanswered by the King James II, his father..."

William III spat on the ground.

When William of Orange heard that he and his wife Mary were to be crowned together as joint Monarchs of the English people, he was furious.

William and Mary, indeed!

The notion was preposterous. But as his own delegation pointed out, the House of Orange was without Treasure. And the throne of England would give him great agency in the affairs of Europe.

Reluctant as he was, there was one more surprise that the Whigs of the English Parliament would present him with. And without his signature, there would be no Crown.

It was a document like no other. Nor had any monarch conceded to its provisions, preferring instead to abdicate, or be beheaded as had happened forty years earlier to Mary's own grandfather, Charles I.

William III, under the supervision of his delegation signed the document. But it would come at a cost, he promised.

The bill was read in Parliament by the Speaker. It was entered by the Secretary on the Ledger as the Bill of Rights.

* * *

Amanda walked to class. The facts horrified her. Not exactly your text book history, she thought. But in biographies and diaries, the story had been pieced together.

No. She would not use it to teach class. That was the preserve or research historians.

Stick with the facts is what her lesson plan suggested... But the human story was compelling. And one thing she knew about history, it was the telling of the human condition.

Leave controversy to the Controversial - she could hear her professor admonishing...

Still, the facts rankled her brain. It was clear to understand.

The French Queen Marguerite, a queen representing a large territorial constituency by title, felt threatened by her husband's new mistress *Diane d'Andouins*. Unlike any other bedfellow, this mistress actually pressed the King of France to make *her* the "Queen of Navarre" - without having claim to any royal bloodline or birthright to the territorial lands of the region of Navarre!

These were fighting words. They implied territorial conquest - with armed assault if necessary to reduce titular entitlement by the mistress.

Yet the rumor gained traction.

Finally, Marguerite of Valois fled to her homeland to instigate an uprising against her husband. Her territorial lands were in danger of conquest and assimilation by interests within the French Court of the Holy Roman Empire.

If the Pope were informed that the King of France Henry IV was annulling his marriage to Marguerite, then there was surely a bigger play at hand...

By the end of the year 1599, having thwarted the Spanish Armada during her reign, the health of Elizabeth I of England was fading.

Sir Henry Neville, sent to the French Court with the gift of a play to auger happy reconciliation for the Royal couple, now sensed danger. As the English Ambassador, he reported on the deteriorating situation overseas. The power shift would have damaging effects for England.

The French King "...goes in secret manner at Zamet's house where la belle grace Claude entertained him and that he was courting Henriette d'Entragues..."

The French King's offspring were now many, and illegitimate. The affair was dangerous business. Plots and relationships could suddenly turn deadly...

Yet Sir Henry Neville knew of even greater treachery lurking in the shadows.

Catherine de Medici, heiress to a vast fortune from Savoy, had arrived in France from Italy. She brought her daughter Marie de Medici to the French Court. By the time Marie received the attention of the French King as his new bride, Sir Neville was in danger.

Neville, a Protestant baron of some wealth, pleaded for his health, and left suddenly the Court of France as Ambassador.

The shadows would move quickly, and history would record the events that followed.

The Royal wedding between the French king and his new bride, Marie de Medici went on for days.

Festivities, parties, feasts, banquets and masked balls all round.

Only a few cries could be heard in the distance. Nobody paused. Nobody noticed.

They had been invited from all over Europe as guests to the nuptials, to celebrate the new marriage of Henry. They were the Huguenots.

Protestants, merchants, descendants of the Crusaders and traders of great wealth in shipping, wool, cloth, gold, consumables… and independence! Many of them central to the Protestant lands of Europe held by Proprietary Right - All of them princes entitled to owning their own territorial rights in an agrarian society - offering opportunities and prospect for the individual whose faith was his own to pursue…

Most significantly, they remained outside the centralized integration of the Holy Catholic Empire: Like Queen Elizabeth of England, they had resisted the Pope of Rome. For in such manner was Europe held captive by appointed kings and queens claimed to rule by Divine Right – as God's anointed, in the service of the Holy Roman Empire.

The Hugenots, who for centuries remained suspicious of the Roman Church, were duped by new overtures of friendship, believing political reconciliation.

They had come as guests, accepting invitations each: All of them assembled in one city, at one time.

And all of them massacred in one sweep.

History would name it The Huguenot Massacre.

* *

Within six months, Neville would be himself in the Town of London.

From there, he would turn his pen to tragedies and dynastic histories of unjust Kings and Queens, his skills at their peak, his name Incognito.

He might even help King James, once he ascended to the Protestant throne of England, translate the Bible from Latin to English.

* *

The loading dock was busy. People, trains, trucks, military troops and sweethearts waving goodbye.

The ship at the dock, with diesel engines churning within its grey steel hull, stood ready for action. Stacked within her cargo bay holds were some of England's stores of precious metals, including valuable commodities destined for Iceland, then on to Canada for safekeeping. A convoy of escort battleships was to accompany her across the Atlantic Ocean and defend her against enemy torpedoes.

"So, you talked with the President's Ambassador coming to England, I hear?" said Len Paloski.

Sir Neville looked at him, his elegant face masking surprise. "Why Yes, I did!"

"Well then" said Paloski, pulling open his watch from a chain of Welsh gold as if he were a Mayor surveying the Court-leet "You must have special intelligence that leaves us all in the dark, I should say, what?"

If unprepared for the question, Sir Nevill was unhurried with his answer. He was never one to fraternize with London's bankers, and it was known he preferred the comfort of his home in the country with his hunting party, his dogs and his books over his Executive mansion in London. But this man was baiting him.

How to explain that on his return from America his only interest was to be home to Enid, his wife of thirty years - an American heiress in her own rights. She would want to know everything about his visit immediately...Not wait for his session of Parliamentary Assembly in London to end. Still, he knew the ways of the Londoners, and he knew the subtle penalties for not cooperating in their spirit of things, war or not. After all, many had already lost sons in battle, many of them looking at the first families of the realm for example and honor. Then again, Paloski would know this, and it was his every intention to make Neville uncomfortable for any social infraction of the day.

 "We discussed matters of common ground, he and I" said Sir Neville, sidestepping the matter of preferential treatment "We... have family ties in the Austrian Alps, he and I"

Leonard Paloski was a man whose currency included intelligence. But he was sophisticated, and ceded the point with a smile. Still, it bothered him that Sir Neville had been invited for a private meeting with the President's key Advisor on matters of importance occurring in Europe. Events that would clearly involve a great deal of wealth.

Sir Neville decided to diffuse any cause for festering. "I regret that we were so pressed for time. Of all the things to discuss, I am happy to tell you the topic of our discussion..." smiled Sir Neville.

"How kind!"

"Skiing! The topic of our brief discussion was his avid interest in skiing in the Alps!"

"Where you have family, no doubt?" pressed Leonard

"Formerly, yes! But...err, alas, I do not ski at all with any skill. Rather, only to protrude from the snow with my legs atop the surface and my posterior beneath it..."

The response did surprise Paloski, and he did laugh.

Sir Neville knew he had purchased time, no more. This was a crafty wolf, this Leonard Paloski.

He moved on to meet with the London Representative of the main bank's repositories. He and his accountants would be securing the bullion cargo on board the ship bound for America.

They had a brief discussion, and Sir Neville joined the group of investors gathered here today at the docks. All of them with a stake on board this vessel. They met briefly with the Captain, even as troops took to the gangplanks for boarding. Many would be briefing in America, then shipped on to the Pacific theater for action.

Next to board the ship were the Nurses and Medics headed for Iceland en route to Vladovostok. Judging from their luggage coming out of the bus, they were outfitted to garrison at the Russian front.

Finally, with all their business completed and accounted for, several chauffeurs brought forward the cars for the party of Investors, and they all climbed in to be driven away from the docks. And not a minute too soon, for the weather had turned cold and blustery. Except for Leonard Paloski's car. His car took a different way and broke from the convoy of bankers and executives assembled to oversee the delivery of wealth from the Bank of England's vaults to the ship.

* *

Amanda made notes of the events. Clearly, there had been too much pain and humiliation for the playwright's work to have any effect on the royal couple.

Amanda read the material twice. Then she wrote and email in response.

Topic. "What's the case for his attainder and confinement to the Tower?" <SEND>

By nightfall, the answer came in.

Re. Topic "For his collusion with the Essex Rebellion, as a reformist!

"The Writ came from the Cecils, who were (father and son) Advisors to Queen Elizabeth of England, usurping their privilege to become personally enriched by fierce competition, corruption, and takings of liberties, trade licenses, patents, wealth, lands and overseas venture."

Best,

"H"

She stared at the screen.

* *

Sir Neville took the news well, considering the loss to him personally.

He retreated to his library where the legacy of his family had been kept for a long time. He sat there alone for days, staring at the portraits that shielded empty vaults. He mourned the loss of all other treasure that his beloved England could not afford to lose. And he mourned the loss of so many men in this wretched war.

He could only guess at what might have happened. To imagine the events was almost too grotesque to contemplate. The question that rankled him was simple.

How had the world come to this? ...
Neither was he alone with the question, as awkward and strangely distant as the enemy was...

"So, tell me son, how do you *listen* for anything?"
The boy looked at his Captain, then wilted back a shade, eyes down.
The Captain lit a cigarette, something highly irregular when underway, and he took a long draw. Then he turned the butt of the cigarette around and offered it to the youth, smoke vaguely rising to perfume the cabin with the redolence tobacco. "American!" said the Captain, by way of advertising the product.
The youth smiled. He resistant at first, but was clearly bowled over by his Captain's favor. He took a polite inhalation then resumed his position. Whether or not he smoked was immaterial. This was a man's thing. A military thing. A patronizing thing.
"Tell me!"
"It's the radar Sir! First, it's the radar that sends it signal... and back. Then it comes and goes with some irregularity, I hear the radar pulse with a beat. Beep. Beep..."
The Captain eyed him with encouraging interest. "Oh?"

"Yes Sir!"

"So, you here this... this *irregularity*?"

"Yes Sir!"

"When?"

"When there is no ship Sir! Then I hear other things. Sometimes a little something of the sea. Ice. Fish, Or floating debris. .."

"Yah?"

" Like sometimes... if there is a storm, I hear a faster *Beep*... As if all the fish were all running away from the storm!"

The Captain smiled.

"A storm?"

"Yes. Like now. We have heard nothing of the enemy. But only sea fish beat!"

Franz Krantz , the youth, was two years younger than he had reported on his recruitment papers. The oversight had not been entirely overlooked. Rather, under-scrutinized. With a name like Krantz, certain dispensation was allowed. Still, if he were not eager and tall... Submarine duty, after all, was serious business for the German Army. Duty service in the Communications Corps was not offered to foot soldiers! But his father's name did carry weight. And within six weeks of intensive training, the youth was fit for duty as a radar operator.

If the youth Krantz was being questioned, it was out of utter frustration by a Captain of a U Boat that they had failed to make any sighting of the enemy. This, in spite of specific instructions, position coordinates and intended destination!

What was even more remarkable for the German Captain, as he told his officers, was that their torpedoes were to be used for no other assault but this commission. No open hunting. And the Atlantic offered opportunities. His target was given as specific and unique. His arsenal was tailored for the task.

The Captain dismissed the communications radar operator and lay down on his bunk to enjoy the rest of his cigarette. Then a thought came to him. *Out of the mouth of babes ...Of course!*

As he left his quarters to return to his Navigation station, he called to his yeoman to bring crystals and wet sheets into his quarters to dampen the air and rid the cabin of cigarette smoke.

He had his answer!

If the target ship left the dock in London headed for the North sea on that course heading...

 Vigilant as ever, it would sail under cover of darkness, then change bearings headed for Halifax to cross the Atlantic. If it were underway for four days at thirty two knots, then its cargo doubtless was insured for several million English sterling by companies across Europe... Why? What was it carrying? Why his instructions?

As a cargo vessel, it was built for heavy duty shipping with crane capacity for loading gear, and rigging for deep draft and heavy seas. If it had a species room it would have been rearranged for its cargo. It supposedly had four Naval escorts trailing it as two different convoys. The First into Iceland. The second across the Atlantic. What did that mean?

His orders were clear. He was armed to attack. Or be attacked... Clearly, he and his boat were *not* expected to survive this sortie. It was clear from the crew they gave him, older, less trained, more disposable. Why? Such conclusions could leave a Captain disenchanted with his command.

Or more determined to survive...

The storm that had developed off the Bering Straights did not cause alarm; their speed was predictable and their radar able. From Denmark an Intelligence message made its way into German hands, and the Captain's submarine took out to sea from the bay of Arcachon in France. It had orders to carry only six torpedoes, one target and a specific timing schedule.

If a Captain were preparing to abandon his mission after days expended on search and destroy grids, and the boy Krantz was missing signals on his listening device because he could hear no sequence that measured for the regimen, then the Captain would be held accountable in a highly restricted mission...

But the boy *was* listening! With both ears. And what confounded the U Boat was that the intended course of its target had been altered by the storm above. It was, rather, *driving* them. ..

This the young Krantz could not have known. But his method of listening allowed the Captain to determine the reason for their failure. Only when the Captain called the youth to his cabin for a private conference did the concept blossom.

"Plot a course south of the coordinates, please!" his told his Executive officer.

The storm had driven the convoy southward. As sure as if the youth had told them. Within 18 hours the convoy under escort was identified. Two torpedoes were discharged, the balance of his arsenal unused. With a vessel still loaded for fire, the submarine was returning to Brest on the French coast, knowing only that its mission had been completed, its targets sunk.

Yet, the suspicion lingered with the Captain that what was sent to the bottom of the sea was critical, requiring him to abstain from all other engagement with the enemy. If that were the case, his cultural heritage instinctively told him that the cargo was somehow indelibly intertwined with the achievements of Europe, for such was the knitting of their history, even including advancements in the industrial revolution of recent history.

Too bad the leaders of Europe had been forced into war, he mulled. And, he felt saddened for any loss his mission might have caused.

Being of an elitist Prussian family, he knew only too well that the Monarchies of Europe had been replaced by socialist dictators, dictators that hijacked the nations of Europe and declared war upon each other. Yes, there was a loss for Europe, a war that destroyed the past traditions by socialists! But this he could never whisper. This was a war too great to stop. He wondered, though ,at the princes of the enemy only now hearing of their losses. Losses he regretted that he had sent to the bottom of the sea.

How had the world come to this? ...

On his next sorties off France, he knew that it was only a matter of time before his ship would be sunk. Within hours of reaching the Atlantic, his submarine was hit by an American torpedo. His last thoughts damned not the enemy that delivered the weapon, but his own leadership.

* *

When Sir Neville received notice by telephone, he had just returned from a hunting expedition yielding deer and fowl for the household. The cargo ship that left the dock at London never reached its destination. It had been sunk by enemy fire, all cargo lost.

It came as little comfort, ten days later, when a letter from the Prime Secretary was delivered by special driver. Yes, it was confirmed that England had taken its loss at sea. However, Sir Neville's particular cargo had *not* be placed on board with the specie as promised. Rather, it had been rerouted to another form of transportation, the Prime Secretary assured him, thereby spared a sinking by the enemy of one of England's most revered literary treasurers, the words of his ancestor...

This news Sir Neville could share with no one. Not that it mitigated those feelings of loss as a matter of principle for so many, and for so much...

Even if he had exercised a measure of duplicity himself by not delivering the original Master work of his household, but sending rather, a fake copy. Such an act would be expected of a Trustee of so valuable a commodity.

Regardless, something had emerged of greater danger.

A saboteur lay within their bosom.

He would go to London and discuss the matter with the Prime Secretary.

* *

It wasn't until the next day that Amanda was fully informed by the Head of the Department whose head would roll.

Evidently, early manuscripts of - some unknown author – had found their way into the University Vault. Unfortunately, the person who put them there was dead. And Amanda was the last to use the vault.

Worse. The police confirmed that the boy had been murdered.

* *

Thirteen

Amanda was dreaming. The words of a most important work revolved in her head. Like a tune that passed your lips at every breath...Who would write such a thing? Why? She was obsessed with the meaning behind the words. She opened the little sheet on which she had written them, copied from an Attachment sent to her...Found, apparently, within the personal estate papers of Sir Henry Neville. He wrote

> This royal throne of kings, this scepter'd isle,
> This earth of majesty, this seat of Mars,
> This other Eden, demi-paradise,
> This fortress built by Nature for herself
> Against infection and the hand of war,
> This happy breed of men, this little world,
> This precious stone set in the silver sea,
> Which serves it in the office of a wall,
> Or as a moat defensive to a house,
> Against the envy of less happier lands,
> This blessed plot, this earth, this realm, this England,
> This nurse, this teeming womb of royal kings,

> *Fear'd by their breed and famous by their birth*
> *Renowned for their deeds as far from home,*
> *For Christian service and true chivalry,*
> *As is the sepulcher in stubborn Jewry,*
> *Of the world's ransom, blessed Mary's Son,*
> *This land of such dear souls, this dear dear land,*
> *Dear for her reputation through the world,*
> *Is now leased out, I die pronouncing it,*
> *Like to a tenement or pelting farm.*
> *England, bound in with the triumphant sea*
> *Whose rocky shore beats back the envious siege*
> *Of watery Neptune, is now bound in with shame,*
> *With inky blots and rotten parchment bonds.*
> *That England, that was want to conquer others,*
> *Hath made a shameful conquest of itself.*
> *Ah, would the scandal vanish with my life,*
> *How happy then were my ensuing death!*
> *—Act II, scene i, 42–54*

Amanda replied.

For an 18th Century guy, where did get notions of republicanism?

<SEND>

* *

"My dear Man!" said the Prime Secretary extending his hand warmly to Sir Neville. "So good of you to come!"

"It's my pleasure Sir, I only wish I were young enough to fight on the front!"

"As do I!" chortled the elder statesman. "But as you see, we are much needed in our own capacities. And each man's contribution to this war effort is essential..."

"Of course..."

The butler of the Minister's office came forward to pronounce dinner.

"Ah! Wonderful! Wonderful" said the Minister, rubbing his hands eagerly. "Please come through for some burgundy; a good side of beef, and then we shall talk upstairs over a brandy" said the Prime Secretary.

The seven-course meal , richly embellished with gravies and side sauces was served with impeccable elegance at Government house. Especially fulfilling for Sir Henry was the Beef Wellington served with a deep Bordeaux and salad , a war-time luxury.

Moreover, the Minister was enjoying himself, having company was a way of releasing those woes of the weary, as he put it. He appreciated Sir Henry's quiet attention as he proceeded from one account to another of the war. That, and the comfort of knowing he could share his confidences with a man of reputable integrity - a man whose family legacy of monetary and commercial development was legendary in the history of England. Sir Henry, after all, was a descendant and Lord of the Realm. In fact, when it was heard that Sir Henry would be dining in London, a message was sent from Windsor Castle to extend to Sir Henry the best wishes of the Royal family.

But finally it came time for the true purpose of the visit, and in the drawing room, the details came out.

"The fact is" said the Minister settling in a winged chair beside the fireplace, "the war is not going well. Our losses at sea have been considerable. We are facing a formidable foe!" he said. His picked up his brandy and swirled "I fear for our country!"

"Surely, the Americans offer great hope?"

"They do!" said the Minister "but there is a problem within our infrastructure, and I'd like to include you in my circle of confidence to help me get to the bottom of it. You see, the President has sent us Mr Harrison as his Special Representative with the rank of Minister in regard to all matters relating to facilitating material aid to the British Empire. He is himself of considerable means, and holds the trust of the President. He has chosen for his staff three key men familiar with the procurements and capabilities of their various supply, Ordinance, Aviation and Manufacturing production management, and his Naval officer as his Administrator. They mean to win his war under the provisions of the Lend-Lease Bill passed by Congress and signed by the President..."

"Is that not a good thing?"

"Naturally, it is. And thank God for our alliance with them. Or should I say, for the President of the United States, a man himself committed to end this wretched war." He drank. "But it is a matter of some concern that in fulfilling the mission, there will be omission of oversight, and, if I deign say it, a temptation for greed and personal enrichment amongst us..."

"Surely not... The cause of the war is upon the lips of every true Englishman"

The man in the chair facing him was not only leader of the present government, but pleading on many fronts for allied support, even as England was being ravaged by an enemy bent not only on military might, but cultural damage. Sir Henry was shocked at what he heard next.

"Thank you! Your words are most encouraging. But I fear we have an enemy amongst us! A spy who informs our enemy of our position where shipments of wealth and cultural provenance are at stake..."

The Minster got up, walked to the sideboard and poured himself more brandy. He turned and raised his glass to Sir Neville " Was it not your 9th grandfather who wrote of seditious temptations

'with this there grows, in my most ill-composed affection, such a stanchless avarice that, were I king, I should cut off the nobles for their lands, desire his jewels and this other's house'...?"

Sir Neville smiled "*Macbeth* 4.3.91-99... You cite correctly!"

The Minister beamed. "Thank you!"

"There is our decision, for example, to ship our sovereign gold to the United States rather than have it fall into enemy hands....Only, *'See, sons, what things you are, how quickly nature falls into revolt when **gold** becomes her object. ..? 2 Henry IV 4.5.64-6,* I believe?'"

"Correct!" said Sir Neville raising his glass. "So, How can I help?"

"I fear we are losing too many ships that carry such cargo. It is for this reason, and I trust you forgive me, that I diverted our sovereign wealth from the last shipment as agreed, to the Bank of Scotland for safekeeping!"

Sir Neville got up and walked to face the window, a dark and unlit world outside to hide from enemy aircraft. *What had happened to the world?* His head swirled at the potential loss of what was his to defend as a family legacy. An arm came to rest on his back.

"You are safe. I had your crates of sovereign gold also diverted to the Bank of Scotland vaults for safekeeping and recording. It has not left British soil...You shall have it back in your keeping at the end of the war. This I shall commit to paper for you to request on demand when you think it safe. My man shall deliver it in the morning."

Sir Neville turned. "Thank you!" Then added quietly "You are a most courageous and thoughtful leader. Arouse your people in their darkest hour. They shall follow your lead! Have faith in all that is good..."

Fourteen

Were it not that the last two weeks were speeding by with preparing lecture notes and a research paper, the Spring Semester had not started well for Amanda.

Neither had the winter weather cooperated. Once she found Jack alone in the apartment, curled against the cushions, and the heat off.

Broken, said the landlord, without any remorse.

But that was not what irked Amanda. Jeannette Bevan was doing little to shield her staff.

"It's not that I don't believe you" she had the gall to say "It's that you are not used to our ways here…Things in the United States are… quite different, you know, when it comes to Universities."

"But not when it comes to murder!" said Amanda, rising from her chair. "Trust me, *American* Juris Prudence is rooted in centuries of English law!" Amanda spun on her heels and left the room.

It was not like her to resort to sarcasm. But Jeannette had a way of provoking people. The Department "Chair" as they called her, lived in a landscape of her own. That, according to the rest of her faculty.

Especially if there was a foreign body within her ranks, they reminded her sheepishly, like a good scapegoat.

 For an official enquiry? She wondered.

Jack listened to her rant with as much accommodation as he could muster. By the time she pronounced they were circling the wagons, he stretched, then bared his teeth and unsheathed his claws.

 "Quite right!" muttered Amanda, that's what I said.

Jack yawned.

What was she supposed to do, exactly. Stop her work? Carry on?

"All right class" She began. "I see the calendar is moving along a bit. "So tonight we will be addressing the authenticity of 18th century musical manuscripts and the integrity of compositions." She paused, waiting for any questions.

"On Wednesday we will examine early modern era books and their publishing techniques....Yes. Yes!" she grinned, responding to the buzz "..We do look at the King James and the Gutenberg..."

"*Ahhhhhh*" they all coughed up with fake admiration, but not inimically. Professor Wells had earned their respect and could share some fun.

"And by Friday..." she continued "we will be covering early playwriting and scripts." She peered over her glasses and smiled wickedly..."with a twist for next week, guys!" *(She must stop using the word Guys...Jeannette had said...)*

Then, for the next two hours, and dressed in a Tweed jacket and skirt by Chanel, with a J Crew T shirt, she delivered a lesson plan that even her mentor would love.

"So, at the end of the day..." she concluded "with musicologists and forensic analysis exhausted, you can feel free to meet the *persona* of the composition. That is, his tweaks and habits, the sounds...in his head, if you will.

Like, does he repeat variations with regularity or punctuations that *purposely* confound the listener? Or... was he trying to impress? Were they a *lively* lot? Or...Did they like surprises? Or was he just background noise...did the ladies' gowns on parade reveal more *decoltee* to his music, perhaps?..."

They giggled.

"In other words, once you've covered all the professional grounds, start using your own intuition, your own sense of deep-down thinking, your instincts as scholars and humans...Got it?"

Some smiled. Others stared. "So. Class Dismissed!" she finished.

They actually applauded her.

It surprised her when the girl from last week, Ms. Nolles came up to the lectern.

"I really enjoyed you class Ms. Wells...."

"Do you play any instruments?"

"I sing!"

"Oh, really?"

"Yes. Schooled, yes. But I'm in a band at the Elm Club. We perform first Tuesday of every month." She stopped.

"May I come and hear you perform?"

She grinned.

* *

By Wednesday, it was clear things were not getting any better with the investigation. She could hardly believe the questions that the Superintendent of New Scotland Yard was asking.

"And you assured the National Archives of the security of the Vault Ms Wells? ...Whatever were you hoping to have them *give* you Ms Wells...?"

 What was he implying? He would be in touch, he said, with a few more matters to discuss, he said.

Thursday was a relatively calm day.

Friday brought the class to a Break in the Spring teaching term. Mercifully, thought Amanda.

"Next week, we look at the case of the Performing Arts...Here's the twist: Following the readings, YOU get to Write *and perform* your own play!"

The idea stirred them to a measure of excitement and fun. Yes! No! They couldn't decide amongst themselves...until one bright soul declared himself the Director. The rest took off for a running start as to who was doing what.

 "Alright.... Alright!" she said finally. "Just six per group, once only, a one- hour play each group, starting next Monday. Remember, I want to see the script of each group early, and yes, props too for the century!"

The room was getting noisy, and someone opened the rear door and shut it again at the commotion.

"...After that" said Amanda over the roar "It's a month and a half of independent work on each of your research papers...which will be due by the end of the term for a final grade. Meantime, one short review paper from each of you, please, sent by email by the

20th of the month! At least one area of examination of forensic study in the Arts."

She left the class, and made her decision. At least her class was a lively lot enjoying the topic. Less encouraging, she noticed from her email, was the matter of the Department's Investigation.

She was pleased with how her class was going.

At home, she and Jack had a good meal. She talked to him.

"Someone will be checking on you daily" she told him as she washed the dishes. "But I...am going to Paris!"

Before packing she went to her computer for one last look at her message.

> *RE. Topic Neville. Republicanism was evidently built into his hereditary genetic code from an early age, and exposure. Read on! He was on the Board of the Virginia Company that settled Jamestown, in the new world...*
>
> *Nor was there much love lost on the Crown, evidently.*
>
> *Best , H*

* *

It's not that he *disliked* the cell he was detained in. Oh certainly, he was a prisoner like the others, and when push came to shove in these parts, the enemy used whatever quarters they could to garrison prisoners of war, but the truth of the matter was that he felt comfortable, if not entirely safe here. Why? Because he knew the premises quite well. Actually, he even felt rather at home, if not somewhat superior to the others because of that familiarity. At best, he knew what spots at this level were dry, warmer and deeper in the recesses of this vast structure built within the mountains of the Austrian border. At worst, it masked the new realities of all that he held dear.

His own family castle was less than five miles away, he told his neighbor.

They ignored him. The enemy had a way of leveling all. Even so, the time in this confinement was less a punishment to him than a chance to heal and recover from a grueling six weeks of resistance fighting, bunker living, and forced march before capture. Something he vaguely understood. Next, evidently, was intelligence.

Not that he had any understanding of what the enemy was after. But he suspected that like everything else in life, it came down to the usual contention of the socially privileged, the "haves" being pursued by the "have-nots". Or something like it, his school master once told him.

Still, the uniforms and the military precision with which these occupiers conducted themselves was entirely reminiscent of the Austrian-Prussian traditions of his own privileged family. So when they treated him like an equal and asked him to seek information and deliver it to them, he was easily swayed.

The question was, what in the world could he possible discover that they wanted to know? And from whom? Why?

Not that there was any activity in the hills and forests where he played as a youth companion to the Master Patrone's son. Not any more, they were long gone, the premises abandoned if not used to garrison Occupation forces instead.

But they knew he was a local with local ties. And they wanted to know about... the *mine?* What on earth for? Out of use, these days, like the rest of the economic activities of the region, but still, there was interest. What should he tell them about the mine. Nobody worked there anymore. It was closed with the war. The owners, the patron of the castle, as he was known, could no longer pay the workers! Everyone had been sent home. Including him and his family!

This puzzled him. Surely they knew this. Now that the war had begun, there were times when he looked up at the sky and saw RAF planes dropping bombs upon every strategic and population center they could find, including factories, foundries, commercial centers and transportation terminals. But certain spots remained untouched. Why?

They asked him, the Germans. What did the Foreman say about the crates and deliveries of the last shipments made from the mine? Was anyone talking? Did anyone hear of any interest for orders from the outside? Or did they receive general information about matters pertaining to the mining operations, like gossip - from former employees, now moved on?

He heard nothing, he said. But they pressed.

Accounts, lists, serial numbers or quantities of supplies ordered for the furnaces before the war began? Who had those documents? How much was smelted, who shipped out the ores mined? After all, so many had worked in the mine over the years! In fact, in that part of the world, where the mine was something of a generational employer, there would be many who still spoke of it. Hints, ledgers, connections with news from outside clients, old business contacts, or stored supplies and movements of shipments...They wanted to know. He was free to go, but he should be their friend, they said.

Then, just when they gave up on him, he discovered something that came from the most unlikely source. Something about the mine that might have currency, and it came from the hospital. Rather, the nurse who worked at the hospital because she was the wife of the Fish shop proprietor. A shop that kept the Occupation forces in fresh cod and place from boats that went out to sea daily - something the cooks relished as a food supply for their new Occupation masters.

Nor was it particularly important, really. Just the babblings of a wounded soldier urging his nurse to pass along news and information to his family, should he die.

A cargo load of processed copper, nickel and tin refined at the foundry was preparing to leave the dock! And when payment came for the workers, of which his father had been one, there would be money for his family...

Clearly, it was a ship quietly neglected at the docks with its cargo half loaded at the time of the invasion.

It's destination was Denmark. From there it was to go to Halifax. The lad thought about it. Should he bring it up? Probably they knew about it. And in truth, why should they not be aware of it? Besides, they had lost interest in him. So why volunteer?

He got away from a passageway that he knew led to an outside well, and he ran to the dock to see. That's when he made his decision.

The old vessel was a commercial cargo carrier showing its age, and no wonder it was disregarded. It had rust streaks; its rigging without halyard and a spreading oil slick at the waterline delivered a good deal of seepage had occurred from neglected pumping. No wonder it had been overlooked.

Until something caught his attention. No much, and perhaps due to the oil, it was hardly visible, but a slow soft bubble burped up at regular intervals. That gave the engine room away. Someone *was* below decks, and someone was preparing to move the old maiden. Not with the kind of normal smoke, flag and horn-blasting of the peace time, but in a quiet quest to leave the docks, at night perhaps.

Tonight, he would bounce over the rails and stowaway to Denmark. That was his decision.

Fifteen

There was nothing more glamorous, thought Amanda, that flying from Heathrow Airport.

Here the rich, the famous and the styles of the world had passed. Or so it used to be. Now it was jeans, shoes off, and metal detection scrutiny. Hardly a place to show off a Jersey knit suite if your bowler needed bomb inspection!

Still, as a child, she remembered travelling to her mother's destinations as an Unaccompanied Minor, they called her, and watching those white-gloved retro suits with matching raw silk shoes and bag. Or Gentlemen with their silver handled canes ushered by chauffeurs through celebrity photographers...If, as was often the case when her mother was conducting a particular search at an archaeological dig in the tropics, men wore tailor whites and Panama hats.

By now, her shoes were in a plastic bucket; her jacked folded under her laptop and her face emollients on full display in sandwich bags. Security measures against would-be terrorists. An ironic legacy, she thought sadly, of a Muslim culture that so cherished a woman's privacy in burka and veil!

Still, for dreamers, as one author said, all the world is beautiful. And dress well she would. Period!

The engines roared, she leaned back into her white pillow and shut her eyes, the fuselage raged at full throttle to gain altitude. This was so exciting. Paris!

She popped open her laptop and decided to do more research on what might have motivated the Neville to be a leader in the American Colonies, the Virginia Venture Company.

Sedition. Bitterness? Flight? Especially after being held in the Tower of London. Why would a Neville be at the heart of the Virginia Colonial Venture to settle the new world?

For ideas? For escape, from what? For Gold?

What motivated him? Who was he?

His family was engaged in minting coin. A Mint. A treasury! His wealth was for...what? A new world... A kingdom of princely dominion? Surely that would mean striking a trademark. A Stamp. Something uniquely of his own brand and currency value...

But what?

She researched the marks of ironwork, minting and silver productions. She found that early Lords found surface deposits of ores on their lands, a resource strictly controlled, but lucrative and if used for the minting of coin as currency. They produced money!

Such lords were given full rights of the soil, and with the Crown's trust developed over the centuries, producing ores for ironworks, armaments, coin minting and ship building. All of them employing furnaces that required vast water drainage systems and wood for fire build-up.

Such it was in Wales and South West England where the Neville's had ownership and rights and liberties for exploitation. Here was the region from which early American explorers and mariners like Sir Walter Raleigh had hailed. Known as "West Country Gentlemen" Or Country Party, they had long ties with the sea trades and mercantilism, chiefly because of the coastal seaways and creeks.

The use of coin for commercial transactions was key to the realm, if new.

During the late medieval period the demands for silver dictated all. However, that which was minted on English soil was problematic for the Crown, and without value.

Moreover, they were on soil privately held since the Magna Carter by ancient lords and barons.

One ancestral family was Neville.

Newly mined English silver was overshadowed by that entering the country as coin or bar in foreign exchange as payment for growing exports - wool and textiles.

"Ladies and Gentlemen" said the pilot "We are approaching Roissy Airport for a decent, please fasten your seat belts..."

The details started to blur. Amanda checked for source minerals. Was there a connection between Neville and the New World ventures that were commercial.

Amanda opened her own notes scratched up from a variety of public information sources and started a compilation of her own.

"At the close of the medieval period lead/silver smelting relied entirely on organic sources of fuel - brushwood in the wind-blown bole hearth - and charcoal in a series of bellows- blown furnaces. At the end of the 17th century the ore-hearth continued to be used in some mining fields."

So how did they know if Neville was involved?

She read on and discovered that at his mines, he was knee deep.

The Crown, evidently, was holding coin hostage as a choke-hold on all who would venture.

She consulted more researched notes...

"However, significant amounts of coal have been found in the residues from what is believed to be an ore hearth smelting operation, treating lead/silver ores, at *Combe Martin*, in North Devon, and dating from the late 16th century through to circa 1690.(10)"

These were Neville's own lands! What was he doing?

How did they process? Who was in search of ore, iron, silver, tin and brass?

She read the works of various scholars. Combe Martin was an archaeological site that shows what was used. Semi-anthracite of 8 to 10% volatile content. Such coals were mined in south-west Wales, close to the coast in Carmarthenshire west of Llanelli. Port books, cargo shipments overseas in the late 16th / early 17th century showed that the use of that substance was coastwise from the late 17th century. In particular, she noted, to the North Devon creeks.

Creeks from where early colonial ventures sailed!

Now she recalled her Early American Readings. What were the Gentlemen Ventures of the West Country asking the native Indians when they settled America? Not gold. Necessarily, but ores!

Further, they needed laborers.

"Their use in the late medieval period reflected the demands for silver mining and the availability of resources, both material and human.

Many, she knew began in regions of Europe from where great Princes of the Palatine had ruled and traded in technologies, arms, metals and other ironworks, including cannon. Many were Protestants of the Huguenot culture of the Crusaders, voyagers and legendary guardians of the wealth as independent campaigns, if once Catholic, so long ago.

But haulage of water carrying together with the increasing cost of labor, plus demographic decline, produced mechanized pumping by 1480.

Both smelting and refining responded too to the availability and cost of labor.

These were matters of resources considered for territorial conquest, power and defense.

Transition would affect the value of sovereign land holdings, and liberties of owners.

Smelting techniques, introduced into Devon from the lead mining fields, were adapted through experimentation in the late 13th / early 14th century. This allowed certain premium processing of the ores mined - resulting in the bole / furnace complex which satisfied the industry until superseded by new technology in the 16th century.."

The steward approached. She had to put away her work!

So, she deduced, while searching for ores in the new world ventures, they needed laborers! If not the Indians, then the need to attract settlers to the new world with the promise of land, as indentured servants! Feeling very pleased with herself for having found a motive, she switched off her laptop.

Except... ? Nothing!

She closed her eyes.

No. There *was* something that mystified her?

 It was dark, ugly and she'd deal with it later, something untouched, unconnected by dots. Yet trailing with blood stains! No! Enough already, she decided.

Only when the stewardess gave the signal to open electronic devices did Amanda unfold her cell phone for messages.

She texted to H: "Minting of coin, *for a new realm!*"

She opened her next incoming message, and her hand flew to her mouth. It came from Superintendent Philligrew at New Scotland Yard, she saw.

Unfortunately, she was at 25,000 ft altitude when she read Re: Investigation.

 "DO NOT LEAVE THE COUNTRY!"

* *

If he had any scruples when he left Hamburg, he would have none left before the end of the war.

Within five months of his arriving he had betrayed the ship that brought him. That was because he discovered what it held, after it slipped its mooring.

Not only did he find the cargo below decks in the hold where he hid, but the species room that held other precious metals, clearly bank collections leaving the country. Which bank? Who owned it? Rather, who had the authority to own it now that it had disappeared beneath the radar.

That is, until he found the Purser's Office, locked up and forgotten in the cold North sea conditions.

The ship that left Hamburg and arrived in Denmark had been allowed to leave the dock because she carried lumber on her top decks, and because she was considered empty of anything valuable. The lumber, it was thought, could build shelter for Occupation forces or for Detention quarters.

Lumber on an old steamer was good. So only a skeleton crew, mostly Polish, were allowed on board to man her; that meant only a couple of ships' mates, deck hands, two engine room mechanics and a cook.

The cook was local, someone the lad recognized from the next village. And by the second day out, when the lad watched the galley for food, he waited behind crates at one deck higher than usual. That's when the cook made the mistake of losing his way below decks in search of the Freezer section. ..

There was a confrontation. More like a conflagration when the cook came upon the lad suddenly, and the lad had no choice. He dispatched the cook and integrated into his role, topside. If anyone recognized the difference, none said so. Perhaps because of the

Luger sidearm in his holster visible just above the belt, where the cook's apron strings tied twice around the waistline. The lad wore it, along with the apron.

On arrival, If he thought he was safe, he was mistaken. The Polish Ship's Crew were rounded up and taken to a detention camp, him included.

That's when the cargo of the ship became useful to his survival. When moving about the ship below decks as a stowaway, he had found the Ledgers, the Ship's Manifests, Bills of Lading and the content of all that was held in the cargo hold. Even the Safe in the Purser's Room. The intelligence of what lay below decks saved him. Clearly, they were supplies and raw materials for Munition factories to be manufactured into wartime airplanes and arms.

But not for the Axis Powers. They were being delivered to the Allies under stealth, the crew executed because no informant came forward.

They rewarded him, the Germans, after the cargo was unloaded and carried off, by letting him continue as cook with a small rank. A rank that would later translate into a peacetime police officer's job. At least he could marry the girl that carried his child. For him, it was a living, even if he lost his soul earning it..That's what he told his family until he died.

What he did not know at the time was that the cargo was not destined for a factory, as was the bulk of the mined ores from his hometown. Rather, they were owned by those in the castle where he was rounded up at the start of the year. Owners that dedicated their resources to the Allies, lock stock and barrel. Even title to the mine. Something for which the owners were condemned, especially since they failed to amplify with details.

In fact, the Allies were sending this shipment to Canada as payment for Lend Lease, an arrangement whereby they paid for American assistance in metals and primary resources. Clearly the lad had fed the enemy a play-book pattern that would define the sinking of countless other deliveries moving across the Atlantic between the Allies. And surely, other spies amongst the Allies were enlisted to refine this countermeasure by the Germans. This, the lad suspected every time news of another sinking was announced. But he was the first.

He would stay in Denmark, he decided. The Luger was his only memorabilia of the war, and that became property of his son when the lad died, a grown man of 60.

That, and the socialist incantation about the monarchies of Europe rightfully overthrown during the great wars. His father had lived in a castle in Austria before WWII, after all. His son should be diligent.

* *

They had agreed to meet in the morning.

It was far into the night when the Dutchman offered to drive him back to Coquelles, Pas-de-Calais. From there, the student had his ticket for the Eurostar high-speed train across the Chunnel in his jacket.

They had chatted at the bar of the Café Grotto. They talked about things, even the women – those arriving at the bar - especially one requiring a little recess for "personal behavior," as the student put it. But in the end, they had decided to drive back to Calais together in the morning.

At 8.30 am, the Dutchman was standing beside his car eating a sticky bun and drinking a coffee. The youth appeared out of nowhere, he had managed a couple hours of sleep on a bench outside the café when it had closed, and was now glad to be getting his ride: France could be cold as the devil, he said, pulling up his leather collar.

The White Cliffs of Etretat would be visible shortly, Segor the Dutchman assured his passenger. "Tell you what...We have a few hours to kill, do you mind if we take in some tourist sights along the Normandy coast? I've always wanted to see those legendary beaches!"

The young man looked at him, puzzled, his face pale. True, the student had come to like his travelling companion, especially after a long night of drinking together. That is, following a successful exchange with the Antiquities dealer!

In fact, it was he who introduced them at the bar, after dinner. *That was Paris!*

Still, he was ready to go home now. He was hungry and cold, his leather jacket collar lifted up around his neck, even if the car was warm. Accepting a ride to Calais was one thing, agreeing to a deviation was another. He hesitated. Then he smiled. "Sure!"

"Of course, it's not necessary if you wish to go straight..." said Segor.

Why not? Besides, how much safer does it get than hitching a ride with a detective, right? "Why not!" he said. "We were all fighting in the same war" referring to the Normandy landing beaches of Calais. He added

"Would you mind if we stopped for a bite to eat on the way?"

The Dutchman smiled. "Not at all. Some good French onion soup with fresh bread, melted Swiss cheese; a good salad and a coffee, Si...? I am *hungry too!*"

They laughed.

"Sounds good to me!" said the young man inching down the seat for his head to lean against the headrest, relieved.

The Dutchman tuned the radio, his thoughts settling in for the road ahead.

The youth was English and offered to pay for the gas as he hitched. *Not bad!* After the Chunnel, he would go from Folkstone to London by train, he said. He was a student there.

The Dutchman was happy to oblige since he was driving to UK himself from Paris. And he accepted the Euros from his passenger for the gas.

They had talked about the Chunnel, the young man remarkably informed about its 31-mile rail tunnel linking England to France. Especially its construction.

"Oh yes?" said the Dutchman.

"It began with the idea of a French mining engineer in 1802 proposing illumination from oil lamps; horse drawn coaches and an artificial island mid-Channel... But it was the Frenchman Aime Thorne de Garmond who performed the first geological and hydrographical surveys between Calais and Dover in the 1830s for Napoleon III. Then, to build, it would have cost less than $7 million!"

The Dutchman laughed "Too bad his father invaded Russia!"

"When they built it, it was a BOOT. That is, a build-own-operate-transfer operation with a financing concession. The Trans Manche Link got the contract with private funding, imagine!"

"sounds like the Suez Canal..." said the Dutchman

"It cost over 5 Billion pounds"

"Really?"

"They cut through chalk marl with tunnel boring machines, and well, you know the rest..."

He did, and the Dutchman nodded.

The long two hour drive from Paris was passing quickly. But then, things can be conveniently delivered with a little patience. For one thing, the drive was pleasant. For another, this route was convenient enough from Paris to Calais without soliciting unnecessary attention from the French Metropolitan Police or traffic cameras. The Dutchman felt pleased.

A short break would suit him fine too. He'd been on deck for 24, and was now on his way back to the UK to brief his clients. What harm was there in a little fresh air? As for a detour along the way to their destination, well...

His intentions, what were they?

Well, in the first place to ply this man with questions, especially *where* he found the stolen artifact, and from *whom* it came in Cairo. Such things didn't crop up too often. He was a detective, after all, and meeting someone in a bar in Paris who knew a little something was rare enough.

But mainly, it was his own iterative thinking that he most relished.

Such as, how long had the item been in circulation? Who was the owner of the stolen property? Who were the principles involved, which museums and who were the antiquities dealers?

Not that his passenger was without brains. He talked a lot, and he liked the mechanics of things. How they worked, how it came about, always framing his thoughts like a scholarly paper to be delivered. He was after all, a student.

And what a coincidence, he was visiting France during his University break, just a weekend tour to Paris and back - he liked a good party! Doing the Paris thing...for a little fun with his "winnings," he said.

Paris had rewarded him well, all that money to spend from the sale of the relic...

Where did he get if from?

The student was willing to chat. It was an ancient manuscript found in the deserts of Egypt somewhere, discovered at a market kiosk bragging old stuff for any tourists who might listen...But it never sold.

Only the student recognized it as a value item! He became a real buyer, with real cash for the item. It came to him through a merchant in Cairo who had a shop in Turkey. And by the way, said the student, the detective should not consider *him* implicated in any malfeasance, of course.

No. Of course not!

Because by the time he acquired it, it had become legitimate and reported. The dirty dealing, so to speak, had been done. He was just a willing to buyer. He paid a thousand pounds for it. Cash!

The detective knew this. Jacques had informed him already how much was paid to the student for it: Jacques had given him close to a million Euros...

* *

"So, tell me what is the significance of this item?" asked the Dutchman, one hour into the drive from Paris.

"Well, it's an important Codex because it is Roman and believed to come from the Library of Herculeum. It is significant because it is the first document that defines a philosophical concept. One would like to think that the Emperor Claudius retired at Herculeum before the volcanic eruption. But we don't know of course"

"Oh"

"Anyway, there has been some forensic study, and the dates do fit. If it's authentic, and I believed it was, then it describes the strategy against the superior force of Greek heroic tradition. It marks the possibility of *cleverness* defeating brute powers, so to speak. And written by a Roman shows remarkable perspicuity, for its era."

"I see"

"Well it's a matter of historical significance, because strategy itself implies control over a situation - something we aspire to achieve today in the business world even!"

"Ahh..." they laughed.

"But it's unusual because we did not know they had such arguments in ancient philosophical literature. Since Homer we have seminal discoveries, like Sun Tzu, the Chinese General who wrote *The Art of War*, a book that celebrates cunning. And we have Machiavelli, of course. But strategic analysis is something we ascribe to the 18th century, like Napoleonic wars, Carl von Clausewitz or Jomini..." He glanced at his driver. "Sorry, I don't mean to be a bore..."

"No. Not at all. Is this of current interest then?"

"Oh yes. In the intellectual community, that is. There is work being done by Lawrence Freedman examining the history of human strategy. And of course, it picks up in the markets of art, books, antiquities, museums, libraries etc"

"So, err... The bidding for such an item must be high amongst these, err.. experts?"

"Oh it is. And getting stronger! That's why I was interested. I'm glad I bought it."

"But you sold it?"

"Yes. I'm relatively a small fish in the food chain. So, I'm glad I got in quickly and out, if you will" he said, tapping his chest where the money seemed to be burning a hole in his leather jacket.

"But legal..." scolded the Dutchman.

They laughed. "Absolutely!"

* *

The meal took place at the old Covered Market in Etretat. Of all things, they ate fish and chips out of a paper wrapped basket. That is, with mustard pickle sauce. Then they stopped at the raw bar and ate muscles. Coffee was welcome, and they meandered through the town like a pair of tourists.

They went to the Benedictine distillery and museum at Fecamp. But the Dutchman was most intrigued by the beaches. They discovered that during the eighteenth and nineteenth centuries, the local economy was so bleak that they burned kelp on the beaches for its iodine. The plumes of smoke from these beach fires could be seen well across the Channel, and many records were made of them by the British. An ominous sign, many thought, if not strange and Frankish. George Inness' painting "Etretat" made the white smoke clear in his painting.

The student was less interested. But the Dutchman insisted. "iodine is a rich mineral deposits found in Chile and it was a ...how you say...a world thing" He reversed the car along the cliff trails. "These cliffs are famous for their white face and sheer drops into the sea" he added.

"What for?" asked the Englishman. "What was it needed for?"

"They used it for soda, potash and iodine for medicines..."

"Ah" nodded the Englishman, looking out the window at a desolate landscape along the top of the cliffs, the wind blowing.

It was grey, icy cold and the gusts ripping without impediment across the high verdant fields that sprouted grass clumps all the way to the edge of the cliff edge.

The view across the sea was stunning. They got out of the car, closed the car doors, and walked a bit..

"You can see the beach, from here!" yelled the Dutchmen above the howling wind.

Down the side of the cliff, at a small dip along the parapet, a small pathway had been carved against the chalk cliff wall down to the beach. Much of it steeply inclined, some in graded steps all the way to the bottom where the seas roared in and out over rocks with the tide. .

"Imagine viewing the ocean ships from here" said the Englishman, knowing well the history of the English Channel and the many wars between the two continents.

The Dutchman pointed. "Over there, see that tower, is a signal. They used to send signals along the coastline for defense!"

They walked a bit, the sea calm, but the tide was clawing slowly at the north Atlantic rocks that lay at the foot of the cliffs. Some areas showed a modest ribbon of white beach sand. The rest was basalt rock and chalk cliffs, stubborn outcrops at the waterline where the sea surged and ebbed with thunderous fury. Few tourists could be seen, and of the occasional car that toured the road to the famed cliffs of Etretat, few lingered in weather like this. It was blowing.

"Windy!" said the Englishman, clearly with a little shivering.

"This? No. Not at all! *C'est rein!*" he laughed approaching the cliff top. It is calm, the tide out. "Where I come from, this sea is tame!" he laughed. "Come, we go down to the beach for a stroll, then you can say you have walked the French shores when you return to Folkstone, si?"

The youth glanced at his watch. Plenty of time.

"Why not?"

They could walk along the edge of the cliff to the recessed crevice where a step-way would lead them down to the beach, there perhaps to find the remains of some Atlantic debris...

The student moved along the cliff's edge, some twenty five feet from the recessed crevice.

It happened with a sudden jerk, and he was off his feet. The Dutchman rammed him from behind in a clean, powerful push.

The student shouted, threw up his arms flailing, his body well over the precipice.

Without waiting for a view of the impact, the Dutchman moved quickly down the steps of the cliff.

He had to rush. The tide was coming in, certainly.

Where the youth would have fallen was rock, ragged boulders that would soon disappear beneath the North Sea Atlantic Ocean.

He found the body face down, pulled the leather jacket off the student, one arm tangling and broken, then stepped quickly with giant leaps across the boulders as the gathering foam rose up with menacing force.

He managed the base boulders across the sand and gravel, leaped across a small brackish ponding from which he could reach the steps where the sea and the cliffs had carved out their own erosion frescoes.

Within minutes he was atop the cliff, he did not look down to see how the body fared. Instead, he observed no viewing tourist group in sight. Nor any cars.

Glad to get back into his car, he tossed the leather jacket on the seat beside him. He turned on the heater.

The tide would be over the rocks in twenty minutes from now, and the body washed out to sea.

He looked at his watch. He would have liked to return to the Benedictine distillery and buy that case of wine he saw in the gallery. But he must get going to Calais and get on the train to England.

He backed the car twenty feet, then over the turf to the road. It was drizzling now, soon it would storm. Thank God for the Chunnel. No gale force winds for a crossing!

He glanced down at the leather jacket beside him. He saw the bulge, and knew what it contained, the young man had pulled a bill from it at the Market to buy his chips. It was all there. Jacques had paid him well. Jacques was a reputable antiquities dealer, he always paid full price to any seller for anything valuable. That explained how Jacques attracted Europe's best prizes from private sellers. He would then offer his items for auction where the world's top collectors and museums would wait for anything he had...

Oh yes. There was some money there in that jacket. . The student thought to take the cash back to UK without having to declare taxes on it!

The Dutchman reached the highway and looked at his watch. Plenty of time to reach Calais!

He would empty the pockets later, then dispose of the jacket in a bin at Folkstone or somewhere.

The body would long be gone. The money taken, and no accounting of it would show up anywhere.

He was pleased with himself. Yes, he knew Jacques, and they often talked museum regulations together over a beer or at a café in Paris. It was his job, after all, to track down stolen items, detectives did that. Occasionally, he even helped Jacques on a lead with an enquiry about a theft from a collector or a dealer.

But this guy? No trace. No accountability. And no declaration of the cash received as payment from Jacques.

Jacques was the discrete one, never divulging information to anyone about anything. And he was always clean. No illegal activities., No underhanded acquisitions of treasure. Just a straight-out purchase for cash from a seller, the item provenance and described for the auction catalogues. He would list the seller as unknown. Always. That was Jacques. A very, very rich man as a result. Even if he paid the student close to a million for it.

This student? Who would know what happened to him? The money would be gone. That's all. Why ever tell Jacques? As far as the broker was concerned, he paid for the item in Paris from a seller who left town. Cash. No need for Jacques to be told anything by the Dutchman.

But damned, the kid was right about one thing. It *was* cold.

*

Sixteen

"Mesdames et Messieurs, Welcome to Paris!"

The announcement came over the speakers.

It had been a stormy landing. Temperatures fluctuating between moderate and unseasonable resulted in rain and lightening.

Wearing a comfortable Gucci cotton bomber jacket and versatile trousers from Uniqlo, she blended easily into crowd and passed through French customs with nothing to declare as a weekend traveler. But she felt troubled.

Once out the gate, she put down her Armani sheepskin bag and rifled through her briefcase to find the phone number of her contact in Paris for the Conference tomorrow.

She was about to flip open her cell phone when she saw him behind an armful of Spring Ephermals.

"Trevor!" she all but yelled.

He came forward and gave her a perfunctory hug.

"I'm a suspect!"

"I know" he said, thrusting the tall bouquet at her and steering her briskly by the elbow. "No luggage at the belt?"

"No. I'm a walk-on"

"Good!" he said, looking down at the remnant of a soggy wrapping.

"Keep moving..." he muttered softly, his smile firm.

Without breaking his stride, he took her luggage and briskly led her through the airport and towards a waiting black cab, her face partially obscured by the excessive foliage she was clutching.

"Trev..."

"Cell phone?" he asked. She handed it to him.

Outside, in the rain, an umbrella sprouted over her head, Trevor nodding to the taxi driver. He climbed in after her, dropping the wrapping to the ground where is slid through a street grill and down into the subterranean drain, taking her cell phone with it.

He sat beside her, crushing the snowdrops and bending the paper whites. The car veered into traffic and picked up some speed.

"How nice of you meet me at the Airport..." she began. The look on his face was something she had witnessed only once before. On a posting in the Middle East, a century ago.

She smiled resolutely, teeth clenched.

* *

"Good morning!" she said.

"I'm delighted to be here to present my paper on the influence of French writing on early English authors..." she paused, sipping from her coffee cup, and noticed only 6 people in the room, two of whom were administrators, and one being Trevor.

"Meme plus sans un gout de café d'ailleure!" she added in good public-spirit fashion.

The elderly couple at the rear chuckled

"*Qu'ell-est-sympatique!*"

Her paper delivered, she felt a little cheated by the early morning slot and lack of interest and sparse attendance.

Outside, in the Hotel Lobby, staff were setting up tables and posters advertising the event. By lunchtime, the excitement in the air would be audibly growing. Those arriving from distant institutions were meeting and greeting to refresh and renew their professional networks.

"So what would you like?" asked Trevor.

She wanted to say that she wished her paper were better prepared. Or that she had center stage in an auditorium filled to capacity with an Oscar winning performance and a red carpet reception. She wanted to whine about being the first paper to present, and ..."

He was pointing to the sign behind her "Hot dog or pizza?" he said.

She glowered at him.

She thought she heard her name, and a stout looking administrator with a large nose approached. He had notes in his hand.

Trevor smiled, spun Amanda in front of him and pointed to the entrance with a quiet "I'll meet you outside!"

"I have two messages and some phone calls for a Ms Wells, if she would be kind enough to wear her

Conference badge...She has some acquaintances wanting to reach her, err Monsieur...?"

"Ms Wells will be here for the Reception tonight..." Trevor was saying as he took the badge. "How thoughtful. Thank you!"

He was firmly steering her through the door.

"Well that was clever...I want my pizza!" she protested like a child. He gave her an admonishing look and stuffed her into a bright yellow taxi. He looked out the rear window.

"Good" he said "You're done. And out of there!"

"Look. Would you mind telling me what is going on?..." He ignored her.

"OK. So. You hijacked me at the Airport, "coincidentally" arrange to get me to present my paper at the crack of dawn – with no audience... get whisked away from the conference -without so much as a hot dog – and here we are in another taxi!"

"Well the paper is entered in the Proceedings isn't it?"

"Now. Officially. Yes. May I ask where we are going?"

"To a Hotel"

"But I am booked in a Hotel..."

"...where it's safe..."

"Safe?... for *what*?"

"...for you to meet someone!"

"Who?"

He opened the door to a Hotel suite.

The white satin, gold, glass and baroque either belonged to a Hollywood movie set or was authentic Art Nouveau, she couldn't decide. Trevor moved to an Inner Suite and knocked softly.

"I brought you here to meet...an old friend" he said, opening the door.

Jacques de Torraine stood up from a group of men, handsome as ever and entirely dressed in black. His angularity and height cut a stunning figure. If a little grey at the temples.

"Cherrie, mon Dieu!" he said advancing with his arms open for a big hug.

Amanda recovered nicely. "Jacques! How nice to see you again. I had no idea..."she began and hugged. Trevor was already shaking hands and introducing the other three Gentlemen in the room, all seated with morning coffee.

"Please, take a seat?" said Jacques, chivalrous as ever.

The chit chat was pleasant enough, but Amanda was uncomfortable.

"We have something we want you to...Well, examine..." Jacques paused to search her face, giving her time to digest the full content of what had just happened.

"It's just that what we have is priceless...and we want to be sure that first, it is authentic, and second, we can insure it and keep it in a safe place...?"

Amanda's face was steady, her eyes vacant.

Trevor stood up to hand her a coffee. *Cream and sugar be damned.* It was a moment more he was giving her to collect herself.

Jesus!

"Well. I'm flattered Jacques..."she began "You are, after all one of the world's most eminent Antiquities dealers..."

"Brokers!" he interrupted, nodding to the collective group as a whole. "Yes. We each have our Galleries in cities all over the globe for private investments and bank securities..."

"But surely there are experts better than I...."

"Non! Non! Pas du tout!" he stuttered. "You are by far the best, the most informed, and the ..the ..prettiest!" he added with a self satisfied grin.

How many languages the other man spoke she could not tell. But they were all nodding politely, except for one, a pale faced man, aged in his mid-something and indeterminable since his head was completely shaven. He smoked incessantly, cool, from the Netherlands, they said.

"You see Amanda. It is a manuscript of the 17th century. A lost work that could change the course of historical understanding...and even create a...a...how do you say?" he looked at Trevor who said nothing "a havoc of trust amongst fidelities in the trade of valuables...you understand?"

The others grinned like school-fellow conspirators, all. As if she were some bloody fool.

"So, err... we wanted to ask if you could study it and give us the benefit of your opinion." He looked up for general concurrence from the rest.

"In secret of course!" he added, looking now directly at Trevor.

She could sense from Trevor that this was no time to contradict this merry bunch of cutthroats.

"Well. If it's alright with my, err... academic authorities to do so..." she laced about with ingratiating accommodation.

"But of course! That is why we have Trevor to assure you of the common interest amongst us all..."

He certainly had the bases covered decided Amanda.

No amount of words was going to change the script in this room today. So she stayed with banalities. Easy to do when in Paris...and allowed the meeting to close with as much grace as she could muster. And the sooner the better.

Before leaving, the Dutchman from Netherlands asked her about the investigation at the University. It took her completely by surprise.

He was with the Police, undercover, of course, since he was wearing a stylish black leather man's coat.

But of course.

* *

Trevor. She would kill him she decided.

They were sitting at a Bistro in Paris, ostensibly au outdoors, but insulated from the winter by a warmly heated porch. The streets were dark now, void of children and winter tourists. Yet Paris was remarkably mild for February.

Trevor had avoided the subject of Jacques the moment they stepped from the Hotel d'Holland, insisting, instead, that they Seize the Day.

Three Museums later, her patience was running on empty and her hands freezing. He had marched her through two shopping districts and even taken a carriage ride around the Champs a Lycee!

They walked, in silence.

She turned to confront him, her breath a coil of warm steam in plunging temperatures.

"What do you think I am...?" she began "my forensic analysis is not for sale!"

"What ever do you mean?"

"I mean you are not to offer my professional services to the highest bidder on the black-market..."

" Jacques...is *not*..."

"Not for anyone! Nor anything! For any price! Get it?"

"Jacques is not without a reputation of the highest integrity..."

"that's never been *entirely* clear!" she said.

"Look. You've got this all wrong. There is a lot riding on this.."

"You mean money..."

"Well, yes. That too. But, wait, it is of interest to our Government."

"Sure!"

"And in case you haven't noticed. It is worth killing for."

"What are you talking about?"

"What do you think that caper into the Vault was about... Even the boy's death!"

"What are you saying?"

"You've been framed. Look. The log book. Your professional integrity is being tarnished to undermine *your* credibility. Because you are a likely target to expose the truth behind one the most incredible cultural assets we've got..."

"What?"

"And I don't want you hurt!"

He rummaged about inside his vest, beneath the winter coat, and pulled out a brown envelope.

"What is this?" she asked.

"Read!...Please! By tomorrow. Just read this thing..."

"Let me guess. At the Hotel d'Holland?" Her anger was threatening to overtake her.

"I just want to make sure that we play good tourists... As a safety precaution!"

"Wait. Why?..."

"Don't tell me...we're being followed...?" she began, almost laughing.

He turned, pulling her forward, their breath mingling in the cold air and he embraced her quickly, kissing her harshly.

It was a good ten minutes before they talked, walking now.

"That was for fun, right?" she said, struggling to read the situation.

"God. But you're difficult!"

"No" she said breaking free, stunned. "...I'm *easy*!"

She took to walking.

"That's not true. You're a strong woman. We are going to get through this. We need to stay calm. Until things settle down in London. We're working on a few contacts in New Scotland Yard."

"We?"

"And I need to keep you sequestered as you read this stuff..."

"Jesus!" she breathed. "Are you serious?"

"Deadly serious." He tucked in her scarf. "Come on. Let's get out of this cold." He put his arm through hers.

"Taxi!" he hailed. "Your things have been delivered to the suite. You're safe there. And it's quiet and private for the duration..."

"The manuscript?"

"This is just the rubric. The rest is waiting for you in my safe."

All through dinner she sat there; he, without comment, sampling culinary treats, wine and a dessert. Money was not an issue evidently. Tasting was.

Amanda watched the night lights outside dance in the winds like undernourished Arctic birds. The music playing softly did little to calm a mounting turmoil within her head.

The evening ended at the door of her room in the Hotel Holland.

"Just read it!" insisted Trevor. 'That's all I ask. Tell me if it's authentic. If it rings true. If it speaks of matters held long ago that have been buried for centuries..."

"How would I know...?"

He paused. "You ... read Elizabethan English with your breakfast croissant!" he said.

"This makes me sound like some religious freak...like reading the King James for daily sustenance"

"Not an unworthy thought! Actually, as a barrister, I wouldn't mind if more of our stranger societal elements would read an occasional holy scripture or two..." he smiled.

"Very funny. That's what the Crusaders said..."

"And so shall you... when you read this testament! He raised his forefinger in wisdom. *'For to understand the language of medieval diplomacy, speak only the language of God'*"

She eyed him suspiciously. He had moved to the windows, and had drawn the curtains.

"That's nice. So what am I supposed to do? Brief you on God's Creation?"

He looked up "No. Just man's New World."

He closed the curtains.

"Please! I'll want the morning sunlight. This is Paris..." she began

He turned. "I want to know who was behind the money laundering scheme of the early 17th century!"

"Oh. You mean *for* the New World?"

"No. I mean to *create* a new world."

"What's the difference?"

"Anachronism! I need a piece of provenance - evidence of some kind to make a case for a larger issue..."

By now Trevor had toured the room. He touched under the art nouveau lamps, peered under their shades, passed his hand across large glossy pictures on the wall like some secret-wristed magician.

"Stop this!" She stamped. "What are you doing? I came here for a legitimate Conference. What's all this conspiratorial behavior?"

"Your security" he said calmly. Then he headed demurely for the door.

"Why not ask an Appraiser?"

"Because...its not insured, it's a private collector's tax-sheltered asset..."

He turned to her. "Look. You're a suspect now. Once New Scotland Yard questions you, the information will be out about the forensic integrity of some evidence we need..."

"*New Scot...?*"

"And yes, what you are being asked to review for Jacques is something people on the black market easily kill for...You're looking at an original!"

"*What?...*"

"And if the black market is interested, then we know it's the real deal...!"

"You should have asked me first...I'm a scholar"

"Precisely" he said, standing very still.

"I'll call you later," he said softly "and be careful with that thing. It's worth a King's Ransom!"

"Why should I do this...?" she said to the closing door. His head reappeared. "For Justice!"

She sat, her thoughts whirling.

Barely had he left the room when someone came knocking, and Amanda flung open the door brusquely. The housekeeper curtsied. "Pour Mademoiselle, si'il vous plait"

She was holding a silver tray. On it was a rose across an embossed card. Only in a baroque hotel like this did such things happen. She smiled graciously at the housekeeper and took the message. Not the rose.

"Merci!" With another curtsey the girl left.

"Oh, Madamoiselle!" called Amanda after her "...de caffe s'il vous plait?"

"Oui Madam!"

The card was an invitation for dinner from Jacques de Torraine. 7 pm. Tomorrow evening.

"Great!" she sighed. *And Why not*?

First though, much as she resented Trevor's pre-emption over her precious hours in Paris, she had some reading to do. She would take a shower first.

Seventeen

The folio was leather bound, laced with throngs, and definitively a 17th century document. How it got itself bound without being an officially printed document, she noted, suggested an owner of means.

Clearly, a Treatise. Old English. Yet French-made, she observed.

Half wondering what language it would be in, she opened the leaves carefully.

When Amanda put down the folio, she has been reading for four hours.

As a PhD Historian, her training drew knowledge from Research. Analysis. Readings. Peer Reviews. Proceedings. Contradictions. Papers. Thesis. Dissertations. These were the tools of her discipline. And if understanding today meant assessing the thinking of yesterday, then she had performed her professional duties faithfully.

But this?

This was different. This was *not* a study of any kind. It was a personal account. A commodity in its assessment, if in today's world.

The manuscript held the heart of the author. It revealed the identity of the author of one the world's most known works. And not just the works, which were remarkable, but the reason for its secrecy - its treachery and duplicity - if not a revelation of the early modern world that it helped shape.

The narrator, moreover, knew what was stake. *Even four hundred years ago...*

Amanda could hardly believe what she was seeing.

 "Blackfriers"

"You may call me what you Will, if you will pardon my pun, for I am about to tell you a story so true that it can only be told as a tale. But be ye warned, for in revealing the world upon this stage, you shall find you mocked, for I unmask a human. A dreamer.

I begin with my Master, my Lord.

Born in the same province as my father, in the year of our Lord 1562 in the household of the Queen's own knight. He was christened in this very chamber, being firstborn to the Lady Gresham, a London Lady of the Commerce, and the babe named after his father, Sir Henry Neville.

You shall know him well. For it is he of whom I speak. First, be mine telling of the happy states upon this stage, for they were many...

* *

For daywear, she'd been wearing a J. Crew Stretch shirt, and while it absorbed the body temperatures of a tumultuous day, it was now definitively ready for laundering. It had been a long day, and she had dozed off a bit.

She was feeing a little stronger. Fresh croissants and coffee had been delivered.
"Merci beaucoup!" she said.

She opened her suitcase and laid out her belongings, perhaps for freshness, perhaps for bearings. She had packed for the Conference.
For her presentation, she had chosen to wear the tweed jacket and skirt, and it was Chanel. She walked into the bathroom and took a shower. She watched the water swirl before her.
Her thoughts were elsewhere.
What was he saying then?

She wanted to return to the manuscript. She walked about. She would lay out her clothes for the evening with Jacques. Then she paused. She found her hair brush.
Ben Johnson, she knew, was involved in putting Shakespeare's name on the First Folio editions of his plays. But that was in 1623, and only at the behest of a college in London associated with the Neville Family.
This, however, was dated *1615!*
She sat down.

"...For it is, gentle Lord, that the monarchies were for themselves in crisis. And in a state of perpetual need. – Nay, did I rather say, greed?"

"Here, the young lad Neville would write, and with me from his countryside, his true identity was unmasked. For I, the lad's country land friend, an actor, am Shakespeare, his friend and troupe master only. He, the author of the plays! Not I

"And know thee well, that this son born to Henry and Elizabeth Neville was to rule the world, as had his ancestors. Theirs was a great kingdom of kingmakers and merchants. A family whose pen would reshape the new world with new words and new ideas. As firstborn to this second marriage, his name would be Henry Neville, after his father, as I have thrice told.

She barely heard the phone ring with her hair dryer on. The French accent was unmistakable

 "Allo Mademoiselle...j'espere que tu est en receipt de mon billet doux?"

"Hi Jacques!" she laughed "Yes I received your billet doux as you must call it"

"Dinner then, at 7. I pick you up...my most delicious Princess d'Engleterre!"

"Jacques. I'm an *American*. .."

"But your grandmother...eh bien. She was Anglais, n'escet pas?"

"Yeah. You got me there!"

"Al'ors, a tout a l'heure!" he said, and hung up.

Geese. The guy had a way about him. What should she wear?

He was a dresser. That was for sure. If not a dresser, then a poet. And hey, this was Paris!

But she'd play it safe, anyway, and pulled out a wool jacket and pants, if Louis Vuitton. Hell. He'd know the color of your underwear with his French eyes. She would have laughed, but as the clothes went on, she stopped demurely to ask herself if this was real.

Was it possible that another man wrote the Shakespeare plays? If so, why was this man so hidden? Rather, what did he have to hide? Or... to give... that was so secretive?

Trevor had called. "Say hello to him from me...will you? That 'll keep him honest!"

"Trevor!" admonished Amanda.

"So. I guess you've got your cozies. And I'll see you...err in the morning?"

Later that day, she found herself waiting. But not for long.

Jacques did notice everything. He arrived, of course, with a bouquet of white roses, which naturally fit the décor of the room.

"Lunch" she said without further adornment.

"Lunch then" he said.

The Bistro that Jacques picked came from a demand made by Amanda who said she was hungry. Or anxious, she wasn't sure which. And no city-touring, please!

No need to replicate the path taken by Trevor, thank you.

"Ahh..I know just such a place. It is for the artists. The writers..."

"...the anarchists.." she interrupted.

He stopped. "Please Amanda! We no longer have anarchists. We have only deal-makers!"

She laughed.

"And good food..."he added as they entered something like a subterranean grotto on the Left Bank.

They were seated across from a stone hearth burning red hot coals. January of Paris, Bordeaux wine and stew provincial filled her veins and her consciousness like a potion.

"So...what are you working on now?" he asked

She told him. "Kingmakers!"

"Oh? Tell me all."

She did.

"Back in the days when England and France were One..." she giggled, weaving together the fingers of both hands.

Like a magician, the world of Jacques was shrouded with mystery and intrigue. He could evoke imagination with the look of his eyes, especially as the candles flickered at his elbow. He was encouraging her, beckoning with the effects of an aphrodisiac ...

"... Decedents of Gilbert who was steward to William the Conqueror, Neville would stand at the side of the king. Alan de Neville was made Chief Forester for King Henry II in the late twelfth century"

"the 12th Century?" He raised his wine and drank. "To the Forester!" he hailed.

"Most importantly" she proceeded "the family married into the royal family, and descended from the marriage to Joan Beauford, daughter of John of Gaunt, Duke of Lancaster - firstborn to the crown of England!"

"Later…" she sipped "in the line of descendants, Richard Neville, Earl of Warwick, was known as the 'Kingmaker.' That was in 1428."

She leaned back, her eyes gleaming.

Jacques, for all his larcenous heart, was rapt.

She went on. "His brother Edward, Baron of Welsh Abergavenny regions, became the great grandfather of a succession of heirs and heiresses close to the throne - one of whom was not only godson to Henry VIII, but rumored to be the King's illegitimate son."

"Well now I *am* interested!" beamed Jacques

"He received an annual Royal Annuity of £20; and subsequently, he was executed in 1539 for implications in the Courtenay Conspiracy – cited as a claim to the throne itself! " she said.

He raised his eyebrow, Amanda proceeded.

"Where …do you go with this story, Amanda?"

"OK. His mother was found with incriminating 'Letters' and an 'appointed' campaign banner with markings: Designed to be paraded around the villages, they were to rouse-up men to rebel against the Crown declaring Courtenay Heir-Apparent to the throne…"

Jacques was polite, but getting suspicious. He poured her more wine.

She proceeded with a tone approaching intimacy.

"Edward's mother, you see, was Gertrude. Someone whom Henry VIII …may have bedded but was later found to be too close to Catherine, a Catholic, the wife Henry must divorce…"

She straightened up. "England was until that moment, as Catholic a realm as any other realm in Europe! And, as you know, the only way that Henry VIII was going to be released from his first marriage by the Pope was to eviscerate England of all her Catholic ties!"

"Ahh!" said Jacques. "I knew there was a reason!"

"He accepted the Protestant Faith for England" concurred Amanda.

Suddenly, her thoughts fled the room and she was thrust back into a fierce reality: So braided were ties with the Catholic past, that England was divided in heart and mind for centuries..."

"and...?"

"Shakespeare included!"

Amanda stopped short.

"Amanda! What is it...?" said Jacques.

"Oh, excuse me. Nothing!"

Little did he guess that she was telling him the identity of the author whose plays she was verifying for authenticity.

Amanda was definitely feeling dizzy, something she knew instinctively that Trevor would not approve. Not here. Not tonight. Not with this information.

"Anyway..." she continued "the boy's appearance - he resembled a Tudor, even to two generations, alongside Queen Elizabeth, all them redheads...?"

"So tell me mademoiselle" said Jacques leaning forward "And what has this to do with your stay in Paris?"

She looked at him soberly, if that were possible. And she chuckled.

"Nothing!" she chuckled. "Nothing at all!" she drained off her wine. "Just English history!" She looked at him. "Boring as ever..." she added, her eyelids heavy.

The desired effect was complete. Within minutes, Jacques had lost interest and spotted someone leaning against the bar.

Actually, someone she had been met earlier.

The Dutchman, introduced to her as an Investigator of the case, was one of the group with Jacques at their meeting. Jacques hailed him over. They exchanged polite commentary about the Police Chief.

They laughed, drank and as the evening wore on, they became acquainted.

Her head was swirling with wine. She turned to Jacques and focused intently on his eyes not to lose her train of thought, a question came to her from a girl leaning over from the table behind them.

She turned to Jacques. "I'm to ask you, from the girl behind me. Why does the Dutchman carry a a...whatummyoucallit..."

Amanda turned to the girl again for the word, wondering *what* it was she had to recite, or why.

"A Luger"

"A Luger?" she repeated.

 It brought a laugh.

"It's a ...novelty!" said Jacques "For...nostalgia" he said, shrugging and draining off his wine. "His father gave it to him!"

She wasn't sure if it was.

Emily broke the spell. A call came in on her cell. Rather, the cell phone that Trevor had given Amanda, because he had lost hers. She had added the number to her closest contacts, Emily was one of them.

She answered. "Ohh...Emily, how *are* you?...What? I'm sorry I can't hear what you're saying...I'm having a wonderful time. Here's where I am!" Amanda looked around and snapped shots on the camera of the iphone. She snapped for the grotto bar; the company she was with; the waiter, the flagstone walls of *La Bastille*, of Jacques...the Dutchman...

"Sending!"

She couldn't quite hear what Emily was saying. Again she repeated her words. Finally she heard Emily's voice. The connection was not clear. Something about Her place... had been ransacked...They *were searching for stuff...* and took some mementos that "belonged to Edward." She didn't feel safe, she was saying.

 "Hide out at my place. Jack will protect you!"

Amanda told her where the entrance key was.

Before leaving the Restaurant, the Dutchman turned to Amanda suddenly. "How well did you know the Vault Manager, Robertson?"

The question threw her. *Who was this man?*

"Why?"

"New Scotland Yard had just issued a report through Interpol that the vault manager, Robertson, has been in a car accident and is dead."

"Where?" asked Amanda, her stomach turning over.

"Wales."

* *

Eighteen

She woke up at two in the morning in a cold sweat, her head throbbing.

If Jacques had had his way, they'd still be in a cavern sipping high priced cognac!

She reached for water and gradually came out of a stupor.

Something was wrong.

She pulled herself to together. The work was still there. Her thoughts ran not to the events of the evening with Jacques, but to the materials in her room.

Why hadn't someone spotted this question of the author's identify before now? Where the hell was the academic community on this one? All those experts; prose specialists; scholars and linguists? To say nothing of medievalists; historians and career scholars whose entire reputation rested on publishing material that...

She drank more water.

Impossible!

She lay resting against the headboard of her bed, already knowing the answer. Scholarship was not thorough. Sketchy at best, hobby-historians and traditionalists ruled the realm of reality. Usually men, lacing romantic storytelling for social value at the dinner table. It could happen. It had happened - where facts were far from the reality!

Add modern-day scams...And you're off and away with the band as her grandmother would say. In such a world, there was incentive and means to produce any kind of result.

Then there was the passage of time...

Yet the study of history could be forensically discerning. If the puzzle fit.

Henry Neville was indeed a member of the London Virginia Company Council that sent John Smith to settle Jamestown: He even provisioned lumber for shipbuilding to carry settlers to the new world!

She read.

"Hence what shall I say of this world? That God did create the Kings as the Moneychangers of the Temple? Or that Christ should come for the lowly to stand upon a rock, free of things temporal and free of things spiritual? And should they not be free to trade, then to start a new heaven and a new earth? A new world?

"From Norfolk they had originated, where the great grandfather James, having as baron, a grasshopper on his shield; a G upon a Mount of Gaunt, Neville Royal, built a great manor house and sailing his ships to Antwerp and the Low Countries for cloth, then adding Bordeaux and Venice to their trade routes."

Even those parts known as the Navarre territories.

I digress...

"His nephew, Thomas Gresham was the Founder of the Royal Exchange, that place of money for all who would trade!

Aye. And one of the best known Merchants in Elizabethan England.

He it was that granted the Gresham College, at Holt, with mission words that would ring long as being the First of all sayings named Gresham's Law, that "Bad money drives out good" to mean by it that money of gold could be hoarded by Ordinary people -even if the governance introduce lesser metals...and thus the power of the poor to trade as ordinary men."

Amanda lifted her eyes from the parchment. What was he implying?

"Aye, and it is that Thomas owned an iron works, that is, an arsenal where he manufactured cannon. A matter of some dispute, I am told, in the Houses of Parliament, and used as defense upon ships of trade, including one commentary by Sir Walter Raleigh for the creation of their new world of the America.

"Also metals, for the purposes of minting coin:

Before times, the Great Bishop George Neville of Durham Castle, in the rule of the early Henry VII did mint coins with his seal of the double rings, and the markings of the letter G. Such were the authority of that Lord Spiritual in England who ruled."

* *

By the time Trevor showed up, Amanda was ready for New York.

Wearing a Donna Karan blazer and pants, she greeted him at the door. "Get me out of here!" she demanded

He grinned. "Is the lady upset?

"Damned right I am!"

He walked over the table with the manuscript and opened his briefcase. "May I?" he asked, his hand out.

She nodded. He locked the briefcase and stood there, waiting.

She gathered her things, and looked at him.

He lifted the sleeve of his suit to check his watch.

"Time to go!" he said calmly. On his wrist was a silver bracelet. He was chained to the briefcase.

She was torn. Undecided about telling him, her thoughts in turmoil.

She told him. In the cab, on the way to the airport she said "Its authentic alright."

It was raining.

"How ...do you enter a world of intrigue...peopled with concepts and words that must hang like jewels in your mind - words that could so make or break your future, and not feel *desperation*?" she muttered.

She turned to him. "The agony, the possibilities of...creating a new world...are here at once immediate and indescribable!"

"How do you mean?" asked Trevor gently.

"It was...a sort of missing technology. Justice. Just thinking."

Trevor looked at her closely.

"*Let me lay my head Westward* said Sir Walter Raleigh to his executioner ...*so that I may face the new world as I die..*" she said, her eyes moist.

Trevor squeezed her hand. "It is on their dreams that we stand today" he said. "Nothing is for naught."

"Do you really think so?"

"I know so!"

Trevor saw her through the Gate.

"Here" he said, pressing tickets into her hand.

"Wait...what's this?" she said.

"Your next flight out. It stops at Luxemburg. Then lands two hours... later"

Amanda looked at him blankly. "Why?"

"Ok" he said looking down to avoid alarm. "So I changed your flight. A security precaution, that's all. Sorry. I should have told you."

Amanda knew better than to question Trevor's security. That world, with deadly realities, was not a safe place.

She took a deep breath for her thoughts to absorb his change of venue.

"They have a decent meal on that flight. And there's browsing in an Airport that sells duty-free stuff" he smiled.

"Like gold coins, mebbe?" she added with a strong urge to antagonize.

"Nobody to apprehend you at the airport when you land at an airport they aren't watching..." he said.

"Ok. So. I'll see you back in London?"

He grabbed her shoulders and planted a conspicuous peck on her forehead for all to know she was not an unaccompanied passenger, adding in her ear "the Ladies room to change clothes is one hundred meters to the left once you get passed the restricted gates. Lose the admirer with the poet's hair who is watching you!"

Forty minutes later she was flying at 35,000 feet, her thoughts dwelling upon the events of 400 years ago.

"But did I speak of the treachery of kings as was done to him? All written as he lay in the Tower, writing the history of Kings. From the forbidden manuscripts of his family tale, the Leicester's Commonwealth whose vision for the new world are said and spoken. And where he made his mark many times upon those sheets with many works.

"In the very Tower of London did my Lord write upon paper thoughts of his heart that would later read in the play. Aye, I did insist upon it, of ol' Henry VIII. For there he was placed, my Lord was, Sir Henry Neville, for the events of that time...And there be the truth of things, even those events of that time. Which only God's Eyes can see, and hear in the beating of man's heart, and witness, to which I do add my testimony for posterity.
"It was to be, I do recall, for the Rebellion of Essex that he was put in the Tower of London for to be beheaded. Which only if he do not tell, his head he would keep.
"Thus many a secret he did keep, in the writing of his plays. Alas, Aye, more than any is his secret name. Falstaff was not a name he named. But one recalled. For it was to be first named Oldcastle. A pun of antonmony from his word "New Town."

Amanda knew the Shakespeare plays. She had even seen an original copy. The real question was, *who wrote the plays?*

People had been led to believe for centuries that it was Shakespeare himself, the young actor...

And if not him...then who?

Why?

Amanda knew that in Feb 1601 several men were sent to the Tower of London to wait for sentence on their fate from the Court Council: A case for treason had been cited.

Treason to seize the throne of England?

Queen Elizabeth was dying without heir. Who was to succeed her? Who stood to gain, she wondered.

Essex was executed for treason.

Lord Henry Neville was also in the Tower of London where he was furnished with pen and paper. Here in this family were secrets that suggested a subverted rule. Perhaps intended to set up a new kingdom of rule...with new *moneys*...?

Secrets to die with Neville? Or secret enough for the family to keep?

The Earls of Rutland and Southampton were incarcerated also. As was Lord Cromwell, who was brought to trial with Lord Sandys in Westminster Hall. Lord Cromwell was fined $3000 and placed under house arrest. Years later, Amanda knew, he would lead a rebellion, the English civil war!

Yes, she decided. This was a power struggle. She read on.

"You must understand this, though said it never was. That it was for us to serve the hearts and minds of the English...as it were...not the Church!

Was God a puppet? No. For my father did whitewash the walls of the church, one day a catholic, another not.

"Now did I tell you how we had the money. And why it was that the London merchants did sail the seas, pay for the Navy and conquer other worlds?

Or should I say, who it was and why my Lord did have his heritage of the realm?

His mother, it was, Elizabeth Gresham, daughter of John Gresham whose family had traded in the oversea venturing for centuries. He was Lord Mayor of London in 1547.

And it was of this ironworks that my master did inherit, and did soon write upon in his ways.

Upon the death of his father and uncle, he did inherit the ironworks, this babe would. He would visit the Jewish Ghetto in Venice; and Elsinore in Denmark in the knowledge and furtherance of his iron and ordinance business. And it is from this moment that he should be so knowledgeable, my lord, to have penned the play called the Merchant of Venice and The Comedy of Errors.

"Indeed, it is in such matters of wisdom that my Lord was so great. He know of the steel, for it is more than many times written in his works, and iron, so many times mentioned. Cannons and Ordnance of many times even Touchstone of metals and Gods gifts to mankind. Even words as dross and uneal'd. These worlds you shall find in his writings of the Plays "As you Like It" if you please. It doth give the little man a moment of importance to hear such ring and tone in his plays, doth it not?

And now it is, with this poor hand, that I testify my dear lord in the Tower, writing for the Lords Beamont, Fletcher and King James I...but never his own name, here concealed... In our Lord's year of Anno Domini 1616."

* *

Nineteen

London, Kensington

Amanda backed the Bentley carefully into the designated garage space.

She closed the garden gate behind her, and skipped up the black wrought-iron stairs to the Palladian townhouse.

The kitchen staff were preparing a light dinner, and she found them.

They both came forward with a big hug for Amanda.

"How long are you staying Ms Amanda?" asked Fred Peters.

"Oh, for the summer I should think. Then I'm off to New York for a three month course on high-tech forensics!"

"God" said Susie, his wife. "That sounds like Fred's cooking!"

"Nonsense!" laughed Amanda. "You're both the best...We're so lucky to have you here!"

"Thank you" Fred said. "Your father is due in tomorrow. He's flying in from Rome at midday. I'll be picking him up in the car from Heathrow Airport"

Mr. Wells was a well know Boston Real Estate Developer. He loved his home in London, especially at Christmas time.

"Have you had many visitors?"

"Tons! It's been non-stop for six weeks" said Fred. "And I can't get Susie away from the donations paperwork to do any *real* work!"

"Good strategy" giggled Amanda "...and good for scholarship funding..."

"I'll ignite the fire" said Fred.

Amanda pecked Fred on the cheek and danced out the kitchen, through marble hallways of the Edwardian house, then up the circular steps two at a time.

She switched on the lights to the familiar bedroom, took her shower and pulled a white mohair sweater from the Louis XIV chest of drawers. She came back down to the library to examine her tray of mail. Mainly journals, books and pamphlets. She loved them all – the reading of the content, the messages, meanings, missions represented... She grouped them into piles, and spread out at her desk where she switched on the computer and a few soft iTunes.

Behind her the lampshade offered a soft glow over her work area. It was an idyllic place for a professional to work warmly. Very soon the logs and kindling that Susie had ignited in the fireplace were crackling.

 The Library, which she shared with her father, was the center of activity in the house. Padded with densely woven Persian rugs; rich high backed leather armchairs with throw rugs and an eclectic collection of books made this a favorite space.

Druce House was part museum, part residence. A gift to the English, her father said, from the Americans! A Foundation established by her father, it held displays and records from early English settlers who went to America. Dress. Armor. Trade beads. Journals. Maps. Gifts. Maritime trades artifacts for native Indians, souvenirs and portraits told the story of early colonial history for those who left to sail westward to the new world in the 17th century. Many who signed the Visitors Log Book said the exhibit was touching.

For Amanda, the day passed too quickly.

Dinner was on.

She took her place at a large polished mahogany table with its centerpiece of silver urn and candlestick and looked at her meal. Tomato basil puree soup; country bread, roast beef on spinach salad with goat cheese. White wine sparkled in a crystal glass. She ate.

A heated slice of yesterday's apple pie and ice-cream followed with coffee.

What she wanted was entertainment, she grinned, and she invited Fred and his wife Susi to join her at the dining table. They moved the large central silver urn aside, and having already eaten, they trailed in with coffee and cookies and sat with her. It was a small gathering of happy chit-chat.

"Had we known you were coming..." began Susie

"Please! Guys! No more fussing. No apologies needed. And thank you for caring... So. What's up with the house?"

Druce House, they told her, was becoming popular with tourists. What with tales of visitors, supplies, events, correspondence and queries, they were having fun with the program. Her father was right. It was meaningful to many...

It was eleven o'clock at night before they rose from the table.

Amanda picked some books for reading, and switched off the lights to the Library. The fire embers would die down during the night, and Susie, she knew, would sweep them afresh in the morning.

Amanda retired for the evening, and she felt a glow of refreshment at having come home. A place to refresh the identity, and replenish the soul, someone great had said about home visits. For Amanda there was a need to retreat from the insanity of a year at the University where she was serving as a visiting professor. The notion that she would have anything to do with theft of a manuscript... let alone the death of a student - was too surreal to imagine!

 Home. A good place for reality. And a few hours of rest, at least. For the weekend, anyway.

Outside the building, the house lights were being watched. Once the Library went dark, a parked Ford finally turned on its engine and slid into the night.

It was less than a month later that Amanda got the call from her father. Fred and Susie had been reported missing. He would lock the place up, he said, until the case was solved.

* *

Ref: Convoy No CO8KC.

Sir Neville received the letter from the Prime Secretary. It was sent by Courier Pouch.

Since the American Representative from America had his daughter with him, said the letter, he was having something of a family gathering taking place. Thus, could Sir Neville do something for him?

The Americans were preparing to enter the war with Lend Lease.

The war was not going well for the Allies, he knew.

In the past two years, the German Army had succeeded in invading enough territory to own Europe. Except for one great and ancient, prize, a country that had long been entwined with the history of Germany, Russia.

In a startling new development of the war, Germany turned on her Ally: *It was preparing to march on Moscow as an invasion force!*

The goal of the Germans was evidently to absorb the vast territories of Russia, just as they had invaded the rest of Europe...

Sir Henry made his way through the bombed streets of London. He closed his eyes at the vision of it all. This war was an abomination of biblical proportions, it seemed.

And now England needed Russia on their side!

But there was a problem. A problem the Prime Secretary claimed that only Sir Henry to solve.
The Polish.
Unspoken and unrecorded, the Minister knew of long legacies and deep secrets that entwined the family of Neville's ancestors with the Polish. There was no need to embellish. But it was tacitly understood. *England was now in desperate straights*, as the Minister put it. The past came suddenly to the forefront...

During WWII, the Government of the Polish people had fled into exile. They resided in London, waiting for reinstatement after the war for their statehood. A statehood that had been taken from them by the Russians at the start of war, allies of the Germans.
Sir Henry was to seek them out, this Polanski discovered.
Sir Henry found them in a district of London where they gathered.
They had cause for grievance, certainly. And as a small gathering of exiled diplomats they remained courageous and sympathetic. But they were known equally, after dark, for their vibrant living and cultural celebration of life, such that they stood out in stark contrast to a dark London deeply in despair for its own survival. And joyous they remained, for hope. For encouragement, for defiance.
 Celebrate they could, with vodka, gin, gayety and betting - even as a people living in Exile. This, Sir Neville understood. But he suspected this to be a veneer for deeper wounds afflicted over a long period of time. And he was right.

Still, as difficult as his mission might be, he had to get through to them. He had to persuade them to embrace the Russians now. The very Russians that had caused the Polish leadership to live as Exiles on foreign soil in London. This was cultural courtesy.

This, Paloski could not allow him to do, at all costs.

 Sir Neville raised his cane and knocked on the door of the lavish house that served both as Ambassadorial residence and assembly for the Governing body of the Polish people.

"Because of your ancestral legacy, may I ask you, my trusted friend, to be my Cultural Attache?" said the letter from the Prime Secretary of the Committee.

Why the Minister picked him to make the overtures was implicit. Sir Henry, though at great danger for entering the mouth of a lion - an injured lion at that, was a man of history. He was a man with a legacy of monarchical stature. Yet there was something that the Minister also knew. The Polish had also been an Imperial dynasty, that is, long before the Monarchies of Europe collapsed under socialist revolutions.

Worse. Theirs had been a history badly exploited, and at incredible cost, especially during the WWI where Poland, newly established as an Independent State, served as a battlefield between powers that that had divided them into Partitions previously, now again disregarding their independent statehood, and fighting for territorial gains and cultural ownership on their soil.

The reason that the Minister sent Neville to the Poles was his identity. He hoped it would work. If not, he was sending Sir Neville into danger. Still, this was war.

Extreme measures, perhaps. But the war was bigger than them all. He hoped it would work. Then again, it might not. There were spies everywhere.

The door opened, and Sir Henry entered a rowdy house party. Or so it seemed. More like a house of brawlers and loose women, nor was the man in charge amused by the intrusion. Anyone walking in on them in the dark hours of London was suspect.

Especially if he were being followed.

Sir Neville was taken aback. He did not know what to make of the mob that glared at him. They said they knew him alright. Anyone in such high ranks was known to them, but for all the underground intelligence that they held related to secret resistance agents in Europe and Russia... they did not appreciate the company of a stranger in their midst, a spy.

"But I am not a spy!" said Sir Neville.

They glowered. Then Sir Henry reeled back in utter shock. A dead man was thrown at his feet.

"Not you. Him!"

"Who did ...this....that?" pointed Sir Henry in total horror.

The leader of the mob stepped forward. He came so close that his breath smelled of alcohol, and he sneered. "You did!"

"*What*?"

"Russian!" he spat on the ground. "He was following you! A spy in our midst, your bring, Sir Henry Neville!"

" Not at all..." he began "I don't understand!" He was sweating. "*Who is he*?"

" This man was sent to follow you. Evidently, he did not like the direction of your Lordship's steps!" said the leader. "In this Polish neighborhood that is nothing but bad news. We are considered murderous thugs to the Axis powers..."

"*...and he would be right!*" chortled someone in the rear.

"The question is..." said the leader "*who* sent him? One your own, perhaps..?" he took a few menacing steps forward.

"Enough!" bellowed a voice. They parted. A gentleman made his way forward.

"This is..." he said, "a man of honorable linage, with a legacy that shares something found within our ancestral heritage. ..." He paused, the room tense. Then he faced Sir Neville and gave him a deeply gracious and old world-bow of homage. "Please come in! We are most honored!" he said, brushing away the mob that had gathered. "Come this way, please!" he begged. They entered private quarters.

The English Prime Secretary was right. The Polish people recognized something within Neville's make up that defined their very cultural identity. For as much as they had suffered over the past centuries there was something deep within their history they recognized - the germination of a concept held so sacred through the centuries - that it had rent them as a people, leaving them as the battlefield upon which others had vied for their resources, leaving them in name only as the "Partitions" of others. Poland, the partitioned state for centuries.

 It was a concept introduced precisely by Sir Neville's legacy whose ancestors authored words of great and famous literature written centuries before. plays that would be known by all at a time singular to the Polish heritage of the same moment when something happened. Something so rare that even the author of the plays would found a new world across the Atlantic while seated as a Member of the London Virginia Company in the early 17th century , a colonial venture in which the Dutch, English, Spanish and others had traded and grown wealthy as expansionist nations.

Simultaneously, the concept first appeared in Poland in 1632 when Poland once dominated the landscape of Europe as a vast central territory. It was known as the *liberum veto.* It evolved during the reign of Poland's monarch *Wladyslaw IV.*

It was to change the world. Like a crucible for reform turning the corner on Medievalism, it gave Europe the nascence of promise, hope and prosperity amongst men. It was a policy of procedure in a Parliament, still in its infancy, that assumed political equality for every "Gentleman" -such that he represented his constituency. And it went further.

It asked for politicians to build consensus amongst themselves in civil and liberal ways, producing as a result unanimous consent for all measures of Parliamentary rule!

In a world of subsistence living, Papal dominion and Imperial Feudal Monarchs, the *liberum veto* was quickly challenged by local princes and by foreign diplomats advancing the interests of their own empires.

Through a succession of wars, deceptions, occupations and constitutional changes for Poland, the territory was divided and partitioned off to its neighbors.

 Finally in 1730 a secret agreement of its neighbors was assembled to put the matter of the *liberum veto* to rest. The Alliance of the Three Black Eagles known as Prussia, Austria and Russia vowed to maintain the status quo. specifically, that the Commonwealth of Poland's laws would not change to include the *liberum veto*.

Only after WWI was Poland given the rights of its Independent State. That is, until Russia reclaimed its "Partition" lands on behalf of the German Army in WWII. That left them exiled. And bitter.

The room was hot, the tea sweet. Finally Sir Neville put down his cup and saucer. He looked at the man seated before him, both of them in a salon of elegant English and baroque furnishings. Here was the leader of the Polish people, like an Ambassador in exile without a country to call his own, thanks to the Russians.

They remained calmly silent, both knowing that something significant was about to happen. Sir Neville faced him and spoke evenly.

"I am here to petition that you encourage the Russians to come to our side" said Sir Neville.

Twenty

Len Paloski kept an apartment in London. He could afford more.

His wealth came from printing shops that distributed newspapers, pamphlets and other government issue public announcements.

It was not the most elegant of professions since it relied not on content, but on the volume and speed with which his shop could produce ink, paper, loading trucks and distributers during the early hours of the day.

It irked him still, especially when invited to a Gentleman's club, that while others read the words of intelligent people, he was the one providing newsstands with paper products, when in fact the legacy of his family in Italy was one of refined bookbinding, artistry and yes, even content writing! In his culture, there was an aura about the printed word. Especially remarkable in his family was the reproduction of musical scores and librettos for the most celebrated talent that Europe ever saw since the great renaissance of the 17the century, opera.

But that had vanished. All wiped out in the last stock market crash when patrons fled from the public halls and theaters, leaving no buyers, no writers, and no liquidity willing to extend a sous to newspapermen.

The printing press saw social disruption sweep through the streets and target the venues of the wealthy. No buyers, no papers. Especially on the night of the fire at the Opera in Milan. It took the lives of hundreds of wealthy patrons trapped by locked doors and barricaded exits.

In a country where words could flow with mellifluous melody all night long, the public newspapers went silent when fantasy turned into reality.

Even the churches were emptied. There was nothing but silent remorse, a mourning as if the last of a rare and beautiful birdsong had been extinguished, afraid to express the sentiment that could no longer be expressed. No print was willing to risk any position that might be incendiary, and incite further unrest.

His father Paulo Paloski migrated to England at the turn of the century and began again as a boy-errand in a print shop - even before he could speak English. Not a bad profession, he often said. At least he could put food on the table.

He made friends with the owner of a newsstand on the corner, and frequently was asked to stand in for him. Usually, when the wind blew hard and few bought papers, he was in the newspaper stand. Then he acquired his own newsstand across town, and Len took his turn selling a few papers and calling out the news.

Pretty soon, it was Len making the decisions on what should, or should not, appear in print. And finally, when his father helped him buy his own print shop. With a few large contracts, he grew it into quite a media business.

Len Peloski missed the sunny memories of his childhood in the Mediterranean. His grandmother, her house on the edge of the sea, and the games he played with his friends in the soft night air of the warmer climate.

Then Italy joined the war on the side of the Axis powers.

England could be harsh, bleak and cold. Endlessly cold, it seemed. Still, it was clear his father was pleased with him, even if his mother kept her Italian ways in the oppressive confines of a small English house, like an apartment.

Mainly though, there was no escaping the language of his family, equally fluent in other neighboring languages like French, Spanish, German, even Greek and Arminian -Turkish. He was prevailed upon for translations. Especially for those who crossed the channel to Europe and back with some frequency, and urgency.

Translations for a few friends with harmless requests about letters and documents came occasionally. But increasingly, translation requests came from regular key men in the city, men interested in a regular trafficking of intelligence material.

At first, they seemed silly. But even as he was drawn into this web of night-time writers willing to pay for the printing of pamphlets, he knew he was becoming central to a mission that was circulating propaganda, much of it going by boat back to Europe. Others did. One such pamphlet actually came to the attention of the authorities. It was alarming, even to him. It professed to know the fighting air superiority of Germany, and how it would bring supreme command of Europe against all enemies. It bragged of Invasion forces.

And as fast as he was printing the reports for his special group of men in other languages by night, he was also printing the fighting stories of the English for the reading public by day. One after the other, the stories fell from his press. He was knowledgeable of the Invasions of Czechoslovakia; Poland; Finland, the Baltic States, Norway, Denmark, Belgium, Holland and France were occurring. Italy, he knew had joined the Axis Powers. Dunkirk and Paris had fallen. Spain, Portugal, Sweden and Switzerland were neutral.

The document that truly alarmed him was for the preparation of a major air attack over England for August 18th, 1940. And a full invasion planned for the 19th August. For this he went home to alert his family. He made his preparations for evacuation, and he chose not to print for fear of retribution somehow. He closed his shop. But the messages for translation still came in. The war was seeping in from every quarter.

Air raids occurred in the daytime hours, mortality high for the Germans, losing over a thousand planes. Details revealed that the docks were to be spared for future use by the Occupiers.

British RAF loses were proportionally counted as six to one.

In the end, the assault failed. The Airfield which were supposed to be disrupted by enemy fire held, and the raids over England provide for the Germans the edge they needed. Fairly soon, Len Polanski did not know which side he was on.

As a successful businessman in London, it was no surprise that he was amongst the ranks of those who could afford private clubs and special invitations.

That he knew Sir Henry Neville was not overly remarkable. But that Sir Henry was trusted by the Prime Secretary and placed in his confidence was of some concern to Paloski. Especially when the Americans came over to London six months later.

What were the new plans? What was being discussed? He wanted to know. He had contacts who wanted to know...

He needed to send this one message back to the continent. Never mind whose side, it was intelligence that he should deliver, now that he was knee deep in the information business.

Sir Henry Neville was not particularly easy to impress. Let alone probe for information. But try he must. If not by fair means, then by foul. His obligations depended upon his information.

Len Paloski had Sir Henry Neville followed by an informant.

* *

Emily was unhappy. The image of her boyfriend was still upsetting.

God, who she missed him!

Of course, by the conventional standards of English society, he was way beyond her station, on the echelon of the social hierarchy. Yet he treated her so wonderfully, as if her tattoos and her black martial arts classes mattered to him! He was so tender, both in bed and out, ever defending her like a gentleman should. Or, as her eternally optimistic mother would say, to hide the silly sides of her family.

Truth is, Emily's father had founded a business and failed. In filing for bankruptcy protection, he brought upon them much public shame and suffering. Still, as he would often say. "Better to have tried to make a business success than never to have tried at all..."

 Still, at the end of it all, her father took to fitness running; bicycling and hiking. As if always on a pilgrimage, he dragged the family to every mountain trail; historical site and boundary line on the British Isles he could find. It was his way of keeping the family together. Of course, they recovered financially. And it was he who encouraged her to apply to University. But it was because the woman of his life, her mother, had taken her vows seriously and remained at this side for richer and for poorer...that it all came together in the end. A covenant of honor that few marriages could boast of in the aftermath of the great economic recession.

Emily got a scholarship.

Even so, she wanted to withdraw into her shell in much the same way that she did at school when the family experienced financial difficulties. At University, Ed made her feel normal. It didn't matter, he told her.

You move on!

It hurt so bad to think of what must have happened to him that such brutality to the hero of her life left her overwhelmed...

Oh God!

Why was his name in the newspapers again?

* *

Twenty One

London, Westminster.

Trevor was getting worried.

The gold in the celebrated case was not consistent with what was reported in the tally sheets of England's Treasury for the time.

Further, several assessments by groups of descendants whose ancestors owned the cargo of the ship was listed on the manifest.

Worse, there were open trade agreements presently being negotiated that were held up until this issue was resolved.

It was central to England's currency, if to be valued at face value - even through the vacuities of history. And the value of futures trading depending on Holdings on the monetary assets of the company.

Trevor must ensure that the trade Agreements between the two countries proceed amicably.

Most troubling were the tally sheets presented by the Office of the Exchequer. They did not correspond with the Parliamentary records of what was delivered onboard the ships in the way of supply.

If Insurance was to establish liability, then loss and theft was not a pretty allegation by any ally doing trade with the same company.

How to reconcile the past with the present, thought Trevor.

The phone rang. His Secretary warned him of his appointment with the Minister of Finance, and the Minister of State. Both would later have to make an account to higher authority within the realm, he knew. So he closed his website, gave Margaret a list of items to search and apply to the online. She was to set up the site and Entry access codes for others working on the case in the support group.

He walked from his office down the hall.   Tomorrow was another day.

* *

Deep within the House of Lords, in the Lords' Chamber Day Rooms, sommeliers filled goblets with sparkling wines of *rose; blancs de noir* or vintage Champagne. On the sideboards lay an assortment of *h'ors d'oevers* - sour cream on latkes with caviar; softly scrambled eggs with smoked salmon; spicy crab claws and cocktail sauces of several varieties. At each end of the long buffets lay open mixtures of cheeses from tart Alphine to aged goat; salted meats, breads and creamed butters. At the far end of the cloister chamber stood large silver coffee urns; sliced torte tatin attended by Sauternes on ice.

The clustering of leather chairs and densely woven rugs offered small tables for drinks, food, documents, notepads and increasingly, electronic devices, laptops and earplugs.

It was a place where Members and staff could gather for repast, and, thanks to close-circuit monitors, listen in on the proceedings of the House of Commons ongoing. Here they gathered - moments of regrouping between the storms. Here, every corner of the Union had at one moment or another been in this room when Parliament was in session, sometimes in battle as bloody and deadly as any for the rights that would define democratic governance.

Several groups were in the room for the morning hour. But it was dominated by Trevor's staff and colleagues.

Trevor's two attendants were Edward Granville from Cambridge, and Stewart Eldridge from the London School of Economics. Both were in their final years of study, and whereas Edward was related to Trevor's mother's family, Stewart came from a neighboring Scottish clan studying International Law in London.

In his offices, down the hallway of the Left wing, Marci, Paul and Jeff were spread out at the conference table surrounded by law books. At the center of the table was a speaker where Trevor's voice could be heard. They were internally wired to each other for internal communications while also watching the overhead screens of the House of Commons in Session.

Trevor switched off the tiny speaker monitor midway down the audio lead attached to his ear. It let the office staff relax when he was offline.

"More coffee, would you mind, please?" begged Trevor to the passing Server.

"...And one here too, please... Plus a mug of water with ice, thanks!" added Edward.

Hearing no sound of chit-chat in the Chamber as background, Marci took the moment to jump up from the conference table in the working office and race to the bathroom and back. It would be a long day of tense work.

Today was not a pretty sight in the House of Commons. Today on the Floor, the British Prime Minister was being heckled badly, they could see.

They were getting nervous.

Especially Edward and Stewart seated with Trevor in the Chamber Day Room.

Edward's shirt had lost its tie, his cap and gown somewhere crushed beneath him, and perspiration was running down his back.

Stewart wasn't much better though the gown of his Junior ranking was backwards slung around his neck. Each of them wearing wire for private talk. They moved about, occasionally looking up at the monitors, listening. Today, all food tasted dry.

Barristers wandered in and out of the Chamber, some to consult with Trevor; some offering material evidence, others just a nod of support. They looked up to hear the Representative from Hampshire, a constituency with close ties to London's commerce.

..."And will the Prime Minster please explain to the House and to the people of this country...how it is that we must pay a penalty for a case that fails to show clearly who the debtor is and who the creditor is to the tune of several billion pounds in gold bullion give or take...from our own Treasury?"

The cacophony of shouting fairly bristled with anguish and outrage. *Bang! Bang!*

"Order!"

"....Will the House allow the Speaker to respond." "Order! Order!"

The Chair beat the gavel hard at a bench above the Great Mace.

The Prime Minister rose to speak.

"It is our intention to fully address the concerns of the parties in this case..."

"...And about bloody time!" shouted one angry heckler from the rear benches.

" and to direct our line of enquiry to setting a precedence..." continued the Prime Minister.

"...A bit late that, two centuries, old fellow"

"Absolutely!"

"Order! Order in the House! I say. Order!"

"...that will not unravel the covenants of the past with this matter of territorial claims..."

"Thief! Thief!"

" ....in international waters? These monies belong to England. And they shall be retrieved!" Bankrupt... is the Bank of England!

"Order!"

The Debating Chamber erupted into disarray and chaos.The Prime Minister had to sit down.

> *"And how does the Prime Minster intend to reward the Insurance companies for lost cargo that rightfully belongs to the Crown?"*
>
> *"Say! Say!"*

In the Day Rooms Lounge, they watched.

"God!" said Steward jumping up, the tension of confrontations unbearable to him.

Trevor stood up and started to pace. He switched ON the speaker of his internal wire.

"Marcy, you there?.."

"Yes Sir!"

"I'll need all the legal precedents on Maritime Law cases involving lost cargo in national waters, and.. No. Make that international waters. Especially the American Insurance claims of the 19th century...I'll need a field of precedents across multiple centuries of Admiralty Law too, got it?"

He turned on his heels and proceeded with his speaking "Paul, you there?... Any news as to the discovery of materials and content of the purser's bourses yet? We'll need an update to establish how those accountings were recognized."

Edward walked up to him and handed him his coffee. He said to Trevor "You'll want the bill of ladings from the Netherlands, the ordinance lists and the letters from the Duke of Savoy's inventories..."

Trevor nodded. "Did you get that, Jeff? - everything Edward just mentioned - and then look at the Scottish

Bills of Lading for the decades prior to...got it? We'll look at historic continuity for money loads"

Steward got up to lower the volume of the overhead screens.

"Steward here" he said into his own mouthpiece, interrupting. "I'd like to suggest that we start bringing some experts on the intrinsic value of the alleged treasures and in the historical integrity of the material goods in the hold...Estimates from museums, historians, evaluators etc...We need to start making up sums and comparable market valuations. We must execute damage control with a cost containment boundary before it blows itself to the sky..."

"I agree" added Trevor "Everybody got that?"

They all looked up at the overhead screens of the House of Commons. The arguments on the Floor were getting out of hand and the Chair was pounding on the gavel...

"Right then" finished Edward "We've all got a ton of work to do...Upload everything up on the files that might prepare for the framework. What was the prevailing thinking of the time? Who knew what, when etc.. We start with framework files. Everybody reads everything...Send me your framework and your assumptions. I shall read them! The case rests on arguments of precedent. Someone is playing with the rules. We need to know them all. Got it, everyone?"

They all switched off their audio feeds and collected their gear.

Trevor was flying down the hallway with Edward and Stewart skipping beside him. "I'm wondering how much longer the standing government can take this beating before calling for a Referendum of Confidence..."

Stewart got off his cell phone. "Apparently there's an expert who is familiar with authentication and valuations..." said Stewart.

"Question him!" ordered Trevor.

"...Her! 17th century, I believe. At Christ... "

Stewart did not see Edward's cringe. Nor did he notice the hesitation in Edward's pace suddenly.

"See to it!" said Trevor disappearing into a neighboring Lords' Chambers.

Stewart entered their own Rooms where the other's greeted him.

Edward lingered.

Stewart popped his head out. "What' the matter?"

"Nothing!"

"You're dragging your feet. *Why*?"

"He has a relative there...At Christ."

* *

The statue of Bodocia overlooked everything on Threadneedle Street, even the Bank of England.

Trevor MacDonnell made his way across Bank junction and faced the Bank of England. Rebuilt by Sir Herbert Baker, the place was better known as the *The Old Lady of Threadneedle Street* after a Sarah Whitehead - whose ghost haunted the garden, it was told.

Nothing beat the original site of the Bank of England in Walbrook built upon an historical site said to have been the Roman temple of Mithras, God of Contracts. Still, it served the auspicious façade of a central bank. Frank Charms greeted Trevor in the lobby and escorted him to the upper chambers of the building where he held his executive offices.

"Nice of you to see me Frank" said Trevor. "It's not everyone who gets to see these hallowed quarters up here!"

"It's my pleasure Trev! And it's not every banker who gets to meet a man doing so much in the House...*Thank You!* It's important work that you do for all of us"

"I'm curious about the history of the place" said Trevor. "It's as if we are forever reshaping our finances through banks' reconstruction projects."

On the door was the title *Governor of the Bank of England*. "Please..." offered Frank Charms holding open his office door for Trevor. Canadian born, Frank Charms was also Governor of a large Canadian Mining Bank.

"Actually, I'm awestruck by the mandates that has held this place together for so long, and so well... Charles Montagu, 1st Earl of Halifax founded this place just three years after a scoundrel adventurer William Paterson offered a million pounds to King William III to open it in 1706. Good investment, wouldn't you say?" said Frank.

"Who says pirates didn't serve their purposes, poor fellow!" said Trevor, accepting a drink. .

They laughed. "And to think that the same man originated the Panama Canal, clever man!"

"Scottish, of course!" chuckled Trevor.

"Speaking of such, thank God the last Governor elected to grant it operational independence over monetary policy. He must have had a premonition of the finance markets needing the bank's Monetary Policy with Committees having the responsibility of setting interest rates in tandem with CPI..."

"I guess he saw globalism coming..."

"Well let's say he saw Ben Bernanke coming and turned the place into a Central Bank like the Fed"

"A place of much vision, perhaps. But I'm not entirely sure for whom...Anyway Frank, it's an old matter I came for. A Trust my father was given to Execute that he recorded here. The next heir to the Trust has recently perished, most sadly. He was a young man at University, and the case is still at hand. My mother brought it up..."

Frank Charms looked at him, and put down his drink slowly. "Yes. I know. I've had to do some digging myself. It has a history, those days of war. With so much unhappiness and so many out of work, it's no wonder that socialist spies lit up the landscape at every dark corner.

The bank box inventory. We shall need to open the vault. Meantime, please have this!"

Trevor perused the file and looked up.

Charms took his place at his desk. "It's hard to draw the lines of where things stood back then. As you know we were shipping all our gold reserves to America for safekeeping, such was the tenuousness of our position militarily. The matter is related to the printing Bank Notes was a controversial issue to begin with. This goes back to around the mid-nineteenth century when the

Bank Charter Act restricted the issuance of Bank Notes by commercial banks , leaving the Bank of England with a monopoly of Note issue in England and Wales."

"Now, the Bank is the regulator!"

"Thank God!...But there was a connection..."

Trevor listened carefully.

"At the first WW, the Currency and Bank Notes Act of 1914 granted *temporary* power to HM Treasury for issuing bank notes. But they were not convertible to gold reserves. Instead, the plan was to replace any gold coin in circulation to prevent a run on sterling and to enable raw material purchases for armament production. The Notes featured the image of King George V. This you know, of course" said Charms.

Trevor nodded.

"The Act of 1928 however, returned note-issuing powers to select banks in varying degrees and for certain denominations. Regardless, the Germans had learned their lesson. By WWII, the German *Operation Berhard* attempted to counterfeit various denominations, producing 500,000 bank notes each month for 1943. Their idea was to parachute the money onto UK soil in an attempt to de-stabilize the British economy. Instead, the notes were used to pay off German spies in Europe! One operator of that scheme was in England, a group of disenfranchised immigrants from Europe, whose name nobody knows..."

"The case for your father was that he became the Trustee of an Asset when Sir Neville infiltrated the group. The Prime Minister sent him to negotiate a delicate and difficult Agreement, It involved the leadership of sovereign states living in exile in London at the time.

"Neville was compromised. The Asset was scheduled to go to the US, but waylaid in Scotland as a precaution by the PM because of the many ship losses at sea carrying our treasures. It was entirely possible that spies were leaking critical information about their cargo.

Eventually, Neville died, That Trust was Administered entirely by your father."

"I see" said Trevor. "These photographs...?"

"Yes. That was the case of Neville's accident itself. The information was held in the files by us because the government wished not to have it aired at the time. Those were very tenuous times, the war, and security always a concern then"

"These documents were put in a safe deposit box taken by my father then?"

"Yes. That, and by a joint release at the Bank of England, sealed with express instructions by the Prime Minister. The London counterfeit players were involved when a counterfeit banknote was delivered to the Prime Minister, suggesting foul play. By implication, it suggested an act of counter terror tactics. That's why the government wanted to limit exposure to the incident, your father, included!"

"I see. Any particulars as to the incident itself ?"

"Yes. By implication, It was speculated that Neville was blackmailed, then punished. There was some talk of a suspects. But nothing came of it. And talk also of internal strife with the political factions of the allies. Or unresolved border disputes in old Europe: Russians against the Germans. As if any of those strategic decision could be attributed to one person's machination..."

"It does sound jingoistic. Neville was on his way to visit his wife?"

"Yes. She was in a convalescent center recovering from a bad case of poisoning. Then, at the scene, the boy, who evidently had been considered dead on impact was abandoned, but survived. The girl was missing..."

"Did my father execute the mandate of the Trust?"

"He did. However, he was bound not to release the fortune that was attached to that Trust and kept it all here in the Bank."

"Oh?"

"He could not release the full endowment or asset. I mean we did what we could, tiptoeing around the asset as long as it remained affiliated with a safe academic institution for viewing etc...and some funds for its management, maintenance and basic expenses. Plus wellbeing of the family. And here it sat, to this day, in fact, until a rightful heir can be proved."

"How so?"

"You see, there was no proof that the girl had died. She just went missing. By probate law, she was the older heir!"

"So, err...resolution?"

"None! There were none found. She just vanished. Oh sure, a few hints here and there that someone knew something.. Neither a body, nor an assumption of anything could be made.! We kept the matter secret so that few imposters could show up. In any event, it's clear the perpetrator of the incident knew damn well what he was doing, and what the fortune was worth." Charms walked to the window.

"We never heard again about anything from anyone after the war. If the motive was money, then we would have spotted tracer issues, questions, enquiries, claimants surfacing. Nothing! That left us to conclude that it was a war-related act.

"The boy in the accident survived. He grew up and married. He is now receiving elder care in his home. He and his wife had one son – that would be Neville's grandson and heir - whose recent death occurred while attending University of City College."

Trevor took a deep breath. "My mother regrets the matter, and cares deeply now that the grandson is dead. Do you suspect any linkages?"

"No. None at all. Perhaps the grandson overdosed, as is want to happen these days amongst our young, I do regret to say. But no hints or claimants as to the disposition of the fortune is at hand. The legacy Asset and fortune held in Trust is sealed still in our bank vaults, put there by your father. Unfortunately, without proof of hereditary to the Neville line of successors, there is little we can do to unseal it. You see, it is only the passage of time   that will unseal the case. Resolution would have occurred if the grandson had patrimony of an heir to receive the inheritance. But unfortunately, the kid died without issue.

"It's almost as if this Legacy Trust is destined to be kept at bay..."

"Destined, or by design...I wouldn't know. But until the natural life of the girl of the accident would be considered beyond the age of natural survival -

assuming she even lived on - the matter of the Trust or the fortune cannot be disposed. ”

“This must have weighed heavily upon my father...”

“It did. But he was impeccably discrete and sincere about the whole thing. Repeatedly, he petitioned for concessions for the family, even if the bulk of the estate could not be released. Those were the terms of the commitment arranged...”

“Is this file complete?” asked Trevor

“Pretty much. Do give me the benefit of your thoughts will you?” said Charms “ I sure hope we are acting in the best interests of the asset and the family...”

“I will” said Trevor. “Thank you for all your efforts on this case.”

* *

Trevor knew the story well.

The Companies Act of 1862 introduced the concept of limited liability, a means of starting an investors trust which could float bonds. It was used chiefly as an instrument to finance the industrial revolution of the 19th century.

It flourished during the American building of the railroads. Securities could be sold to European investors who had insatiable appetite to buy American bonds in developments of the Industrial Revolution. Even during the worse economic depression, railroads like the Pennsylvania Union Pacific and Atchison, Topeka and Santa Fee ran on investor's money, and did well. But it required a constant cycling of cash back and forth across the Atlantic.

Other investments flourished with investor money, such as investments in the Anglo-Persian Oil Company such that banks like Pierpont Morgan, Schiff at Kyhn Loeb and the New York Warburgs became international financiers.

But if the few did well, many did not. Europe was in turmoil at the turn of the century, and it was only a matter of time before war would settle old scores and uneven distributions of wealth.

Old perceptions of national survival within limited territorial boundaries was rooted in agrarian economies able to sustain themselves.

Now, new pressures of growing populations; industrial centralization; labor demands and technological advancements left smaller nations dependents of trade agreements amongst uneven economies. Here, seeds of destruction were here sown and spread to Europe.

In a 1931 plot to seize Manchuria and its rich resources, Japanese men attacked the South Manchurian Railway dressed as Chinese bandits. They staged a fake act of provocation. It resulted in an attack by the Kwantung Army (Japan's field army in China) with the aim to occupy the whole of the province.

The League of Nations did little to protect China from Japanese aggression. Japan began a full assault of war against China in 1937 and within a year conquered much of China's eastern seaboard.

The worldwide economic slump of the 1930s hit many nations hard. Especially those who had come to depend on trade between nations and the production of goods for export.

Those with strong Trade Agreements, like the Imperial and Colonial powers had international political and economic standing. But lesser nations were neither recognized, nor supported by international communities, especially those having poor supplies of raw materials; growing populations and limited resources.

Neither was Japan alone in their aggression. Inequity spread nationalist sentiment like wildfire, and the wars followed, one after the other for the lack of resolutions, such that dictators toppled monarchies, one after the other.

In England, following the initial growth of industrialization, socialism took root in aggregate amassing of laborers unemployed.

The House of Lords, formerly upholding the interests of the landed wealth and monarchies of the realm, came under scrutiny, their power curtailed. Whereas the Appellate Jurisdiction Act of 1876 to the House of Lords allowed Law Lords, known as Lords of Appeal in Ordinary, to perform judicial functions as the highest court of appeal, their role has been largely limited and reformed. A legacy of their function remains intact, that is, they served the purpose of reviewing bills passed by the House of Commons.

More significantly, and because of the economic turmoil that roiled Europe since the wars, peers of the House of Lords remained conservative guardians of England's monetary and sovereign assets. But it was a grey area of dispute.

This matter, however, because of its age and circumstance, had been left at their doorstep like an unwanted baby.

More often than not, it was often said, when monetary policy produced winners, all peoples were content. But when losers came up short, it was time to reform the House of Lords!

Yes, he decided. The Companies Act of 1862 was a winner. It changed the world with industrialization.

Twenty Two

The case was expanding. Trevor was in his study reading.

An elegant home of the Regency Period, it was the place he used when working in London.

He poured himself a scotch from the sideboard and settled into his favorite armchair, his legs up on an upholstered footstool with a laptop on his knees.

Quite aside from a discrepancy in treasure, the matter of sovereign ownership was becoming troublesome.

"...In the Reign of King William and Mary..." He would read up on the framework of history very quickly, especially if it served to frame a legal argument.

 "1694: Parliament, having invited William III of Orange to England to rule, now faced an old enemy supporting his predecessor, James II..."

Trevor knew the account. A number of important laws of the land changed when Henry VIII divested all Catholic monasteries and declared England a free and Protestant state.

The legacy of the Protestant Tudors was enduring.

James IV of Scotland ascended the throne of England and the King James Bible was translated from Catholic Latin to the English language. Shakespeare completed his plays, and a new era of mercantilism flourished. In seafaring trade, the English colony of Virginia was settled, and the spirit of Martin Luther's individualist agency, as theology, prevailed.

But it did not last. Regicide followed a disastrous English civil war and a penitent new heir to the throne betrayed his realm. Parliament languished, the era of Restoration perished and England was drawn into war. Finally, eighty six years after Elizabeth I died, Parliament settled for a new monarchy.

It was called the Glorious Revolution. William III was invited to ascend to the throne of England.

The wetness of that autumn day was nowhere more visible than in the muddy streets and wooden houses of Brixham, it was said: Every public house, private estate, barnyard and tavern was garrisoned with foot soldiers.

By the time the ship *Brill* approached the dock, a large ceremonial canvas and pavilion had been erected for the great disembarkment.

William III, in full battle regalia, came ashore declaring *"the liberties of England and the Protestant Religion I will maintain."*

He must have eyed his Aide, wondering if he had pronounced the words correctly. William could not speak English.

More importantly, a fleet of 100 warships, 400 Transports carrying 11,000 infantry and 4,000 horses stood offshore. He came with an invasion army.

In the surrounding fields and pastures, he read, soldiers had made camp and quartered their horses, sending long roads of supply running to and from Brixham in endless motion. The provisioning alone, according to the ledgers, fairly depleted the English Board of Victualling Storehouses, it was recorded.

More soldiers filled boggy fields. Billeted in make-shift tents, they were hungry, belligerent, fully uniformed and crowded. They had made a harrowing crossing of the Channel in tall ships and shallops.

Supplied with Arms, and standing on English soil with their own William of Orange from Amsterdam, none could speak English.

Less than 10 weeks later, William III summoned a Convention Parliament at Westminster Palace to discuss the terms of his kingship in England. His Aide was his translator.

Mary, his wife, was glad to be home again. But she had doubtless begged William to spare the life of her father King James II now fleeing to France, and vacating the English throne.

Parliament objected to William's reign as sole monarch - even with his own lines of succession of royal blood of Europe allowing for his English ascendancy. William III of Orange looked appealing. He was related to the English monarchy, and he was retrieved from a Protestant line of succession in Holland...

Trevor stood up, facing the window. *How long and how often would the treasure of this island be used for political gain?*

Trevor turned to the files on the Framework of case studies, and downloaded on his laptop.

The head of a large mastiff raised itself for Trevor's hand to stroke. Otherwise, he remained very still at his master's feet.

The English: Oh, the English! So tolerant, so hardy against those who took arms against her!

He read on, like one waiting for the familiar and happy ending of his tale.

 If at the end of the century Parliament was conflicted, in one bold stroke both Whigs and Tories asserted never to allow a Catholic to rule on the English throne: The oligarchic character of the monarchy was forever changed from sovereign dominion to modern Parliamentary Reform and a modern rule of law!

Trevor smiled. He always did. He read on down his legal briefs, knowing that under the Bill of Rights, the king could maintain a Standing Army *only* with the consent of Parliament...

Yet to accommodate, an annual income of £600,000 was disbursed to the monarchs by Parliament, with additional grants for *specific* purposes, when collected as taxes from the people.

A series of laws, written in bold and courageous words constituted the Acts of Parliament. *How proud he was of them!*

The Mutiny Act ensured Parliamentary approval of the armed forces on a yearly basis.

The Bank of England was established to deal with financing the government. ..

Finally, the Settlement Act of 1701 established the supremacy of Parliament: Above all else, it disallowed all wars without Parliament's consent. Thus, while embracing Scotland to become part of England, it engaged reforms that would shape a democracy!

Still, England stood alone and the world was far behind her.

Meantime, the matter of heir to the throne of England remained unresolved: King James' Catholic offspring with Mary of Modena would be barred from the throne. The crown was to pass to the descendants of Sophia, granddaughter of James I and niece of Charles I, who had married into the German Protestant House of Hanover.

Indeed, William of Orange from Holland looked appealing. Even if Europe was ravaged by wars.

King William's Wars were a series of continental battles fought primarily to advance Protestantism in Europe!

He was invited to rule England. And he accepted.,

But as Trevor knew, things went terribly wrong:

Not the least of the reasons was William III's hold on Parliament - even as his power eroded and disaffection set it.

Trevor looked up.

Or was it that he was so disenfranchised from the English in ways that none could imagine?

Why?

The matter of the case before him now was shaped by motivation. A fleet that sank was no small event. And it had bearing on the material facts.

 For six years, France had been in protest against William III. They supported his chief challenger to the English throne - the deposed English Catholic monarch, James II.

France was relentless. Louis XIV supplied and provisioned James II to land with an armed force in Ireland.

The English Royal Navy was neither successful in attacking his French supply ships, nor able to retaliate as the French torched the English town of Teignmouth on their way home.

Moreover, a French invasion fleet was gathering off Normandy and provisioning for a mass attack on English soil.

Trevor read the last page of the historical record placed in his briefs by his assistants:

> *"Thus, when William III sank the entire French fleet off the coast of England, there was little he could not ask from Parliament in his cause against France."*

"Ahh" he muttered, draining the last of his scotch. Of course!

...Improving the Royal Navy was something William III would exploit the fullest, even if was to deplete the Treasure of England for his private ambitions, thus far hidden...

> *"With Mary now dead, King William III of England ruled alone. And he had his English Navy."*

Here Trevor appreciated the efforts of his staff to supply him with the Research. He read on, even as the phone buzzer went on in the next room. It could wait, he decided.

> *...For thirty years Samuel Pepys kept a diary. He was a naval bureaucrat, and answered diligently to his King.*
>
> *He had replaced the ad hoc process of merchant's contributions to a maritime fighting force with regular programs of supply, construction, pay and command.*
>
> *He introduced the "Navy List" which fixed the order of promotion. In 1683 the "Victualling Board" was set up which fixed the ration scales. Trevor put down his glass and sat up. He did not like what he saw next. And it explained the approach to the events.*
>
> *...But in 1693, Parliament was outraged that the King was not bringing home the fleet. He was to send it to winter in the Mediterranean for outfitting.*
>
> *Worse, since he was spending little time in the British Isles, Parliament became suspicious of his intentions.*
>
> *Protected by the Bill of Rights which they had made William III sign for free speech, there was growing hostility and outward protested against his appropriation of large sums of English coin sent to "Foreign Princes"...*

Trevor got up to refresh his drink. If ever in the history of human behavior one could deduct the hidden intentions of a criminal, it was through his motive, means and opportunity. Like any good legal case.

How then to figure for the intentions of this king and this secret mission? Especially to determine the legal powers of rightful *ownership* of the cargo?

He read on.

> *"This was a new world of mercantilist economies. And King William III had his historical connections with the Monarchies of Europe.*
>
> *"The HMS Essex was one of the biggest ships ever built. Even larger than the 74 gun ship, it had three decks which gave the vessel rigidity if not stability. More importantly, it was armed with more cannon. The Essex, as flag ship of the flotilla carried 80 guns?*
>
> *Trevor thought this a little abnormal. He turned to the pages of fleet descriptions.*
>
> *"Normally the ship of 180 ft. in length or greater carried twenty-eight 32 or 36 pound guns on the lower gun deck; thirty 18 pounders on the upper gun deck; and sixteen 9 pounders on the upper works. Only a few of the 74s were built for 24 pounders instead of 18 pounders"*

So, he noted that the cannon of the *HMS Essex* was not only greater in number due to the increase in the ships length, but in the increased capacity of battle. In fact, it took 500 crew to man the decks of the Essex.

The man who owned such a fleet might consider himself invincible...having powers beyond those allowed by new Parliamentary reform laws. That sounded like a man with an agenda, thought Trevor. He read on.

The *HMS Essex* was a flagship of a massive fleet. Unfortunately, no one - not even the Fleets Admiral was concerned about the technical details of the arsenal. The ship was overloaded in weight for the hull's design due to cannon and cargo.

He checked the maritime survey report of the ship. The 24 pounders were "old" but "well maintained".

The report annotated that they could remain in commission for up to a century. Many items had been recycled and refitted for the newer ships. Their bore and power was unique.

But in this case, there were remarkable features of identification. Only one manufacturer, historically, had made such cannon on this ship.

Trevor paused.

Was this worth pursuing? Did it mean anything? Where goes-the-cannon, goes-the-cargo, surely?

Or *why*, even?

If the cargo...*why* the canon, exactly? Was this a mission of commerce or of war? Whose? He wrote in the margin

> *Is there a relationship between the two elements here?*

Trevor leaned down and petted the dog who all but rolled over on his belly.

What was William's hidden agenda?

> *"The Grand Alliance of a European coalition, which began in his own countries of the Netherlands - and now England - was designed

to arrest French expansion, and defend the Palatinate...."

The... what?

"The Palatine regions. Dutch, German, Bavarian and Rhine Territories comprised of vast agrarian lands, which embraced the concept of mercantilism, trade routes and empire-building.

Once, it was the Crusader's quest to defend Christianity in the Holy Land, and the Huguenot of that Legacy to advance the spirit of individual liberties...

Not exactly, your Catholic way, thought Trevor.

"One Prince, subsidized by William III, was the Duke of Savoy, a relative."

Just what England needed, smirked Trevor.

...*"From a Marriage in 1438 of the Ludwig Pflalzgraf with Mathilde de Savoi, daughter of a Prince of Alpine Piedmont - Amedee de Savoie: This titular Prince of Achaiai and Geneve constituted the Dukes of Savoy who held title as Kings of Jerusalem and King of Italy.*

Trevor toured his study for another drink. He returned to his reading.

"William III admired Savoy for his new strongholds and bastions in the Mediterranean sea, including his secure hold on territorial structures and foundries used for the minting of gold coin.

...*But Savoy needed gold."*

William has an English treasury to offer, thought Trevor.

> *"William extracted promises from the Duke of Savoy before promising English money.*
>
> *Savoy was to stop the persecution of the Valois peoples to whom he was actually related by title.*
>
> *Savoy was to not ally himself with the French against the English.*
>
> *William III of England he sent his fleet in with gold for Savoy, ostensibly, pay for his troops and money for refitting his fleet in the winter.*

The English fleet never left its shores for the winter. Or for refitting, Trevor knew...

He stood up and gathered the rest of the material to take upstairs in his bedroom.

The dog retired to his sleeping bed by a warm kitchen hearth. There the entering staff would find him waiting in the morning.

Trevor switched off the lights downstairs, his thoughts distracted. Something seemed...out of place.

What?

His thoughts wandered as he moved from room to room. The name of Valois rang a bell in his memory, from somewhere in the 16th century. Was it not the family of a French Queen divorced by her husband? Henry IV? Margaret of Valois...

From Navarre?

Did not Shakespeare write a play for her marriage to last, *Love's Labor Lost?*

* *

The image of Ed was never far from her. She was calmer now, coping. But barely.

It was murder.

Just beneath the surface an anger smoldered. It surprised her, and it left her feeling nauseous: It could leap from within her soul and tear at the possibilities of what could have been accomplished...

Or was she just so tired?

Only slowly did the dust settle on the memory.

For Emily, a strong woman with a university career in prospect, what raged was the need to find out why such a thing could have occurred... Questions popped into her mind like, how did the killer *find* him?

Why?

Had the incident been provoked by a random act of terror and confrontation? If so, *when*? The questions emerged, over and over, without logical answers!

He was last seen in the morning at class, according to his friends. She *knew* he had gone to a rowing practice at the boathouse because he called he...

That would take most of the afternoon. Then he would shower; hang out for a half hour of drill; hull-rubbing and then perhaps even a beer at the pub with the guys. But they said he never appeared at the pub.

So, he must have been diverted. Or gone somewhere else?

The debris found in his car suggested he had gone to the Library. True. But that was usually his habit anyway for any day, because as fast as the weekends could pass with partying; rowing competition and travel – that is, if not making love at Emily's for the night, at least his foundational research and his citations were garnered from the library for his University class work assignments: A good working habit that Emily had inculcated in him. In fact, that was where they had met!

In the library - back when he was an aimless college student, a dreamer, and she...in the library with Amanda Wells setting up for the evening class...

Oh God!

Why? Why did the killer find *him*?

That evening, a thought came to her.

If it were not coincidental, then it was *purposeful*. That meant the assassin had an interest in Ed. Something they/he wanted from Ed. Perhaps something he had. Was it on him? If so, *what*?

Money?

What if they were involved in illicit narcotic distribution? Or, what if...

Check his phone numbers, *contacts for leads* to discover sources...suppliers of...

Wait. She stopped. That was another habit that she had disabused him of early on in their relationship.

This university had zero tolerance for users. She had worked too hard, she told him, and for too long...to jeopardize her enrollment at this university...No!

Ed was clean. Of that she was certain.

Something else? Maybe there was something she missed?

He had been honest with her. He loved her, and she believed him. *"Even with your tattoos and Gothic black hair..."* he laughed.

"Yes!" she had answered demurely. *"It's my ploy to cast my spell over the others!"*

How could she forget?

"Well, you got my Castle, my moat and... come here you wicked vixen!" he would say.

Emily's eyes were moist.

Never once did he mock her imagination springing from her voracious reading of *V*ampire books. *Witches, dragons and werewolves, too!*

Then later, he would say *"I won't tell a soul...about you!"*

The memory of it all hurt. He was sincere. He was trusting. He was the dreamer of great and wonderful dreams, she decided. *He!*

When did his assailant make contact with him? There, at the site of the car. Or earlier?

So. They were *waiting*....

If so, what was the reason? What in the world would a college student have that could possibly be of interest to them? If it were premeditated, then perhaps he knew them, or perhaps he had communicated with them?

She doubted it.

The questions never left her mind. No: They were *waiting* for him outside the Library because of what he had.

What?

It was two days before she remembered it all. And it came back to her clearly. Moment by moment, she replayed the events of that day. Of course.

The envelope!

How could she not remember?

An envelope of a manuscript! The same one that they had worked on for Amanda Wells...

Yes, she decided, they had been *waiting* for some time...?

Should she talk to Amanda about it? The police?

A coldness gripped her heart.

A goddamned manuscript cost him *his life?*

* *

Twenty Three

The Legal Offices of Igoravich, Cahn and Smythe were on the 71 st floor of the black glass National Building in New York City.

It was a casual assembly of partners, each with their notebooks and laptops at the conference table. They knew, from years of experience, that when they were off the record and ... in a tie-less Sunday gathering like this, the case was too important to discuss during regular business hours.

Today, with the streets of New York blissfully empty, Senior partners were meeting. For while their "in-house warriors" were amongst the best attorneys of international law, there were some core decision that had to be made first.

"So. What have we got?" asked Gore, as they called him, short for Igoravich.

"The Brits are fighting the case that gold at the bottom of the sea belongs to the Spanish, since it was theirs in the first place   -before it was stolen by the English Queen" "stolen?" asked Cahn, incredulously, his mouth playing with a smile.

Smythe threw him a look. Anything in law was plausible, if had anything to do with human behavior. They all knew this.

"The Dutch claim that the Fleet was under the command of *their* Sovereign, as all the Dutch fleet was...and that the money represented an unpaid IOU by the Brits, therefore they make the case that it belongs to them...in trade and commerce"

"But if in the commission of wartime activity" began Cahn

"Exactly!" finished Gore.

"to be given exemption from any particular Nation while trading in international waters"

"And the Maritime Laws of the 17th century are not clear on legitimate trade, let alone piracy and cargo claims by insurers. For all we know, it could come under the same entitlements as prize money"

"Stu. How about you?" nodded Gore to the silent one at the end of the table.

"Insurance is a fine line between financing and owning. The company did both at one time. Especially during time of war. Converging interests. And conflict of territory. Such as in South African gold."

"Well. I don't give a damn about who wins the case. Not even if the Brits sustain a huge liability repaying a king's ransom for a sunken treasure taken from the Bank of England..."

They all nodded, knowing pretty much what was coming next.

"But I don't want any of the laws cited to tamper with our rights and leases over the last two and half centuries" He picked up his water glass and drank.

"...To open up or question our contracts, commitments and covenants on any of those mines is to set a precedent. Open up one and you open up the rest. If we start reexamining our Agreements and Leases in Europe, insured, invested, repaired or damaged by events of *any* nature, sovereign or private, then we unravel the lot like a ball of string. That's not an option!"

They all looked down.

"Now I know what you're thinking. Easier said than done. There are some pretty sharp lawyers and researchers out there...But we cannot allow them to open up the vaults to our past investments. South Africa. Australia. Asia. Remember, the Chinese are our biggest competitors right now. So, not opening of the records in our Swiss banks, Vatican accounts, German or Bavarian interests. At all costs.

Get it, people?"

They all nodded. "Right then. Let's get back to our golf games. It's Sunday! And no stupid e-mails for Congress to subpoena if there's ever a Hearing!"

* *

Trevor's secretary came to his office door with a strange expression.

"There is someone here to see you. She says she is a friend of your mother! Olga Parkenski Shall I see her in?"

"Yes. What?"

"Well, she's...she's Err..."

"Oh do come along Susie and let her through, any friend of my mother is welcome!"

"Yes Sir."

* *

Trevor decided to take the train into Waterloo Station. On the train he opened his briefcase. He had some reading to finish up.

> *"The Royal Fleet. February 27th 1694. Ship's Log: We called to morning muster. We proceeded underway at the signal of the Flag Ship. After a short stopover in Cadiz, the fleet entered the Mediterranean."*

* *

At the Straits of Gibraltar a weather differential occurred. It was winter, and sailors greeted the Levanter warmth with glee. The air had been stable, and the spread in the Atlantic between England and Spain had occurred without incident.

But the clouds, locally, were unusually low. Fog curled off the coasts, and other than tropical feelings, there was no cause for alarm for the Watch of the helm on any of His Majesty's Ships.

 Only the Turkish crews were restless, knowing these waters. But they said nothing in a ship's compliment of 500 crew. All to serve the Admiral as Flag Ship.

From the topmast watch tower, it was noted that the characteristic banner cloud atop the rock of Gibraltar could *not* be seen.

"No flag sighting!" It was entered in the ship's log.

This particular Levanter cloud might stretch for a mile or so to the west. That meant that the wind speeds were below Bft 5. A tad or two over that wind-speed, and the Rock of Gibraltar was known to create eddies and turbulences, often resulting in violent squalls and gusts, stronger even than the prevailing winds. It made for unpredictable sailing at this strange juncture between two continents.

Thus, when the westerly Poniente winds were mysteriously absent, and the residual choppiness of Mistral winds were abating. No signal was made of the *decreasing* pressure and the rising temperature.

The Turks could not express their concern to so great ship of the sea, since clearly, pressure was rising only slightly.

The *HMS Essex* was a Third Rate ship of the line. She had been launched at Chatham Dockyard just one year prior, and was the pride of the Royal Navy. She was under the command of Admiral Sir Francis Wheeler, setting sail from Portsmouth on 27th December, 1693. She was escort to a fleet of 48 warships and 166 merchant ships.

The Admirals' orders had been written on November 22nd.

He opened the sealed commission, and read his instructions, knowing that onboard his ship, the King had placed 10 tons of gold coins, including bullion and antiquity objects from the Treasury of England. The orders were read and recorded.

'Nov. 22. Kensington. Instructions for Sir Francis Wheeler, knight, commander-in-chief of a squadron fitted out for the Straits. As soon as you join the Spanish armada, pursuant to the instructions of the Lords of the Admiralty, you shall act as most advisable for the annoying of the French, and shall give the Duke of Savoy notice of your arrival in the Mediterranean; and in case he desire your co-operation in any design against the French, you shall use your best endeavors to bring the same to a happy issue. During your stay in the Mediterranean you are to correspond as frequently as you can with Viscount Galway, our envoy extraordinary to the Duke of Savoy; and, as far as may be consistent with the service you are employed in, to act according to the advices you shall receive from him.

By the time the steep pressure occurred, it was too late. The Levanter weather pattern had collapsed. On 27 February the violent storm hit the flotilla near the Strait of Gibraltar and in the early morning of the third day, HMS *Sussex* sank. Of the 500 crewman on board the Sussex, only the two Turks would survive. The body of Admiral Wheeler, was found on the eastern shore of the rock of Gibraltar in his night-shirt.

William of Orange, his anger never quelled at having signed the Bill of Rights that would give to the individual an agency of independence - *republicanism* as it was called in the purest sense - plotted to lure away from the shores of England a Naval fleet for refitting in waters warmer for wintering. In so doing, he had taken with him all its Treasure, only to have it sunk.

* *

"My God" said the barman "Who delivered that hulk of Scandinavian blond amongst us?"

"I have no idea... But she is gorgeous!"

The woman discharged her raincoat, and held it over her arm revealing a dark tight dress and high shoes. She tossed free a main of hair tucked beneath the raincoat.

"I could pour her into a bottle and call it eau de sexuality!"

"Is anyone here eating, or *what*?" admonished the attending waitress. "It's rude to stare at customers..."

"No. It's rude *not* to stare at creatures like that..." giggled one college student at the table.

"By the looks of that Mercedes out there, you don't have a chance!" nudged another party at the bar.

"Oh My God. She seems to be *waiting* for someone" said a girl.

"Would that be for *me*?" said the college student. She dug at him.

"No! A date, stupid! Perhaps they are dinning together in the Main Dinning room...then drinking at the bar, then staying at the Inn... for the *night*, do you suppose?" persisted someone.

They laughed.

The words were barely out of her mouth when in came the party they were waiting to see.

The man entered, gave her a respectful greeting, if not a diplomatic public hug, then proceeded into the Main Lounge, he at her elbow.

He took off his heavy coat and scarf, and sat across the fire in the great stone hearth with a fire, drinks being ordered. Clearly, a reservation for dining had been made.

The waitress appeared to take their drink orders. The man turned around to look up at her.

The surprise on everyone's face at the dinning table was less about the blond but that the man she was with. They all recognized him.

Slowly, with every head turning away, or turning down, they glanced at Amanda at the other end of their table. "Oh My God…" muttered someone quietly into his soda straw.

* *

Twenty Four

By the time Jeannette Bevan showed up with her office party, the place was already jammed. She was hard pressed to find enough seating for her everyone, and although the menus had been pre-arranged for a large order, there was quite a bit of shuffling that had to be done. They were placed outside the dinning area, just beyond the pub service bar where the waiters and staff could attend to such a large party in for lunch. Sixteen people, all dining together.

The occasion was to commemorate the University Award given to Chairman Bevan's Department of Anthropological Studies for a year of outstanding research and publications. Such accolades went far to advance the interests of the University, and certainly, its public funding. Chairman Bevan was to be given credit, and all were to attend the lunch as thanks.

That is, all who contributed to the feat of academic excellence. That included Amanda Wells of course, with her findings of a literary work that had been forgotten for three centuries. Evidently, it was lauded everywhere as nothing short of brilliant sleuthing. . No way could she dodge this lunch, try as she might. And while she knew that she had brought a large measure of the loot into the Department Vault as a government query for answers, there was a dark cloud at the absence of Ed, a fellow student.

Still, in the spirit of lifting morale, this was a bright step forward. Even Emily had agreed.

But what surprised Amanda was that Bevan could actually be decent and behave graciously. As did all the students who engaged with the event. After all, Amanda was a favored lecturing professor, even if American, they all teased. "Wow!" said Emily coming in to take her seat with a light kiss to Amanda's cheek. "You do clean up nice!"

"Thank you!" smiled Amanda, knowing that such compliments came few and far between from someone like Emily. Especially someone grieving.

The starters came out, shrimp in cocktail sauce, then entrees turkey; roast beef, gravies and sides, much of it with beers all round and an occasional soda. The meal passed easily enough, and before long Amanda realized that this was an occasion for Bevan to draw attention away from the crisis at the Department, and the sad loss of one of the students. All seemed drawn into the ploy, but Emily who remained subdued.

The hour wore on, and after some in the party had left for class, including Bevan, the drinks came on in greater quantity, and Amanda found herself surrounded by a class of drunken students by mid-afternoon.

Emily got up and excused herself to go to the powder room. Amanda had to shuffle back her chair to let her through, and it was just at that moment that she looked up and recognized Trevor coming out of the dinning area.

"Trevor!" she called out happily, waving.

The class looked up, and he acknowledged the table of academics with a smile. But it was awkward.

"Isn't that Trevor MacDonnell..." asked one "the Member of Parliament?..."

Not that everyone didn't recognize the name from the calls he made as member of the government enquiry, or the calls made by him into her office. He had focused on Amanda, even sending flowers on one occasion.

"Oh" offered Emily, the diplomat "Our Member of Parliament with a penchant for *our* lady of the lectern!" They laughed.

Amanda raised her hand to wave hello. It was only then that Amanda noticed something, her head a little light from a beer.

It was the expression on Trevor's face that remained blank, his posture - that of civility bereft of warmth. Then she saw the girl at his arm and watched him help her with her coat. Trevor ignored Amanda as he ushered the blond through the Restaurant.

Like an innocent, Amanda was left proffering a friendly wave!

The detail was not lost on the rest of the table, and Amanda felt stupidly humiliated. It was enough to kill the festive feast, and one by one, they excused themselves and left.

Amanda suddenly realized that they had begun to clear the table, and she sat there feeling abandoned. Except for one person.

Of course he had other women in his life, you idiot!

"I'm sorry" said Emily   "I caused you the embarrassment with my big mouth...I never saw *her*..."

"No! Not...not anything to worry about. Certainly silly of us to assume anything!" she said.

"True. But didn't you just spend a weekend with him in Paris?"

"I went for the Conference..."

"Sure you did. Judging from all those phone messages, billets-doux and flowers at the gate..."

Amanda suddenly stood up. "Please!" she said, and walked out.

By this evening it would be all over campus - a silly rumor about a stupid assumption.

* *

It was a particularly contentious affair. To believe in something you've just said, and then to give it up. Especially as a young adult.

Amanda tried to forestall him. But forestalled he would not be. Not with half the girls watching, and the other half holding wooden spoons for a play.

"That stuff is a load of pretentious drivel..." he had said archly about one of the 17th century paintings on the screen showing wealth of trades for the Empires of Europe. He was referring to the exhibit of a fellow student.

Amanda folded her arms and paced, calmly, from her position on the platform. She gave the student time to continue.

"How could painters paint such beauty... and... their masters go outside and burn a...a..woman!"

"A witch!" volunteered a voice from the rear of the class.

"Yeah. Like you" chortled another voice from somewhere else.

"That was one of the cultural dilemmas of the era" explained the fellow student whose exhibit was on display " The immersion of a society, funded by patronage -- if often unyielding, engulfing and marked by rebellion –offer shelter and protection"

"Cool" said someone.

She continued. "Imagine the outlet that such a liberality would present to a world of peasants! Most of them ruled by feudalism, the hopes for individuals a forbidden sin..."

"But not if you were a witch!" persisted the voice of protest from the rear, determined to humiliate the girl giving the presentation.

Amanda looked up. Time to take action.

"The statistics on witchcraft..." she said to the protestor about to receive the Award of the Class Lollipop for disruption "was considerably worse in the New World than in Europe."

And before she could bring up the house lights, he stood up and shouted "That's because women are bitches!"

The female student he addressed gathered her exhibit to leave.

So much for good teacher supervision Amanda thought to herself.

The boy would never like Art history for sure. But why so defensive? So she gathered all the authoritarian leverage she could muster and marched to the lectern. "Neither! Sorry Mr. Nolles, but you are quite mistaken!" It was something she hated to do to a student, but his personal outburst was unacceptable.

"Actually. Witchcraft *was* an instrument of social compliance   exercised by the Church, less for evangelical reasons as for political ..."

Sneering.

"..Given that only with the blessing of the Church did Royal sovereignty rule, the Ecclesiastical reins of the Church was precisely the geo-political axis for social enforcement. Given that the femininity of the women related to childbearing and pagan ritual was already infused with suspicion and mysticism..." she added, noting the young man still burning with embarrassment "was precisely the point of contention and threat to the social order..."

 "... So, if we re-consider the notions of women helping men at great works of art, if it was a woman's hand in a painting -- precisely during the age of banking patronage and emergent commerce –it was always *his* name that was signed on the bottom of the tapestry! It may not have been fair. But it did, at the very least, feed the family of the artist. So, think more generously with your...judgments! "

As far as Amanda was concerned, the class could not have been dismissed a second sooner. Her own feelings were a mess, let alone what just happened.

She recalled the words of a famous author who once said that if an undergraduate student in whom he had faith submitted that comment, he would have called it "high falutin'". If a graduate of promise did it he would have called it "Pretentious Arrogance". If a trusted college would have uttered such comments he would have said "Bullshit!"

She tended to her papers. And she was definitely in the last stages of frustration with this class. But nothing near the underlying cause of her malaise tonight. Her thoughts started to wander.

 When it all started, she couldn't quite tell. Except for the moment when Jeannette, who had this effect on everyone, started to draw out as much drama and pain to fan any fire if it advanced her career.

It was the report.

In it Amanda had written about her sequence of imaging the documents of the early 17th century play *inside* the vault began steadily enough.

 She had signed in. They, that is, Emily her assistant and she had talked with Roger, the Security Guard, before entering the vault. The document was signed out of the box, as the log required, and carried over the illuminated table for negatives. Still in the vault, the lights of the deck had been switched off, and the natural lighting from the windows was considered sufficient for Nikon imaging in high resolution - sans flash.

The pages were each written up by Emily at her side on the laptop. All 28 pages. When finished, Amanda felt her cell vibrate and left the vault while Emily put it away.

Nothing unusual. Emily had been interviewed and her exit was minutes behind Amanda according to the logbook.

But when Jeannette handed Amanda the images of the vault taken "before" and "after" entry of the from security cameras, Amanda felt her heart stop. And somehow, she had managed not to show her hand to Jeannette. After all, Roger had been disallowed back into work the next Monday. So she was indeed the last one inside the vault, Friday night.

There on the image, like crumbs from a meal at edge of the imaging table, was something that was not there when she left!

But she had seen too many of them to know what they were. Blue and gold banded, savanna colored tobacco thin cigars. They were leftover smokes from Emily's boyfriend, Edward.

She remembered looking out the window rather than face Jeannette. The blue sky, pale and fading into the night without cloud. Something in the weather that belied plunging temperatures into a rare, but not unknown, Arctic night, occurring only when the warm jet stream off America failed to journey the Atlantic and caress the shores of England.

Amanda shook herself from her reverie, and refocused on the matters before her.

And she almost missed him, filing out of the room as the last of the class to leave.

"Peter!" she called out. It was the student provocateur. He looked up, his face still brindled with red and hotness.

What she might have appropriately said, in a place of learning like this seemed suddenly to elude her.

She gestured a nod of acknowledgement with a brief wave.

He understood, smiled, then looked down.

The blip on her cell was unmistakable. Finally, an answer from Emily. What took her so long?

She viewed the text message. "Not feeling well. Left town for a while..."

She placed her hands on both hips and looked down.

* *

It was impossible for Emily to accept. *You don't kill people over a manuscript, do you?*

Somehow, the question popped out her mouth in class when a similar topic came up as to provenance. The Instructor was the Department Head, Bevan.

The question was greeted with laughter all round.

"In Medieval times, heads were lost for lesser deeds" quoted Bevan, taking a stride to respond.

"Hardly fitting for men of learning, though" insisted the girl in the front row of the auditorium.

"Well that depends" replied Bevan. "The motive of money and fame have informed many a novelist. After all, academic fame can translated into treasure in the world of publishing or perishing. It's like works of Art. We struggle for authentication, preservation and care for the public to learn from...But in the hands of private collectors, art is worth great fortunes. Especially considering the millions spend in Insurance and Museum Collections..."

Jeannette Bevan had a way of sneering with her cleverness. It always had the same effect on her class. A somber silence stilled any further questions. Yet it rang in Emily's head like a crystal bell. Of course, Amanda Wells had much to gain from fooling around with that damned manuscript! If Ed had not volunteered to come in and help...Oh God! Not only did Amanda Wells have something to prove academically, but she was professionally being consulted on something in her "area of expertise" might reveal to some very important officials in the government....Some claim or other. It was good for her career. She was ambitious. She had promised the safekeeping of it all in the Vault of the University while she "gave it full analysis and thought..."

Amanda. Bloody academic snobs, she decided. And she felt angry. Ed was dead.

* *

Twenty Five

Two days later, as Amanda assessed the damage done, she realized she had been caught up in an unfortunate moment, and reacted inappropriately.

Worse, it damaged her credibility as an Academic.

But what she regretted most was her abruptness to someone still sitting beside her and grieving the death of a friend. As it was, Emily was on shaky ground. To push her away at this time was not fair to someone in so fragile a state.

She made her decision.

It took her all day to find Emily, but she did. At the boathouse, and in full tilt with a few friends whom she did not recognize. Whatever the details, it was clear she was baiting boys, and drinking.

She approached.

"Hello Emily" said Amanda. "Can I have a word?"

Emily did not appear to have slept, or changed even. She was desensitized, if not altogether disconnected.

"Sure! Why not?" she slurred, veering off to the porch of the boathouse. "So. What's up?"

"I came by to apologize...To say that I overreacted, and should have overlooked the coincidence of seeing someone we all knew, I should have focused on the lunch company of some very wonderful young people..."

"Ok" said Emily, taking a healthy swig of beer "So you overreacted...So bloody what? And if it helps you to know, I do accept your apophasis...apologies...yeah, apologies, whatever!"

"Emily...How are you doing?"

"Ooooo! I'm fine. Just fine!"

They called for her "Come on darling, we're leaving now. Common an' ave another beer. To Tommy's place! Get on with it..."

Amanda noticed that these were not the normal friends that she and Edward had shared. They were a disparate bunch, friends of a wilder sort.

Emily grinned at Amanda. "Gotta go!"

"Emily!" said Amanda. "Wait..." She smiled. "Have you had dinner?"

"Dinner? You must be joking...As in, proper food and a joint of lamb like?" She laughed. "Oh yeah...we're having our joint of fun tonight...And more!"

They called her again. "*Emily...Darling!*
La..La..La...Common on!"

Amanda didn't like what she was seeing. Clearly, the boys were circling for a night of play. And Emily was impaired. The morning would only bring the dullness of regret. Emily was not in control of her emotions yet.

Amanda was torn. Take a hint and leave, like a polite individual. Say you did your bit...Or jump in and save a girl drowning in the emotional whiplash of a brutal assault on the boy she loved, someone she could have no claim on.

Amanda decided to jump in. It was too recent a trauma to have reconciled. But she had to fight the girl for a hour just to get her in the car. Ostensibly for dinner. But she brought Emily to the apartment.

They fought.

Emily was full of anger unreconciled. Amanda was an easy target.

"So...err...you got all those accolades, you and them... over Ed's manuscripts Huh? I hope it was worth it...To advance your careers! You and that Bitch Bevan." She sank in the armchair, tossing aside the coffee and sandwich Amanda prepared for her. But she did pick up the cup of soup and swallowed the hearty stew between sobs and outbursts.

" And...*What* was in those manuscripts that you you you *prized* to so much? That he had to protect? What, what, what was so worth dying for? He was the only man who cared about me..."

"Emily..."

"I never wanted to get *involved* with anybody!...I wanted to...I wanted. Oh God!" she wailed. "He was so sweet. So kind...I want to die. Tonight, I'm going to end it all, you'll see *Goddamnedyou!..*"

"Emily..."

The brutality of it all was more than Emily could handle. "*Why. Why...*" she wanted to know sinking to the floor in a pool of tears and regret.

"All you frozen-faced academics!" she thrashed. " It would serve you right if you were trashed academically for the price you people want for your *accolades*! ... What was he doing? You're heartless! You, and Bevan...and your bloody two- timing Member of Parliament...Ed was not like that! He was tender. Real. Sincere. He cared, while you...you...take advantage of his sincerity and his world...."

"Emily. He *was* in his world! He was happy! *You* are the one that gave him happiness!"

Emily was too angry to manage. Twice Amanda received calls from her neighbor about the noise. Finally she slipped a sedative in her drink.

Emily snoozed, then threw up. Amanda fairly dragged her into the bathroom and cleaned her off. Then walked her back to a bed.

* *

Scotland 1672

His plan was impeccable. His hat, flourished with a large plume, long ago dated, served his purpose.

He stood there in a red velvet wardrobe and leather belt. He was most convincing, especially the way he described himself for this mission. This he must have told his fellow clansmen. Perhaps on the moors of Scotland. Certainly in his thick Gaelic dialect.

Trevor read the letter in evidence.

He could imagine the moment as he read his account.

Paterson was presenting a plan for the Isthmus of Panama, high on the banks of the Caledonia Bay. Where they had decided to construct Fort St. Andrews, equipped with fifty ship's cannon.

In the letter to William III, he told of the Fort. He explained how it would be defended by fifty ordnance.

In it, he wrote, would be a small harvest of yams and maize. They could pay the local Indians to assist them in farming, with trade items like combs and trinkets.

Across on the mountain, on the opposite side of the harbor, they would build a Watch House. Close to the Fort, they would erect the huts of the main settlement, calling it *New Edinburgh*.

From there, they would dig a canal through the neck of land that divides the Caledonia Bay from the great Ocean, at Panama.

It would require, by Patterson's accounting some £400,000 to be raised by investors in London for the Company of Scotland.

For provisioning, they should stop at Port Royal Jamaica. Such support would need at least five ships of the line.

Trevor looked at the manifest.

Patterson had succeeded in procuring financial support for the missions.

From whom?

The first expedition of five ships (*Saint Andrew, Caledonia, Unicorn, Dolphin,* and *Endeavour*) set sail from Leith 14 July 1698, with around 1,200 people on board. Their orders were *to proceed to the Bay of Darien, and make for the Isle called the Golden Island ... some few leagues to the leeward of the mouth of the great River of Darien ... and there "make a settlement on the mainland"*

Trevor noted from the logs that after calling at Madeira and the West Indies, the fleet made landfall off the coast of Darien on 2nd November. The Settlers christened their new home "*New Caledonia*"

What Patterson could not know was that this letter had been interdicted. Hence it had been preserved!

So, the Spanish *knew* of his arrival. In fact, his plans were used for their battle response. Clearly there was a Spy...

In England, the failure of the Darien scheme was greatly contested.

Some said it was the impulse behind 1707 Acts of Union in which Scotland was forever weaved into the fabric of England.

Others said that the Scottish establishment realized that it could never be a major power on its own and that if it wanted to share the benefits of England's international trade and the growth of the English Empire, then its future would have to lie in unity with England.

But most significantly, the Scottish economy had been bankrupted by the "Darien Fiasco" and Westminster had been petitioned by Scotland to embrace all debts and save the currency – so deep was the damage.

Many in Scotland were personally involved. Especially those that had invested heavily in the Darien Scheme...expecting compensation for their losses.

The 1707 Acts of Union, Article 14, granted £398,085 10s sterling to Scotland to offset future liability towards the English national debt.

Trevor consulted the very map used. New Map of the Isthmus of Darien in Central America, The Bay of Panama. The Bay of Vallona or St. Michael, with its Islands and Countries, Adjacent. *A letter giving A Description of the Isthmus of Darian*, Edinburgh. It had been written October, 1699.

* *

Emily had agreed to feed the cat.

She sat heavily on the sofa, stretched out her legs and took a drink from the Heineken.

It's not that she could fault the Chair of the Department for asking questions about things...it's just that she hadn't liked the *way* she asked the questions. Know what I mean, she asked. But then again, perhaps that was how those in the rarefied echelons of power did things. Or perhaps she was imagining things.

She took another swig.

Without Edward there was no new normal, decided Emily. That is, she would chat with him for hours, and he would re-order matters for her. Like the time he bought her a bracelet, and called it an Amulet, like a poet would. Or how he could explain the shapes of a painting, and what the beauty was behind the things *she* painted and loved about Art History...He gave meaning to her life, in ways she could not always articulate.

God, how she missed him!

 It was almost too much to bear, the loss of no Edward... a world without him...

And as for Robinson's deposition which had to come into evidence with his comments about Edward being in the vault to take pictures using the Department's camera. Well that was hogwash. When would he have done all that? Without Emily knowing?

Bullshit!

Unless Amanda had actually asked him? But wouldn't she have said something?

Anyway, what was Jeannette Bevan asking her for? It was the Notes on Amanda's research paper that she wanted, after all. Which of course, she was entitled to ask for. Perhaps to help Amanda.

As Department Chair she was in a position to monitor all research, findings and papers. She was in charge of the Faculty, the Staff and the budgets. She hired students. She fired students. She gave scholarships and she gave internships. She could also withhold funding.

"So, are you saying that you *saw* Edward on the day he was killed?" she had asked.

"No! I hadn't heard from him for days. As I told the Superintendent"

"Oh. I see" said Jeannette Bevan "Ok..." harmless like. Then "But Mr. Robinson says he was there, didn't he?"

"I didn't know that, did I?"

"Oh. I see" (again) "So, then, Professor Wells was the last person to see Edward alive?"

"I guess" Shrugged Emily, masking her dismay at not knowing that he was in the building on that day.

"It's just that..." continued Jeannette with an irritable tapping of the pencil against her glossy nails

"Well, I don't know. But if Mr. Robinson said he was in the vault on Thursday evening...then he must have been helping Professor Wells with her project in the Vault, wouldn't you say?"

Emily wanted to leave the room and shuffled against the door jam.

"Umm..." lingered Jeannette with the thought.

"So...if that's the case, then Dr. Wells must have been the last person to see Edward alive, would you say?"

That was when Emily left with a disinterested shrug. Actually she ran down the hallway and entered the bathroom. She threw up in the toilet furthest from the door, where an old window could be opened for air. January air, icy, cold.

Lonely air for Emily, with Edward gone...Now.

The light had faded from the apartment altogether. She sat there still, in the dark.

To just imagine that Amanda Wells had been the last to see Edward was just too bleak . She had gone with her to their house. Helped clear it out. Hell, she had brought her back here!

Jack was staring. It shook her back to reality. No Way! She got up, locked up, and left.

The last thing she heard Jeannette Bevan do was pick up the phone to the Superintendent at Scotland Yard.

Did Amanda Wells actually set up Ed..? Like Bevan said...Surely not.

Then again, manuscripts of indescribable imagination and legacy had been hers to read, evaluate and comment on. The burden of proof was upon her to procure a solution for so many officials...What if...what if? It would, for starters, give her world celebrity status, just to set something like that up for discover...

She wanted to throw up at the thought of it all. And she trusted her!

* *

"Look, Amanda, I'd like to talk with you!"

"I'm up to my armpits in research, Trevor. Sorry. It's almost impossible..."

"It's about the Asset related to the boy Neville. And the players around it. I can't explain it over the phone. There is so much to tell you, and I do want to see you..."

"Sorry, Trevor..."

"Amanda, this is important!"

"No!"

"It's also about that luncheon at the Roadside Inn...I'm sorry, I should have..."

"No problem. You owe us no explanation! As you saw from the luncheon, we all have our work cut out for us...It s a serious challenge, the analysis coming up on the case before us for the government. We are about 75% into a report. I'm busy! "

"Damn it, that is MY case! You're right. But I want to talk to you about something else related..."

She hung up. It felt good.

Damned if she was going to wait on his apologies, excuses or explanations about being seen with another woman! That was just *de trop,* as the French called it. Besides, hanging onto men was not Amanda's style. Neither was it her style to be in a position of worrying about whether men liked her! In fact, she was angry at herself for putting herself in a vulnerable corner with any man. Nor was she going to let this dominate her thoughts.

She proceeded with her chores, angry at herself yet for even allowing there to be any suspicion of anticipation with this man...Trevor was, well, Trevor. A playboy! And he was no longer her boss. Or her anything else, for that matter.

The next day he left a message. He called to say he had a problem. The case was not going well for him, and there was a matter related to the Neville family that had to be resolved.

The story that came out that evening was almost unbelievable. They had drinks at the bar downstairs, not far from campus.

 "The boy was baptized with my father as proxy godparents. There is a legacy in Trust that we were to execute on his behalf..."

"When did this knowledge surface?" she asked.

"My mother" he said simply. "You don't know her!"

"How does this bear on the matter before the government, now?"

He avoided her eyes.

"Anyway, we are to provide evidence that the family had authentic ownership over the assets with continuous accountability since the Trust was set up ..."

"*continuous accountability*? ...So, in addition to needing my help to provide evidence for authenticity of ownership of a 17th century sovereign project, you also now have a personal family inheritance matter related to the boy Neville? Is that it?"

"Pretty much. Yes!" His cell phone purred, he averted his eyes.

"*Yes. I can do that, tomorrow, then...*" he was saying on the phone.

Amanda recognized her cue to make an exit. "Let me guess. The-bony-blonde and you have a date tomorrow of the utmost secrecy..."

"...With the solicitor, the Trust Committee and the Bank of England. I get to decide if she is lying about her inheritance."

"How sweet!" said Amanda, sliding off the bar stool "I'll tell Emily that her boyfriend might be a fake, and that something he was killed for didn't even belong to him because his very identity is now challenged by a long lost aunt's 23 year old daughter who gets to inherit a valuable literary treasure; the estate and even his family title..?"

"Amanda!" he called.

She left Trevor standing. It was all she could do to not to tear up. The damned irony of it was just too much! First Emily losing herself over the boy. Now Trevor saying the boy's identity and legacy never belonged to him, yet something he was killed for...

* *

Twenty Six

"The conclusion that I hold is that *she is* indeed the heir to estate" said Trevor facing Charms.

"You do realize of course that once you make that determination we shall open the vault and break the seal on those files which, as you know, cannot be re-sealed..." The Assayer's Accountant was sitting across the table and representing the Assayers Report for the Bank of England.

"Let's be sure you have been properly informed" said Charms. "We shall need an investigation as to her identity and pedigree. We might even ask for a DNA blood type for identification purposes."

Trevor raised his hand. "Wait just a second, please, if you don't mind, Jack..."

He uncrossed his legs and leaned forward. "It's not that I don't appreciate your need to be certain, - of course we must be, and you are quite right to insist on it. But to ask for a DNA blood sample would be, maybe, just a little *too much*, don't you suppose?"

"Yes and No" said the Accountant. "I agree, it is tipping the matter a little beyond the normal. But on the other hand, this is someone who claims to be the daughter of someone who disappeared for a generation, and stands to walk away with a great deal. ..The circumstances do tip the balance! I agree with Frank."

Trevor looked down. "Perhaps so. But if she is the rightful heir, and I do believe she is based on the information she gave me, what a shame it would be to have her start her life with a proof of her biological composition as the only means of true verification. It will leave a bitter taste in her mouth forever! Especially as she must take her place in society and make a contribution to the wellbeing and care of the legacy asset...It is, after all, a national treasure!"

"Umm" said Charms. "I understand what you are saying. Especially since so much is at stake, and the details of the past require some discretion once these files are opened." He paused "In the hands of an disenfranchised party, it might do some irreparable damage both to the innocent, and to those in the past who were in charge of a very difficult war..."

"And Treasure!" chirped the Assayer.

"...If not the political damage to those trying to solve problems today, let alone the leadership dealing with older issues of some social impact..."

"Not at all" said Trevor, standing up. "People today are smart! Give them the facts, and they can figure it out.."

"Yes, for all but the gullible" remarked the Accountant.

"Tell you what, then" said Frank Charms. "Let's leave it as a position of last resort! First, let's take her deposition, examine the details, and come to some conclusion on our own. If there is any doubt, then we will insist upon it, and beg her to understand our concerns. ..How's that?"

"Agreed."

* *

Karmoski threw off the joy sticks and slammed at the desk. The others looked up.

In the working quarters of the control room of the *Vienna*, a 153 ft research vessel, there was little room for isolation let alone frustration. But before they could ask, Karmoski was on his computer Monitor again, with sweat wreathed across his forehead.

"She moving like a terd in these waters!" he muttered. "Can't see a damn thing in this turbidity and the R-pincer is behaving like a bludgeon"

The ROV at twenty five hundred feet below the surface surveying a debris field strewn across half a mile of shadows, over crevices and uneven seafloor.

It was a shipwreck in various states of collapse on an unstable perch, and had accumulated a prodigious flora of slimy sea grass. That it was teeming with sea life was perhaps its only redeeming reward for the team that was operating the deep sea exploration.

Only if the manipulator arms were split by the two joy sticks, could they work at full capacity. Unfortunately, both were powered by the one joystick, even with a five degree area of deviation. The R-pincer could lift its remotely manipulated claw up to 60 degrees without locking when the two arms were at equal elevation. Plus, the bottom was uneven. This precluded any tandem effort by both arms at the same time for any productivity. The going was slow.

There was no way he could know if, deep within the housing of the wiring, the critical wire that programmed the R-handed pincer at full capacity was crossed and crushed by the line to the L-pincer when both were in full operation.

While the programs would allow for an item to lift off the bottom like a tea cup with a pinky, it could only do elbow lifting for a camera that called for both pincers to exercise pinpoint precision and tactile dexterity.

"Someone should design this manipulator for a left-handed thinker!" he admonished.

His invective was ample.

But Karmoski was not about to give up. He abandoned the claws and used the suction cups to lift the coins off the bottom and place them in the suspended baskets waiting close by.

It would take several hours to surface the material, and before cataloguing could begin, it was the crew's one treat to see firsthand the fruits of their labor.

Today was no exception. The find was fabulous. Inscribed on the gold surface of the coin was the insignia of William III Rex. 1694

* *

Amanda was driving.

"What did she say her did, as a child, you know, the habits of a household, like watching her mother cook, or sew, or her father gardening? Anything like that..."

Amanda knew that historians had ways of reconstructing the past out of details that could speak volumes.

"Oh...I don't know" said Trevor, staring out the passenger window and letting the green fields and pastures pass over his thoughts. "Normal things. Yes, gardening of fruits, flowers. A trailer park in the Netherlands, by the sea, upon land owned by the Church..."

"She must speak several languages, then?"

"Yes. French. Flemish, Italian, Spanish, Polish, English...you know, the general mixed bag that comes out of northern Europe"

" Umm" said Amanda taking the I95 route North.

Amanda looked up into the Rear-view mirror and smiled at their passenger.

They were driving Trevor's mother back up to Scotland. And as she sat in the rear, it had been agreed by both Trevor and Amanda that they should not burden her with the matter. She should not be left anguished for the lack of memory that might bring clarity of the case. "

Trevor turned to face her. "How about a bite to eat, Mother?"

"Oh, yes please let's do so! Can we make it to Mrs Hilda Trevellian's? She has been after me every day for a week to spend a day on the way north. It's not far off the Lake District"

"Will she have scones and clotted cream, Mum?" grinned Trevor , and Amanda realized the trip was erasing from his face lines of fatigue and anxiety.

"Oh God. Of course!" sang out his mother

Trevor turned to Amanda. "Would you mind...?"

"Not at all!" she smiled. Then added "All of us descending on her without warning...Would that be an imposition?"

"Not at all!" he smiled. "She has a staff to help her every need. Don't worry!"

"For clotted cream and scones, I shall drive you anywhere!" laughed Amanda.

"Oh good" said Mrs. MacDonnell. "That gives her the chance to catch up on three years worth of news...what gossip!"

"Mother!" admonished Trevor.

"Children..." admonished Amanda

They laughed.

Bold blue skies clouded up occasionally with white puffy cumulous creations that skimmed the mountainous landscape, then vanished suddenly with a fierce blow of wind. It seemed that what passed for villages, towns and fields was only the playground for England's grand sky dance. The miles advanced quickly, and sometimes in peaceful silence.

"Oh but this is a beautiful car to drive!" said Amanda, referring to the Bentley

"It is, isn't it...with her sweet touch and deep power purring just below the bonnet... She's a dream!"

Amanda smiled. "Spoken only like an Englishman!" She caught him looking at her.

"Left...at the gate, then right and straight through!" instructed Mrs. MacDonnell from the rear seat.

And it took Amanda's breath away. An estate stood at the far end of a deep valley threaded by a lake. It fairly reflected like a castle in a fairytale. She paused.

"Hildie's!" said Mrs. MacDonald, almost clapping her hands in glee. "She's expecting us...I called her this morning!"

Trevor looked over at her, then at Amanda. *Oh dear. A hidden agenda!*

Amanda took a deep breath, then adjusted to the unexpected turn of events, and eased on the pedal to drive slowly through the estate. "No problem!" she said gamely.

Trevor's arms reached out across the seat and lightly squeezed her shoulder, appreciating her grace.

After dinner, with the table cleared away by the Butler and the ladies still chatting, Amanda strayed out onto the stone terrazzo with a drink in her hand. The view was stunning. The lake at dusk was surrendering a purple hue mist steaming with rain forest birdsong and frog drilling. Trevor joined her.

"Nice detour, wouldn't you say?"

"Stunning!" She gazed at the coloring and took a deep breath. "Funny thing..."

"Umm?"

"...the languages. All Romantic languages, but one..."

"What?"

It took a few seconds for Trevor to come out of his reverie "*Languages*?"

"Polish..." said Amanda simply. "It's a Germanic- root language!"

Twenty Seven

"The girl was found and considered seriously injured. She was taken to a nearby hospital and treated for little more than head injuries..."

"What?" said Charms.

The solicitor went on reading from the deposition.

"The woman who adopted her became her mother. This mother told her that with the war over, they could return to their country of origin and be free to rebuild. Or so she claimed. Because the years went by with little mention of any details, other than it was an accident. She knew that her mother was married. A Dutchman who later went into the police force."

"Her schooling , as far as we can investigate, checks out. Her mother arrived on the scene with a six year old after the war who needed to enroll for classes at the local Catholic school. Her citizenship was given as Dutch; but then again..." he looked up over the rim of his reading glasses "who checked for much after the war?"

"Her *grandmother* - that is, the mother of the woman who adopted her - spoke only Polish, her aunts and uncles, Italian.

"None of them of local citizenship except as new settlers after the war. They liked music, reading, radio and knitting for entertainment in the evenings. And they all loved to listen to Radio Luxemburg for music.

"By the fifties, the mother had a job in a print shop producing calligraphy and stationary for specialty custom orders. Her father was vaguely gone on mission, apparently.

" Her memories of the war are undefined. Except when she was on her way to college, her family told her she had a claim and family connection in England. She explained that the story was told her by her mother who gave her these items as proof..."

The solicitor put down the document and the room went silent.

Before them were the shoes and dress-coat of a three year old girl. Pink, lined, buttoned and stitched with bows and a buckle. If faded, it appeared to be authentic, with little creases of wear at the back.

Somehow the very nature of the objects brought home the ghastly reality of an era fraught by tragedy, and a war that had taken the lives of so many. And here before them, a child's belongings, strewn on the table. The sense of regret and loss was almost palpable. The clothes that the girl had worn were clearly before them, and matched the descriptions of the account.

" If this isn't evidence that fits the description of the clothes the child wore, then we have little choice. We open the box, compare it with the contents, and give her Title to all that Sir Neville claimed, ahead of the boy Neville, deceased. She then, was is in line of seniority position of inheritance through her mother. Including the assets of the family legacy!"

"We've been over this a dozen times" said Charms. "The investigative team and insurance solicitors all agree. We are at the final decision point now."

"Right   then!"   said   the   solicitor.

"Let's open the vault, unseal the file, review the evidence. And if all reconciles, then she is the rightful heir!"

"We'll proceed next week under a formal enquiry for the record?" said Charms.

"Ten o'clock, next Wednesday then. We shall sequester ourselves in the bank vault conference room, with an honorable member of the Bench presiding over the procedure."

They all agreed.

Trevor felt relieved to be coming to some conclusion. It brought closure. And frankly, he was beginning to feel pressed for time. But it was necessary to provide solace for his mother, if not for the estate itself which had to be Executed by the Trustee, his father, now deceased. Besides, the matter of the missing child was finally getting resolved.

His cell buzzed.

Things were heating up on his case. He had a pile of critical work to get to...The sooner this was concluded, the better to proceed to other business.

Thank God!

Still, he left the building with a feeling of unease. Uncertain as to why, he decided, it was nothing.

A missing link somewhere.

* *

The expression of distaste did not leave Trevor's face until he put down the account he was reading.

He looked out the window from his office at the Palace of Westminster where he was working on the case.

William III's effectiveness as a monarch pretty much ended after the sinking of the Fleet...with money aboard, and an angry Parliament citing the King's rule and questioning his loyalty.

Even more traitorous was the Duke of Savoy himself, the "foreign prince" to whom William was sending the gold of England!

Worse. It took Savoy less than a year, after the fleet sank, to betray the English and ally with the French... even as William promised him a second shipment of money!

Henry, his Assistant popped his head in the door "Hows it going?"

Trevor was glad to talk. "I can't help returning to the central question of ownership...Or even the allegiance of the King of England – a foreign prince himself -- as he was sending English money to his cousin! ...The motive must have been a strong one"

"Indeed it is. Clearly he had found the means. The Fleet had never been outfitted in the Mediterranean before. Nor had they wintered out of dock. And someone was paying for the seamen..."

"that leaves opportunity. what was the connection?"

"I wish I knew, Sir" he said.

"Still. I've got some ideas. But thank you! And by the way, tell Stu I'm pleased with his report. Nice work. Both of you!"

Trevor turned to the Salvage Files. The Exploration Team was on a ship called...*Vienna*?

"Yes. Bought and paid for by the Swiss winner of the America's Cup sailboating event. Rather a contentious affair, I'm afraid. He took the Deed of Gift, or rather the spirit of the thing and turned it on its head with high tech gear, design and killer- take- all- strategy..."

"Not very Corinthian of him..."

"No. But the Americans will find a way. I'm sure. They love their sailing!"

"As do we!"

"Yes Sir"

"He funded the project. But is not part of it" continued Henry. "The salvage company had experts in deep-ocean shipwreck exploration, and had developed quite a following on the American stock markets. Everyone with deep pockets had bought stock options. They provided research and shipwreck search and survey services."

The support team listened carefully. They waited for him to complete his report.

"Recently they received a large US Federal Contract to search within the Gulf of Mexico to identify sunken vessels and known wrecks for proper identification and interpretation. It was a lucrative contract, shared generously, with history departments of the University of Louisiana. Doubtless favored regional status given post- Katrina, for that Congressional district."

Trevor consulted the Assets on the Fiscal syllabus.

"They had Rights of Retrieval. Plus anticipated sale of coins or artifacts; repayment for salvage costs and fees; 78% net revenue in aggregate up to an additional $25 MM."

Not bad, thought Trevor. He looked up. This from one Salvage alone. Not bad for a business!

He then turned to their representatives.

* *

Twenty Eight

"I can't image why I forgot..." said his mother over the phone, her Scottish brogue no less distinct now that it had been all his known life "But the closet in the Attic had to be cleared out. And I found the suitcase that your father kept from the war..."
Trevor was listening, but with one eye on the clock near his desk. Susie came in, and he motioned her to step forward with the letters he needed to sign. He did so as he listened.
"I do hope it didn't fill you with distress, mother. Dr James will be after me if it did, you know that, don't you?"
"Don't you be worrying about me lad. I'll be fine. Just fine. And quite the contrary. .."
The other phone rang.
"In the suitcase..." she continued "your father did keep letters sent to him by me; and even a rose he sent, Many, many wonderful moments of tenderness

between us, you know. It was because he valued love for keeps!"

"You were the love of his life..." said Trevor, spinning around his chair to face the window.

"Nay. But *you* were his bairne..." she continued. "At any rate. I found a package that said there was a file in the Bank of England that would offer the proof of the case of the missing child. He said that what was in the file was evidence. And he had a picture of evidence."

"Can you see it?"

"Oh Aye. I have it in my hand, and I'm reading. It says *Debris from the burning of the car. To be verified against the evidence in the file.*"

"Oh?" said Trevor, signing off on two more letters for Susie.

"You've had it in the Attic all these years?"

"Oh aye... I shall send it. By the way, how is that lovely girl you were with? I'd like to give her my diamond brooch" said his mother.

Trevor's thoughts went to the young woman who had presented herself to his office, less than two weeks ago. Trevor at first would have responded that she was just a Claimant who came forward. Tall, blond and beautiful...as they all pointed out at Frank and Janet Charm's party last night.

But he realized that his mother was referring to someone else.

"Well alright mother. I look forward to receiving it."

He would have like to chat further, to assure her that something was happening on the front of the boy Neville. That there was resolution coming soon...But he decided against it. Besides, Susie was pointing at her watch, suggesting that he had a meeting of barristers down the hallway in less than ten...

"Thank you for calling me, Mother" he said.

* *

There was something that had bothered Trevor for days.

He was shaving when it hit him with sudden clarity. Words that his mother said at Claridges. *"Why was the coat not worn by the child in an open car?"*

His cell buzzed. It was Amanda who informed him that she had just uploaded some fresh information on the general web site cache, for his perusal.

"It seems I have a match with the manuscript in the possession of The Lord Neville at the same time of the Virginia London Company when minting money was much needed! It's the emblem of the family seal, similar to both! That takes us one step closer to providing a provenance for the sovereign wealth project"

"That's good news!" he said. "Well done!"

"A little magnification, a little augmentation, and a little imagination..." she said

"That, and a great mind, - The Lord Neville of the 17th century."

"Yes" she said "And, how are things going for you?"

"Well, as you know, I'm working on the veracity of a case related to Sir Neville of the 20th century. His ancestors, now many generations later, were actually friends of my father during WWII."

"Oh?"

" the Neville family presented my father with a challenge. He was the Executor of Sir Henry Neville's Will. The accident left the legacy of the family treasure in jeopardy, now that the boy has died. So, we're trying to prove *who* the rightful owner is..."

"Or *why...*" she interrupted.

"Alright. Or why!" he conceded. "Anyway, the hearing is tomorrow. We shall find out if it all fits when the vault box is opened."

"I'm sure you'll make the right decision, Trevor" she said lightly "And I must not take up your time..."

"Oh, before you go, you should know that my mother just called and asked me how the girl in my life was doing..."

" Oh" laughed Amanda "She's tall, bony- blond and beautiful, of course!"

"Actually, Olga was in the office and did meet my mother on the day I delivered her back to Claridges for her Spa. Facial treatments! I thought the two of them would never stop comparing notes!"

"Ha! That's wonderful!"

"By the way, it wasn't Olga my mother was referring to when she asked me about the girl in my life...It was you!"

"Oh dear..."

"Yes. She evidently wants to give you her brooch. That means she wants me to marry that girl!"

Amanda smiled. "Give her my best. Bye."

They had giggled of course, but it made Amanda wonder how she would feel if Trevor shared his mother's sentiment.

She smiled.

* *

There had to be a different approach: Something that was directly linked, yet lost by time. A strong piece of evidence had to provide the link.

Historians fretted at the paucity of documents that survived the Middle Ages.

But like any other forensic analytical process, the details would reveal themselves, if not in the heart of individuals, then in some innocuous administrative record!

Where to begin?

Amanda spent the evening going over the elements of the case that would best find a motive. She made pencil marks and notes along the margins. She would have to start with the beginning.

Queen Elizabeth. What was her story?

Why was Queen Elizabeth so favorably disposed to this family of coastal England who became raiders or Spanish ships, explorers of America ...and colonial ventures...?

No. She wrote in pencil at the margin.

Queen Elizabeth I of England. That might inform the linkage to the events in the next century when the Sussex fleet sank.

Father. She scribbled.

As daughter of Henry VIII, Elizabeth was disposed against the Catholic Spanish. Why? Her father's first wife, Queen Catherine of Aragon gave the Pope of Rome continued dominion over England.

Indeed, Queen Catherine of Aragon was the daughter of two famous parents. Queen Isabella of Portugal and the Duke of Savoy who sponsored Christopher Columbus to discover the new world for the Spanish. This allowed vast plundering of South American Indian gold that would enrich the Catholic domains.

But Henry was without a male heir to the English throne. Only Mary - a girl.

Motive?

So Henry divorced Catherine of Aragon. Unheard of in the Catholic world, leaving King Henry without the kingly sanction of the Holy Roman Empire.

Ok.

So he turned England into a Protestant state. And he married Anne Boleyn, Elizabeth's mother!

Mother

Movements in Europe that began with Luther included the Huguenots, a Protestant faith hated by the Catholics – mainly because they had proprietary rights outside the Catholic domain... And since the language of change was the language of Church affiliation, many died in the name of religious persecution.

Politics.

But specifically, when Protestants in Europe presented the Catholic church with competition for commerce, trade, wealth and craftsmen...many of them became persecuted and vilified by the Catholic hierarchy, there was something else at play.

Competitors?

* *

The vault door opened with an abominable creaking.

Out came documents. They were unsealed in the presence of the Magistrate.

Piece by piece, the evidence came forward. The report. The medical coroner's examinations. The accident details and summary of the events of that day. Also, eyewitness accounts of those close to the case. Even a letter from the Prime Secretary was enclosed with two recommendations.

Finally, with Olga's full testimony and deposition entered in the log before them, they unwrapped the package.

Dark and crisply burned scraps of leather, upholstery, papers, paraphernalia and remnants of the fire emerged.

Trevor opened the envelope that his mother had sent him, an image of an item in the vault. The photograph showed charred remains on a vestment found in the car after the fire. A child's coat.

Olga the claimant was present. Wearing a white suite and hair pulled back in a knotted chignon, she looked like an heiress. She got up, citing a need to be excused. The drama of the scene was evidently beginning to agitate her, noted Trevor. As if embraced by a lover from whom she must escape, she wanted to disentangle herself. Her eyes never lingered on the child's clothing, as if fingering an old memory.

Finally, she was escorted out by a police woman who stood waiting, and the room fell silent.

So many years had elapsed since the tragedy occurred. If justice was due, now was that time.

Three solicitors; one forensic analyst; two bank executive and a Magistrate pondered the question for a final decision. The moment of authentication had arrived. In matching the evidence, they were to pronounce the claimant to a vast fortune, and to one of England's greatest treasures.

The day wore on, the recital continued.

"The claimant, Olga was daughter of the child who had gone missing from the scene of an accident which took the life of Sir Henry Neville in 1944. She came forward in response to the notice of the death of the boy Edward Henry Neville posted in the newspaper recently. She produced the dress worn by her mother on the day of the accident. Her mother Mary was the older sibling of the two children in the car, therefore had preeminent claim to the legacy over Edward Henry Neville..."

"Your Honor" said Trevor, suddenly having some doubts "We have no death certificate of the mother Mary. Further, I should show you the contents of a package sent to me by my mother just recently. It belonged to my father who was the Executor of Sir Neville's will at the time of the accident. He was also Trustee to the Neville's estate legacy during the war, should anything happen to either Sir Neville or his legacy. As you know, my father is deceased, and I stand in his place today."

"Proceed"

"Following the death of Sir Henry in his car during WWII, his son David survived and lived to be an adult and assumed the title of Neville VIII. His sister Mary was not found at the time of the accident.

In 1963, David married Lady Ellen, and their son Edward just recently died while at the University of

College City. I am here to dispose to the right heir the Asset held in the Trust of my family."

"Let the record show that we examine the contents of the vault held in the Bank of England. The contents includes evidence of the accident which was sealed in 1944. We do so now to establish the legitimacy of a claimant to the title, daughter of the child Mary who disappeared at the time of the accident. And she being the elder sibling of the two children of Neville"

The Magistrate opened the contents of the package; the images, and the small fragments.

"How say you, Mr MacDonnell as to the claimant's assertion that she be the right heir to the estate and daughter of the elder sibling?"

"In light of what has been brought to light, I find no reason to dispute the assertion" said Trevor "Unless a contradiction to the claimants assertion is discovered in evidence .."

Olga returned and sat demurely behind a desk at the midpoint of the room arrangement, with her solicitor at her side.

Behind her, and well behind the judicial barrier, Trevor and Frank Charms had seats waiting with their solicitor at their side.

The contents of the vault were examined at the Magistrate's bench. As each item was lifted, they huddled and discussed the matter amongst themselves.

The Magistrate looked up and said "Gentlemen. As you can imagine, we have much to look at. This may take some time. Please help yourselves to coffee and water at the back of the room if you wish!"

Another half hour went by.

"You'd think they were exhuming a body" whispered Trevor to Charms.

"In a way, it is the same thing!"

Finally the Magistrate spoke. "Gentlemen...

"it seems that the contents of the vault are in order, and in keeping with all that we expected. Just as you suggest Mr. MacDonnell, your father went to great lengths to record, image and detail the matter...both in the vault sealed, and in his personal possession."

They all took their places to hear the rest of his conclusion.

 "Mr. MacDonnell. We value highly the good faith and judgment shown by your family. The image you present us today, is in fact, the image of a piece of evidence found in this box. ...It is the image of the charred remains of the dress coat that the child Mary had at the time of the accident. It appears to have the same threads and composition of the dress produced now by the claimant, thereby corroborating a direct linkage to the accident scene.

"However, since the evidence was sealed and the coat preserved, we wonder at the evidence produced by the claimant. Why bring a dress coat that matches the dress, when a coat exists?...

"Further, there is some discrepancy with the dress. Whereas the coat in the car, although badly charred has the same markings as the dress and the same lining of the dress, the two match, suggesting they were tailored at the same time. But evidently, the coat was not on the child when she was taken from the scene....

"The claimant's provision of a coat here which also purportedly matches the dress. Why? It does not have *the identical lining* with the dress, and could have been manufactured to match the dress...*after the fact!*"

"I don't believe it!" said an indignant Olga." All these years..."

" This is what the team of experts are suggesting. If this is proven, then we have an incompatibility and a mismatch of the two articles of clothing. A second coat was evidently manufactured! This implies manipulation of the truth, offered as evidence for a case. Clearly, the clothing was preserved and kept for an intended purpose. Obviously, it was not anticipated that the coat in the car survived the flames of the fire. The intention of the evidence produced, therefore, is suspect. Especially since we have the remains of the original coat in the vault box!"

Trevor's hand clutched the image made of the coat by his father. It crumpled.

"Yes!" he thought. Evidently, the old man knew foul play was at hand. And the coat, or picture of it, was his only proof. Perhaps he had received a message from someone...Or perhaps not. Regardless. Trevor felt relieved.

"That's ridiculous!" said Mr. Gladstone, the solicitor

"Is it? Not if you consider the vast fortune that such a child's coat could acquire!.."

Olga cried out, embarrassed by the implication. Her solicitor stood up "Who would have kept the girl's dress - a dress that matches your *coat* – if they were *not* legitimate, and in the possession of the subject family?

The Magistrate took off his glass "Who indeed? Come now, Mr. Gladstone. Surely you have witnessed many cases of an imposter showing up with evidence belonging to another..." He reinstated his glasses

"Therefore, it is the decision of this bench that since the linings of the two articles – the one brought in by the claimant don't match, and the charred coat *does* match with the dress, the truth was manipulated, even if the dress was authentic. There is sufficient doubt that we might have an imposter, and a counterfeit claimant. The evidence was tampered with. The claim rests on the assertion that both the dress and the coat belonged to the child Mary. In other words, there is sufficient doubt to preclude a definitive conclusion.

 "Wait!" said Trevor. "What of the boy, left at the scene of the accident. Is there any connection?"

"Clearly, the assailant left the boy for dead. That implies a pre-meditated motive behind a plan. A plan of long range vision. For all we know, the girl Mary was abducted and might well have been alive at the time. Or killed. Regardless, her dress was kept for later purposes. If so, the assailant performed a deliberate act, and not only knew his victim well, but had a plot in mind all along. The two coats leave questions. We might never find proof of the girl Mary, sadly. That a daughter of hers should appear at this time, with a dress that was worn by the girl Mary as evidence, leaves us to conclude that this was a war-related incident, with crime in mind."

"That's preposterous! " exploded the solicitor.

"Mr Charms, Mr. MacDonnell. I'm sorry, but we have our doubts. We have no heir present!"

Trevor was already striding down the hall when Charms caught up with him. "Have the blood tests ordered" he said angrily "Just for the record. We known the boy Neville's biological information. There should be no doubt as to hereditary linkage...Science can tell us. I fear we have an imposter. We've been duped by a master mind!"

They reached the elevators and Trevor hit the button, frustrated that his sense of decency had betrayed him. "No blood-match, no heir!" he offered, the elevator doors closing to take him down.

"Why was the coat not worn by the child in an open car?" * *

Twenty Nine

New York

"I don't give a damn who is trying the case" said Gore to Timmy Smyth. "Find out what their case is built on and get to the records first."
Timmy protruded his neck from a tight collar, but was actually exerting his assertion.
"You can't exactly re-write history Sir!" He paused. "The facts are out there. And it's only a matter of time before they figure out that the parties that invested... are the parties that *insured*..."
Gore looked up from his blotter. Even sitting down he could dwarf Smyth.
"Europe was re-divided by Stalin, Roosevelt and Churchill after the War. Millions lost their lives. Others lost their lands. But the *contracts* stayed intact. Either remove the records that can be challenged. Or remove the challengers. I don't care which!" he scowled.
Smyth resisted the temptation to ask if he were dismissed. Instead he turned on his heels and left the room thinking the man was a bloody warrior.

He picked up the phone. He didn't like doing it, but it wasn't the first time this group had protected its interests in less than civilized ways. By the time he put down the phone he had determined to do one more thing. From home. Next week.

He would call the Security and Exchange Commission. *God Damn it!*

* *

Evelyn, Trevor's personal secretary, pushed the door open and popped her head into his office. "Ready?"

"Umm" he said, getting up from his darkened oak desk and reaching for his cape, cloak and wig.

"All Rise" announced the Bailiff of the 17th century chamber.

 "The Right Honorable the Lords Spiritual and Temporal of the United Kingdom of Great Britain and Northern Ireland in Parliament assembled ...."

They filed in with all the dignity of the Realm. One Lord had a pony tail peeking out from under the wig. It was a woman, Lady Carlyle - trained as a female barrister, standing in for the vacant seat of the Baroncy, presently without male heirs.

The Lords Temporal were held in place as life peers. They had been appointed by the Monarch, as advised by the Prime Minister. Such memberships, once a right of birth to only hereditary peers, was now a highly selective process, and included many from the corporate world.

Here they assembled to perform their duty in the capacity as the last court of the land, or Supreme Court.

Perhaps they were each wondering how in the hell it was that the Prime Minster of England got them here in the first place to hear this daft case...without using a civil court room to process it.

It was all Trevor could do to suppress a giggle, which threatened to smite the room with contagion. But by the time the Bailiff was pounding on his great staff to announce the Lord Chief Justice of the House of Lords The Lord of Northumberland, who followed dressed in full length weaved wig and paraphernalia, the immediate impact of their sovereign state was before them.

This was no laughing matter.

Britain had invested heavily, both in treasure and in mission, in golden ventures and overseas expansion. Its monarchs, still not quite relinquishing their hold on the purse, had been dispensing commitments in places that were only now being discovered. To lay precedence of challenge against those claims today could open up liability issues of investments past and present, some fabulous and infamous, including territorial claims, resource rights, trade contracts and social covenants, all sealed in centuries of laws, gold, blood and banners.

Amongst them were territorial rights in places far from the Homeland. Places which held British sovereignty today, like the Falkland Islands. And vast reserves of natural resources.

All twelve Law Lords were present, and would abide over the case as Appellate Committee sitting in the Lords Chamber itself of Parliament. For even while limited in today's authority, and badly damaged by socialist governments of the last century bent on eliminating the House of Lords, its function, in the end was to hold the Supremacy and Oversight of the Government.

 Only when such cases of imminent danger presented themselves did the liberal thinking of Acts essential to egalitarian consensus reveal short-sighted value given to deep traditions for the British Isles.

And this was just such a case.

At the moment the Government, in hyper inflated terms of gold bullion, was looking at one fifth of its value sitting on the seafloor off the coast of Spain. Sent there by early Bank of England investors, including one of Trevor's Scottish ancestors.

Trevor stood up, bowed to his Colleagues and opened.

"My Lords, I will give you the testimony of Parliament at the date of William III as he outfitted the Royal Navy in the Mediterranean in the winter of 1694.

"I shall read the manifests of the vessels, their cargo, and their Ship's orders.

"I shall further enumerate the accounting, supply and operations of the fleet and its manpower to show its intent.

"I shall walk through the great Acts that shaped our parliamentary laws; our Admiralty law and the hereditary rights of a citizenry that pay taxes - of their sacrifice and industry to forge our heritage and marshal our resources at home and abroad...And I shall show that if the court's ruling stands without Redress, it will hold danger to our national interests.

"Not only with perils that might end archaeologically sound practices of recovery and conservations, but more significantly, show that the cargo of the vessels that sank on that day...were in service to the state in tandem with a commercial venture, and should be subject to the laws that govern them. "

A muted round of feigned "objections" buzzed. But this was not the House of Commons, and they held their peace in deference to the Lord standing.

"Further, I wish to show that if only ships of war are to enjoy sovereign immunity from our jurisdictional laws, then what of non-combatant vessels carrying harmful and deleterious effects that might cause environmental and social damages, or have consequences of national security...

And finally, I shall show that contractual rights and logistical considerations in the operations underway of a salvage with regards to ownership...which cannot be rewritten at sea, by anachronism, or by facetious descendants of early claimants!

These and other issues shall be addressed by evidence, witness, amicus briefs and experts that are informed as to the laws of the land, and the precedents of history. "

Trevor looked down at his team along his aisle, himself alive to the intensity of his public outburst. Evelyn gave him the nod that he had covered the bases. The faces of the others on his team were resolute, with every evocation of support they could offer.

"And with that, I beg the Lords rest..."

"As well my noble friend may..." said the Chief Justice presiding as Speaker "For I see that it is a ponderous burden of proof that the Scottish Lord does carry! And he shall be heard, with the question put before us in due course for Closure"

What he didn't say, at this juncture was that the damages against English coin induced by corporate investment claims could reach astronomical proportions for the Bank of England.

Or, as the Chancellor of the Exchequer put it "You realize that Her Majesties Government will have to raise interest rates by at least half a point to cope with this loss if we forfeit the loot and the central bank has to pay Reparation damages..."* *

Thirty

Amanda got a call from the Sports Department Coaching Staff. The director apologized for disturbing her but explained that he had someone in the boathouse who had collapsed and needed help. "I was about to call the Medical staff...But she insisted I call you!"

"I'll be right over. If she needs further medical attention, I'll make sure she gets it..." said Amanda.

With her hair disheveled and a Tee shirt under a rain coat, she hopped into the car and drove directly to the training facility.

Emily was in bad shape. She had thrown up all over the bathroom in the boathouse and was shivering, if not almost incoherent. She had asked for Amanda.

"What happened?"

By the time Amanda took her back to the apartment, Emily was dehydrated and close to feverish. Unfortunately, nothing would stay down in her stomach for very long, and a case of dry heaves left her collapsed in a corner convulsing. Amanda called the Medical Center.

Apparently, there was little that Emily could explain herself with, other than a good coffee and sticky bun before breakfast, Then out to the boathouse to watch the team compete in a crew regatta up the river.

Amanda felt a flood of relief. No relapse for Emily.

 The weather had been bad, and whereas the athletes of the sports event managed to keep themselves warm, Emily was severely underdressed for the damp mists that rose off the river.

 "the flu..." she said, her voice broken and fatigued.

Amanda got her to bed, got some Seltzer in her which stopped the heaves, following ginger ale in slow sips. Later, when it became clear she had a slight fever, Amanda gave her a lightweight Tylenol.

"I am not your mother!" admonished Amanda to an apologetic Emily.

By evening, Emily had slept enough to feel a little relaxed, and managed to drink tea and soup.

The next morning found Emily freshly showered, if still a little shaky, with a little orange juice and toast in her hand.

"Today, you are staying put, young Lady. Mother says..." Amanda was picking up her books and bag for a day at the college. "At 4 o'clock, you have an appointment to see the doctor. And if you keep down your supper, I'll drive you home tonight, ok?"

Emily nodded mutely, an expression of relief across her face, Amanda thought.

"Back to bed with you for an hour or two more of rest!" ordered Amanda before leaving.

Trevor called Amanda as she got into her car. He wanted to know how she was doing, and if Amanda's time was still given to medical care-giving.

"She's fine! Nothing seriously wrong, and no real fever. Maybe a lot of pent up apprehension finally releasing itself. It seems that the boy's death took its toll on her, and she felt helpless about it. I feel she's coming around to reconciling the loss. You know, she loved him very much."

"Evidently, she feels safe with you!"

"Thanks for the compliment" smiled Amanda. "But with education being so expensive, any professor holding your grades hostage is cause for good behavior!"

"Seriously. She trusts you!"

"I'm on my way into the office now. She's going to see the doctor at 4 o'clock. And we'll have a nice dinner together before I drive her home..."

"I'll call you tonight then..." said Trevor and hung up.

* *

Trevor was browsing the Financial Section on his way to Westminster.

"Can I stop and buy you some coffee Sir?" said the driver of the black Taxi.

"No Joseph. I'm running late as it is, and munching on a muffin as you can see back here. But thank you!"

Joseph would follow Trevor anywhere around the world. And if driving a highly polished government security vehicle that looked like a cabby was what it took, then so be it. Trevor had done well by him and his family. They'd been through a lot, together.

Trevor spotted the article half way down the page.

"The Westington and Perkins Asset Management Group of London is proud to announce its newest acquisition of a marine entity for its merchant banking and corporate property finance sectors. This Entity is recently in possession of a large deposit of gold bullion from sources to be disclosed.

Marketing for the sale of the bullion, including the legacy and public relations associated with the discovery will soon be made public. The group's core areas of expertise include venture capital, project syndication, corporate finance, mergers and acquisition structure, project development, new venture and global business structuring. It has made acquisitions in mining, exploration and resource management of natural and manmade resources.

New stock will be offered for sale and can be found on the Nasdaq. OMEX with its corporate headquarters in Delaware, US."

It was later in the day when Trevor got the call from New York. Tim Courtney always asked about the English weather first.

"You seen the article yet?"

"Yes."

"Some bloody nerve marketing our money like that!"

"How do you explain the structure of the case?" asked Trevor.

"We see Sovereign markings all over the bullion...But no traceability yet as to who was the source of origin behind the king's agenda. What if the claim stands unchallenged?"

"I'll have to deliver a case for an Appeal that sticks..."said Trevor.

"Well that's your problem, I can see. William was playing with private money; courting foreign princes and outfitting the Royal fleet in Spanish waters when it took down the British Treasury. You'll have to prove that it was English sovereign money on an English mission of war"

"Yes" answered Trevor, cautiously.

"Look" breathed Tim on his speaker phone. "That's the trouble with you Brits. You're still arguing over Scotland and England and I'm up here arguing for our insurer's claims on your losses!"

"Correction Tim. It's the *Bank* of Scotland. And the *Bank* of England that we're looking at in 1694 to lay the foundations to the claimants' case..."

"Whatever. Only hurry it along will you...its rough selling stock in a company on Wall Street with articles like that flaunting their baubles in the goddam Financial Times!"

"I understand" said Trevor.

"Have a nice day" was how Tim always rang off.

Trevor downed his Scotch and looked at his watch. It was six o'clock, and the offices at Westminster were emptying out.

Time to check on Amanda.

* *

"They're circling the wagons Trevor" was how she phrased it on the phone.

Apparently she had called Emily soon after Paris. They had their giggling moments, and Amanda told about presenting her scholarly paper at the conference – at "*8 in the morning with a full audience of exactly two people*" as she put it.

Then it came out what Emily really wanted to say.

She had been snooping in the office of Jeannette Bevan at the University. On her desk were pictures left by the police department. Exterior Security cameras at the entrance spotted a man in profile who is believed to be the suspect. He was walking off the premises at approximately 9 that evening -- *after* Roger had locked up the Vault at the Library.

Amanda had asked for some elaboration. Emily told her that the suspect was walking away from the camera shot, and that it was impossible to see all his facial features clearly.

There was another man walking out through the gate next to him at the time, but he was entirely coincidental and unidentifiable. Evidently, he had spoken somewhere. Because a yellow post-it was attached to the picture on the police report said "French"

"I'll meet you for dinner" said Trevor.

* *

Five men abreast striding down the West Wing of Westminster wearing silk stockings and buckled shoes clamored against the slate floors. Behind them lagged scribers with scrolls, parchments papers, and inkwells, scrambling to keep up with their masters.

With the Royal Fleet sunk off Gibraltar, and the gold with it, this was not a Parliament happy.

The news had just arrived.

Outrage ravaged in the Clubs of all Gentlemen. The Bankers and Merchants remained closed. All paperboys issues pamphlets from every corner and in the halls of power amongst those Assembled in Parliamentarians was talk of armed betrayal.

The streets of London bristled with carriages wielding whips as they raced recklessly down cobbled surfaces and narrow alleys, the sounds of hoofs alarming and dangerous. Running footmen and maids were rushing to prepare for households vacating the city. It would be safer in the countryside, they said.

All day, there had been looting. Incidents and accidents went unaided. By nightfall, the rain fell on mud and the shops shuttered without lighting. The news was now sufficiently conflagrated to suggested an England under siege...

"Treason!" bellowed two Parliamentary Members in describing the behavior of the King.

With London in full panic and all taverns locked, the London Merchants met at the home of Thompson of the Virginia Tobacco Trade Company.

They argued, gas lights flickering and the streets taciturn. Tomorrow, the House would meet for a vote. Tonight was open furor and discussion:

They had been duped. At the center of commerce in London, there was no flow of capital. Everyone was outraged. What of their need, they said, for shipping of agrarian woolen products to Holland for weaving? Florence for dying... Spices for internal consumption? Even jeopardized was domestic production from imported raw materials, let alone redistribution of food and produce to other nations in ships waiting at dock!

What of cultivation of colonial venture - their plantations and coin foundries in the summer isles? What of ships at sea? The bodies of the slavers? Where the Spaniard?

What was the king doing? Malfeasance!

With the Treasury depleted, was there no way to raise capital, they demanded to know. The taxes!

"I know a man..." said the Exchequer, his face hot and afraid of where the conversations might lead about his master's reign.

They looked at him.

"His name is Paterson. He is rooted in trade venture, and called upon us for the establishment of a colony at the Darien Bay"

"Aye. And we turned him down!" said one with surly disgust.

"As did the Dutch. And the Spanish.." said another

" Panama?" said one incredulously

"Aye. It failed for the favor of the Spaniard. But he....He did not cease his venturing with the Merchant's Trade Company!"

"Nor with the West Indies and his slaving ships..." added another.

They looked at the Exchequer. Short, balding, perspiring under the vestments of the day.

The Exchequer had calculated this moment for a long time. Better to create something new and generous than to betray the Royal bourse that had fed him. Nor the plundering of the English treasure without accounting...

"He has enjoyed a large measure of success from the Scottish. He can make account of what he might produce for a new Bank of Scotland. It is he who would be the man to underwrite a Bank of England"

The words reverberated like a crystal bell. *A Bank of England!*

"Can he make an account of this ...this...intended Bank?"

"He can!" said the Exchequer, breathing now, and praying that Paterson would remember him kindly from his overture about the Darien Scheme, knowing that he had been denied once before for his Darien Peninsula colony.

He straightened himself, and adjusted his leather belt.

"And he shall. I give you my word. Within a month!"

"Make it a week!" barked one from the pack.

He bowed his head slightly.

The Royal Charter was signed, approved and granted on 27 July 1694.

* *

They decided on a strategy, Trevor and Amanda, over dinner at the *Lion's Tooth* Pub on Long Street.

She was to stay out of Jeannette Bevan's way. She would go in super early. Work-out at the Fitness center on campus...Take out her work with her to the cafeteria, and, having left a good mess on her desk, and would proceed through the day from one class to the next without necessarily going back to her desk!

Her evening class would receive an electronic blackboard notification asking for progress reports on their research from all students. No class attendance needed!

The Janitors would simply shut down the classrooms at 10 pm for the night as usual.

"No need to jump for conclusions about any French-Connections Amanda" said Trevor.

He reached for her hand across the small dinners table and squeezed. "So don't panic. OK?"

Two beers came down from a passing waitress. "Just stay out of Jeannette's way in accountable ways if you can. She's too damned political to come looking for you in classrooms. She figures you'll show up sooner or later. "

"Well, that'll give me about a week. Then she'll start leaving messages for a DA".

Trevor looked up.

"A Demand Appearance!"

"She sounds charming" said Trevor accepting a salad from the waiter.

Amanda put her arms on the table and looked at him demurely. "Is Jacques a problem here Trevor. Yes or No?"

"No! He's working with Interpol on this one...Although..."

"What?"

"Never mind. Forget it. ..Cheers!"

Amanda was ravenous. Come to think of it, she hadn't eaten all day. Breakfast was a coffee. Lunch a packet of 6 peanuts. There was nothing that looked better on the wooden table of an English pub than their two bowls of Lamb Stew topped with melted Swiss cheese and two full glasses of Bordeaux wine accompanied by salad vinaigrette, goat cheese and fresh baked bread.

Suddenly she looked up and paused. He was staring at her.

"You look beautiful tonight" he said simply.

"Thank you!"

For the evening - as protest against winter coats, scarves, boots and wool hats - she had chosen a Satin dress by Prada. It fairly glowed in the candlelight between them.

 She picked up her wineglass, tipped his way with acknowledgement and said "And how are things going for you at Westminster, Your Lordship..?"

"Ah!" he smiled. Then "Um..." and a distressed look darkened his face.

She waited, sipped, then put down her wine.

"Well..." he began.

Amanda knew the consequences of a case defeated before the Lords. Especially this one which had become a particularly vilified issue between the ruling party and the Labor Party.

The dispute had become a contentious battle of words between the two parties. One implied malfeasance, the other treason. For a young barrister, Trevor was caught up in a vortex of panic, defamation and legal dilemma.

Amanda could only imagine that it had been no less difficult for the men of the time...

He cleared his throat "A rift is widening as we introduce other Nationalities in the Case.."

She waited

"It's as if... William can illicit modern-day party animosity! His very claim to the throne is a matter that stirs the blood. William of Orange's claim to the English throne, and his personal Dutch allegiances when he took England's treasury on board the fleet that sank to the bottom of the Mediterranean leaves the sovereignty issue unresolved for many, still, legally speaking. Especially since the coin was issued by the Bank of England but minted with Spanish gold! "

Amanda sat back, puzzled "But if an English King...then what's the question?"

"Well the Spanish say it's their bullions since its theirs, and sits in their territorial waters"

"But if its English money on an English ship...doing what, exactly?"

"What that's not entirely clear either."

"And... the Bank of England says?"

"the investors of that time were from the Bank of *Scotland...*"

"So..?"

"Well the Bank of England wasn't officially chartered until late in 1694. And Scotland wasn't unified with England until seven years later...1701. Which makes them private investors, technically. Nor are we entirely clear what the mission of the fleet was when it sank holding the treasury of the English realm..."

Amanda looked into his eyes, and they were troubled. Finally he reached for some wine.

"So. This didn't bode well for the Monarch. His secret caches of treasure, for various regents and foreign princes in Europe, was exhausting all reserve capital. He was falling from favor with Parliament. His war against the French was losing credence"

"they were ready to hang him I should imagine!" She could hear them now.

Amanda laughed. "What happened to reformed Britain? Did not the signed Bill of Rights confine the King to an annual budget?"

"You'd think" he said, chewing.

Then Trevor remarked "You know. This Royal beggar has his own agenda rooted in the Treaty of Augsburg, which extended the European sovereign plans...Right?"

"Possibly" she said" He came from another axis of power whose assumptions I must examine yet.. Remember, the Dutch ruled the seas, and overseas colonial trade was designed for Imperial expansion. William couldn't even speak English, he had to share the throne with Mary...and frankly, it appears he used the English Treasure and Royal Fleet for his own ends.

It was commerce, it had to be on Dutch ships. Hence the Act of Navigation"

"Only it wasn't even English treasure to begin with..." he added

" But whose wars was he fighting? Was it not the prerogative of Parliament to stand an English Army?"

"Yes. Only this was also considered a winter-outfitting of the English fleet in the Mediterranean, as Parliament said. Unauthorized, in fact. And he knew it! "

A waiter brought in some coffee and cake.

"Worse..." he proceeded "It appears that a second shipment of money was promised to the Duke of Savoy by King William of England, his Dutch cousin. However, before it could be secured, William III found that Savoy had allied himself with the French Louis XIV, Britain's Enemy."

"A vulnerable time!" observed Amanda.

"God!" Amanda took a sip of her wine, then put it down slowly.

"By the way" he said, "I noticed that you haven't made any entries on my case log files. You know you are invited to do so at any time Amanda. I value your professional opinion..."

And so does Jacques, she thought, who would clearly be monitoring her every transmission to Trevor about the historical integrity of any documentation what so ever!
She smiled. "I will"

A well fired crème Brule presented itself with two long tasting spoons, and two coffees.

Trevor was stirring coffee, idly in thought.

She knew that look. "But that's not everything is it?"

Amanda finished with her food.

He shook his head solemnly
"Then what?"
"It's the contract laws that follow the acts of monetary policy – after the event – that establish precedent. If the money was foreign owned, then so goes the credibility of the Bank of England!"
They sat in silence for several minutes. Finally she folded her arms.
"...And you ...want me to help with the research, is that it?"
"I have something for you..." she said before they parted for the evening. "Here!"
He looked at the Mason jar, sealed with rubber gaskets, designed for pickling produce.
It was a jar of sand, holding shells from the Chesapeake Bay of Virginia, the New World.
"This tiny shell... is the first shed of a Chesapeake Bay Blue Crab. Here, a tiny Horseshoe Crab shed from the Atlantic beaches, and here is a cherrystone clam shell from the salty waters of the southern Bay!"

He would keep it in his office, he said. Sand from the New World..

* *

Thirty One

New York

Marguerite Shutters was not the head of a Department at US Treasury for nothing. She had an uncanny way of being charming while challenging. This she showed in numerous incriminating Senate Hearings, with her clear eyeglasses and parted school-girl hair.

She had heard of the case. And wanted to call the British. Instead she called Bureau of Maritime Commerce.

"Jim. I have an interesting case I'd like you to look at. We're really too young to know this kind of stuff, since the event took place prior to our nationhood, so to speak. But I'm getting a little concerned about the laws being tampered with. They could have an impact on us. We base much of our contract law on early Maritime precedent as you know. And most of it comes from Admiralty Court.."

She let him talk with expletives on the glut of knowledge at his disposal.

"Exactly. So, err...I hate to put this on you, but if you find anything that suggests special interest or dispensations for European banks that hold license to trade in the States....?"

"Yes. Yes. It's just that I don't want to be caught off guard by any other global interest that could end-run us. If it's benign, then fine. If's profitable, then even more fine. But if it's strategic, then I want to know, ok?"

* *

Bill, at the National Archives had been forgiven by Amanda.

 He was too easily distracted by the crisis to much remember what he had done when he tossed her into a serious meeting of officials without warning.

Anyway, he was a man always proud of his mess.

Strewn across the entire conference table - the same as that of the day of the Inquisition – as she put it, were historical records books, numenastical records, receipts, letters and other unknown documents that would inform the details of the Paterson deal with the Government in 1695.

The main Parchment, folded by its legal bindings and covers, was annotated " A Brief Account of the Intended Bank of England"

"In it" Bill was saying, " Patterson proposed a loan of £1.2m to the government. In return the subscribers would be incorporated as The Governor and Company of the Bank of England with banking privileges including the issue of Notes"

"It's uncertain how he got that money, but he was trading heavily in the West Indies and in the Merchant Taylors' Company. He may have had several ships at sea belonging presumably to the Dutch – and coin might well have been more readily available to him. Plus other ships berthed in the Scottish regions of trade. He appears to have his own currency, governance and leadership 'infrastructure' if you will"

"So what was in this transaction for *him* exactly?" asked Amanda.

"Patronage of Credit, really. It was a very patriarchal and materialistic society, remember. All that silk, satin and slippers they wore, let alone the furnishings and housing. In fact it was an era much given to capital construction and Renaissance expenditures. Remember the Courts of the Stuarts disdained Elizabethan parsimony and embraced Papist ideas of opulence, baroque and unbridled expansionism..

 "With an economic depression that followed" she interrupted.

"with an economic depression that followed" he repeated.

"Still, it was a tenuous world at best by the end of the century. Even if Charles II did rebuild London after the great fire of 1666. Nor did the Commonwealth civil war of England usher in popular liberties exactly...I would say. So it was the Glorious Revolution which brought in our William III as an attempt to reinstate monarchy as a sort of hierarchical order. And they did get the Bill of Rights. But clearly, it was an expanding domestic economy that underwrote the need for a patronage system of credit. Don't you agree?"

"Very much so! Was he a Lord, this Patterson?" She asked.

"No. He was born in his parents farmhouse in Tinwald Scotland and lived with them until he moved to Bristol for err... shipping in the Bahamas. That's when he first devised his Darien Scheme. To Create a new colony of trade on the Isthmus of Panama. He used this knowledge to introduce himself to all the key empires interested in colonial efforts. But was turned down repeatedly.

Regardless. Patterson was in a position of Trust. Most likely with the Merchants of London. And look what he negotiates for...with the advantage of his coin! He wants *banking* privileges and Note holding leverage for the subscribers. Plus *Representation* on the Boards."

"What does that mean, exactly, in real terms?"

"Well. It's hard to quantify in the whole, entirely. Scholarly Arguments suggest that England was now viewed as a good place to invest in. London Merchants made the City of London their personal Empire. It's entirely possible that these were efforts to monetize trade without export duties, taxation and royalty ownership. A petition for more Independence for trade for the Individual Investor. (In other words, get around Crown takings on all their venturing).

"There was the Navigation Act ensuring monopolies that only the mother country, England, Spain and the Netherlands, could enjoy the profits of the carrier trades. None could trade amongst themselves. Though clearly they did!

"Thus, when they wanted free trade, they had their eye upon *Representation* in Government...to effect change!"

"Politics?" she said.

"Politics!" he laughed.

"I'll spare you a lecture on the English Civil war. But slowly gains had been made in the separation of powers at that time. After all, there had been too many wrangling over kings, God, and wives producing sons and heirs for the Lords of the land. But this gets interesting if you examine the particulars.

"What they were lobbying for was free trade! To break the hold of the monarchical hierarchy on trade was to produce your own sovereign minting."

"So procuring either the stamped coin, or the metals that would manufacture those coins was a significant step towards that end..." said Amanda "Which bordered on treasonous acts.."

"Including those already long ago operating outside the realms of a Holy Catholic Europe like the Protestants and Huguenots." Bill paused. Then moved to the far end of the table.

" It's no wonder that Parliament had a different view to monarchs, after William – himself a Dutchman dedicated to world trade! So, if there is one thing the English learned, is that Trade made the Empire!"

"Only whose empire?" mused Amanda.

"Well, that's the question. What was William III doing pursuing with money the Duke of Savoy in Italy?"

"Serious enough for making wars. What followed was the Iron Century, remember. And not because of its discovery!" said Amanda.

"Right!"

"Anyway, here are all the documents. You are most welcome to them. Let us know if we can provide you with anything else..."

* *

The tussle between her and Jack never ceased. If she chose to sit at her desk to work on the computer, Jack would elongate himself between the keyboard and the monitor. Until she browsed - whose shapes and colors aroused him to pace the breadth of the screen and obstruct her view with intermittent crossings...

Occasionally she locked him in the bedroom - which was met with a dexterous pinging of the door-cleat spring that could hammer like a pernicious child throwing a hissy fit.

The lap-top computer on her knees was an open invitation for key-board sitting. So, with Jack deeply seated in her lap - one hand stroking his ear, and the screen perched far out on the edge of her knees where it wobbled precariously, Amanda read the proceedings in Parliament. Mostly, it worked.

The matter before them, the minutes showed, presented little dissent. Rather, some excitement in a negotiated agreement. It resulted in a poll count. Within a few months of the fleet sinking at Gibraltar, on the day of July 27th 1694, a Royal Charter was granted for the creation of the Bank of England.

Also, she noted, the Bank of Scotland.

Less than eight years later, she knew, William III was deceased. In 1707 with the swiftness of Reform swirling through the Parliament, the English would move into modern history.

* *

'My Lords....
" We have no proof that the coin found is on a non-commercial venture!" said the barrister behind the bench of the House of Lords. In fact, we can say, in all solemnity, that the coin was the personal belonging of the House of Orange, and such, had no authority vested in it from the English..."
"Impossible!" interrupted Trevor in full gown and regalia of the Scottish realm. "If it were a personal possession of the House of Orange, it would indubitably have the stamp of the Staadholder of the Netherlands. But it is English sovereign markings on it. And as Monarch, possession of the English."
"Order! Please, Gentlemen?"
"I must say" said one Lord rising to Trevor's left "...that if the Bill of Rights did restrict the Royal purse to 600 pounds at that date, then the gold treasure would have been beyond the allowance, but within the purveyance of the Privy Council to grant him?"
"Here! Here!" incanted voices from the upper benches.
"Except...that it did not come from the Royal Treasure!" said one.
They looked up at the voice that was descending the steps to the Chamber floor.
"It was a gift!"
"What?"
"A gift from a friend of the King!" He paused.

The Chair, in full wig and robe, pled him to proceed with his case in open gesture "Please!"

The House of Lords proceeding was not conducted in judicial fashion common to modern Court Rooms. It held rather a traditional tone. It was a gathering of Lords to discuss the matters of the realm. And all held equal rank, with the exception of the Chair, who might arbitrated.

"Whom?" asked one barrister from the bench, her blue eyes peering from beneath her wig.

"That we cannot know"

"Would the Honorable Gentleman Sir Nigel from Ireland please... *speak up!*" bellowed another.

He rose, the newcomer to the debate.

"How can that be known?" asked the Chair

"Because I have in my possession, My Lords, a letter from the Holy Roman Church, with the seal of a Cardinal's signet, to his mission church in Ireland..."

"Bloody spies!" growled an echo from the upper chamber

Sir Nigel paused "Perhaps... But it stipulates in Latin that the Treasure to be of Spanish origin!"

"Please bring forward your evidence Sir Nigel" said the Chair "...and allow us to inspect it with our experts"

"I shall indeed, your Excellency. You will find the markings on the sovereign pieces to be made from a Spanish mint, with silver alloy of the 17th century~"

"This we must have our people examine!" said the Lady from Lancaster.

"You are welcome to do so!" and with a pause in the general noise level, he added

" And then, if you please to find it fitting, allow the gold treasure of the Essex, sunk off the shores of Spain, to return to the Spanish. For, if a gift, then the giver is identified. And if identified, then the gift considered lost can be returned to its former owner..."

Trevor groaned inwardly. They were behaving like school boys playing at a debating society.

What was at stake here, was a value of $350 Billion that would be owed by the Bank of England for reparation and damage to some flake...if this damned fool was allowed to carry on. Bugger historical integrity and his flashy bowing and scraping... Something the Exchequer's Office could not afford and should better use in the service of the government already beleaguered by a global recession.

Jesus!

He took a deep breath and waded in for the dual. "My Lords! My Lords!"

"With every respect for my honorable friend and colleague from the noble Irish lineage where its history is well known to be closely tied to the Holy Roman Church... I do beg to disagree Sir!"

The room was preparing for a good battle. And the anxiety level was high.

"Then how says M'Lord?" The arrogant long nosed Irishman with a house on Cape Cod, a boat in Barcelona and a law degree from Oxford was grinning. "Does the document declare the intent of the gold Sir?" asked Trevor MacDonnell

"It does"

"And to what end is the gold to be brought forth, may I ask?"

Sir Nigel consulted the document "For to put an end to the English ...." He began

"Ahh..."interrupted Trevor "Then if the intent is for warring, then the mission is for battle then?"

Sensing danger, Sir Nigel began to rise for a formal protest, but Trevor never gave him the chance.

"In the first instance, If the battle to be commissioned with that gold failed, then its intended delivery must be considered moot.

"In the second instance, since no battle was commissioned on the day of the sinking, then we can assume that the fleet was not at quarters, nor in the commission of battle, and not Authorized by Parliament for official wartime acts as the minutes do so well show.

"Finally, in the third instance, if not for battle, Sir, then in the commission of commerce and trade. Thus, to be adjudicated not as a sovereign coin, but as private coin subject to the laws of the civil orders of society!"

"What?"

"Gentlemen!"

"Will the Lords....Please!"

"Here Here!"

"How so?"

"Order. Order. I say!" insisted the Chair.

"The gold. If it was not for battle, it was for commercial use, and belongs to the proceedings of civil ownership, not of military admiralty...and the rule of sovereign immunity does not apply! " Trevor sat down on the wooden bench beneath him, his delivery made, the Chamber now in an uproar.

The case, he knew, was at bay. For a while, at least. Finding a Spanish minted coin in the cargo of the ship was all the Spanish union bankers needed to make a bloody case...

What he needed was a scotch, and he headed straight for his office with as little handshaking and discussing as he could get away with down the halls. He passed through the front office with a quick stop at Heather's desk.

"Uplink the feed of the proceedings to my list of selected networkers, will you please Heather. I'll need all the feedback and support I can get now..." and before she could answer, he was through the ante-room and into his own office.

One of those on the selected list was Amanda's computer.

He sat down to his computer and opened his email. One message floored him.

It was from his mother. She was in Scotland

"My dearest Trev...she began.

She spoke of the boy killed at Cambridge. Though Amanda had mentioned Ed Henry several occasions, the full impact of the boy's identify had not sunk in. His full name was Edward Henry Neville, descendent of a long line of Nevilles.

 She expressed her feelings of loss at the incident. As did the whole community. He was such a spirited young fellow, with a promising future, she said. He'd been in the Boy Scouts Troupe just a few years ago before going to University. And being the only heir to the estate, there was much local concern. Was there anything Trevor could do to salvage the Earldom before the family legacy became dormant, including the Castle and grounds that might fall into disuse...?"

Trevor gazed out the windows of his office at Westminster. That, he knew, was something that only the House of Lords could do. And given the present political climate, even that tradition was tenuous, at best. England these days, was hobbled by indebtedness.

The letter was still in his hand. The boy Edward Henry Neville, as his mother pointed out, was officially his godson.

* *

Thirty Two

Karmoski was not a fat man. But neither was he thin. Just 'corpulent' as he would tell it, especially when talking to the chicks at the bar, he said.

However his pale skin, rimmed glasses and height did little for his cohorts in the confines of the vessel. Particularly when he moved about. He was a klutz. His forehead found the bulkheads. His feet snagged on corners. He dropped cups. Things rolled off his desk. And his invective could be called spectacular, said Tim. But peering into a console of pixels at 2,500 ft depth beneath the surface and feeding instructions into a computer monitor, he could dance wonders of delicacy with a robot on the seafloor.

"I'm going topside for some air" he announced, leaving his station.

They stared at each other, Oliver and Stanley, as he called them, wondering what in the hell had come over him. The monitors were on. The bottom was black. The robotic lights were on and the arm was lifting and sucking, lifting and sucking - all of it filling up cargo baskets hovering closely.

Finally Stan went up. He found Karmoski at the stern, smoking his cigarette . The sea was shimmering in the moonlight, calm. Which is why they continued deep-sea salvage ops through the night.

"What's up?"

"Huh? Oh...Something's not right..." Karmoski mind was far away. "See. In the Bermuda Triangle, they say there's a dispersion path that runs up the coastline with the Jet Stream. Right?"

"Right"

"What if we have the same here, only underwater, and in reverse. ..?"

"How?"

"The Levant winds. They collapsed in December, right?"

"Right".

"So, what if there *two* storms, one from the North Atlantic and one from East. Where would all the energy go if not in a vortex that would subverse the flow of underwater currents?"

" South?"

"Well it sure as hell ain't North" said Karmoski throwing out his cigarette. " 'Cos what we're finding is chicken crap"

 "Oh...I don't know..."

"It's West, Stanley. We haven't set a grid for West. And a wider dispersion pattern with a taller peak"

"But that's Spain. And last I looked, that's terra firma!"

"That depends on where they went down now, doesn't it?"

"What are you saying?"

"Someone onboard may have seen the storm coming and tried to change course. They spun around!"

"What?"

"What if they tried to *head* South...?"

"Well that would put their Westward dispersion pattern half way back out the Straits of Gibraltar!" laughed Stanley.

"Exactly!"

"Oh. No... No Way! That's a deep trench. There's no way we're going to search...Turbulent and flukey as hell with the wind whirling from every point of the compass. To say nothing of placing this research vessel in harm's way between two continents... Plus every Cruise Ship squirting out the Mediterranean for an open Atlantic."

"Yup!"

* *

It took two days for the Salvage Company to get the authorization to change the site - and *another* two days to weather-wait as they repositioned the *Vienna* before Karmoski got off their backs.

The Robot landed on the side of a mountain at a forty five degree angle half a mile underwater.

"God I hate boats" said Stanley.

"I hate Karmoski" said Pete.

"Now boys! Watch this..." said Karmoski.

He was searching for wider dispersion field, far from the wreck. First he would need to find identification for the wreck as evidence. Then critical items of interest. What they had before was a bucket or two of salt, he said.

* *

Emily had stopped calling two days ago.

Seven messages had collected on Amanda's phone. One from Trevor.

The very brevity of his words made the message alarming. "The coins are Spanish minted..."

She wrote. "If the identity of the source of funding behind the wreck could be identified, then that would establish or dispute the legal claim of any insurer, or entity seeking reparation."

"As a private investment, then that would rule out a Sovereign stake – *or* a sovereign obligation for reparations today even if the case for commercial activity were made..."

Conclusive evidence must be forthcoming.

"I shall begin with an investigation of the authenticity of the documents. To find, and prove, the true author of the documents, is paramount to the argument!"

Amanda Wells.

<UPLOAD>

It would change the case, she knew.

* *

What had started as a routine week had turned quickly. Like a cold front from the West.

Avoiding Jeanette Bevan had been alright until you got the Royal Summons. And that required some finesse to avoid.

Actually, it wasn't that bad since Amanda could minimize the impact by staying calm.

Being cooperative to the Officers at New Scotland Yard was an easy enough task. She peered at her calendar marked. Tomorrow 11 AM

So she had 24 to get ready.

She picked a black blend blazer and pants, both Donna Amanda with a Lambskin Cummerbund belt by Bally.

"So Ms. Wells. Can we say that you will assist us then, in finding the culprit?"

"I will, of course" said Amanda seated at a desk in the glass walled offices of New Scotland Yard.

"In his Deposition, the security guard said that you were the only one to enter the vault on the evening of January 25th Is that right Ms. Wells?"

"Yes."

"Did you consider it...well, a clean facility. Swept. Orderly?"

"Excuse me?"

"Clean. As in sanitary? Healthy? Managed by Janitors etc..?"

"Yes. Of course. It always is" she answered him squarely.

"No trash... Food... Dirt, or residual build up of dust of any sort...?" asked the Sergeant.

"Not really. No"

"But how do you account for these, then?" he said producing cigarette butts that Amanda recognized.

She stared at them, her hands clammy and cold.

"I don't know"

"You don't know?"

"No."

"So. You don't know if you were the *last* in the vault, the *only* one in the vault, or if these were there *before* you went into to the vault?"

The implications came roaring in... *How did you not see them?...Miss Wells...do you know whose they are ...if you were the last to leave as you say Ms. Wells... It's that young Edward was dead before the last entry in the Vault was made...Did you mean to leave a trail to a dead man by planting his cigarettes there...having cleaned them up from the girl's apartment....*

The door opened. A female police officer presented a note to the Examination Officer.

"Well, it appears Ms. Wells... that I am to ask you no further questions!"

Amanda leaned forward a tad, as if gripping the ledge of the desk. "I had no idea you wanted detailed observations Sir. I would have offered a full report if..."

"....if you were able to do so. It appears, Ms. Wells, that you have diplomatic immunity!"

Amanda was stunned. She almost said "I do?" but knew enough to shut up, even if her expression was dumb.

"Yes. You are a United States Citizen and your Embassy has issued us a notification of your intent to remain silent while you perform your service on our soil"

"My service...?"

"Yes Madam. Your Service as Cultural Attaché.

The British police officer, a woman with red curls peeping out her hat, was leading her out of New Scotland Yard.

Bewilderment must have been written all over her face. More like a screaming heart. She felt so alone! What had just transpired. Cultural Attaché to *what*? Who pulled that one?

She would call her father.

The halls were endless, connecting by architecture continuous worlds of information gathering, organization, manpower management, deployments and chattering technology.

Glass doors everywhere may have closed off sound, yet people were everywhere.   From elevators flowed streams of disconnected levels. And here was Amanda being escorted out with perilous question and unanswered events...as if surrounded by help she could not access.

No. This was different. Definitely. Polite. Cold. Effective.

At the far end of the of the Visitors Parking Lot the Police officer stopped. "Here we are! " a smile across her face "Do enjoy your London stay. Goodbye!"

Period.

She stood there. Just like that. She would call her Dad. She would....

It was damp. The clouds, low and moving fast, offered swirls of tropical wind, like an impending storm.

She turned, stuffed her hands in her pockets and started walking. She would call a cab. Hell, even if Emily came in her impossible Mini wearing frayed jeans and gothic hair, it would be assuring.

Then she stopped.

Less than two hundred meters away, a car was waiting, the door held open. For her?

It was not Trevor.

This was dark windows and steel. There was no *Not-getting* in.

Ford. Black.

**

Thirty Three

The man holding the door to the car was Jacques de Torraine. Not that a Ford was alien. But here, now, for Amanda, it was ... intimidating. There was no mistaking hostility, even in this square of London's wealthiest.

"'Allo!" he said in simple fashion, his French accent barely masking the resolve behind the voice.

"Please get in!"

Amanda looked up for just a moment, and saw the police officer disappear into the building.

She had glanced back and waved even before turning away. But she was gone.

"To get in. Or not to get in..!" she incanted in full jest as she climbed into the rear seat.

Her options were nil, she knew.

"But of Course!" said Jacques, playfully slamming the door behind her and coming around the other side.

 "Chez moi!" he said to the driver as he got in beside her.

"The papers you were to inspect...In Paris. Will they be authenticated?" asked Jacques.

"I believe they are. But forensic analysis is still underway" said Amanda. It was the least she could do. Considering Trevor never showed them to her again after he disappeared with them locked in a briefcase that was attached to his wrist with a steel padlock.

The house Jacques chose to call his own, these days, was a brick factory edifice now rehabilitated for residential condos.

 Parked along the side idled several cars with chauffeurs, waiting for their call.

The door was opened by a housekeeper who let them into the front room. Arranged in much the same fashion as Paris, the same three men sat over coffee.

Two stood up. The Dutchman Amanda recognized. The third just waived casually from his seat.

"Amanda confirms that she believes the manuscript is authentic" announced Jacques.

They looked up, one pulling at his turtle neck for relief, the other wordless, except for the crackling of his black leather jacket.

 "For ...*Insurance* purposes, you understand" he said turning to Amanda as afterthought.

There was little mirth in their eyes, clearly now shuffling with cups to indicate that it was time to leave.

 Except the Dutchman.   He tossed his bonbon wrapping back into the confectioner's bowl, and lingered.

"Can we be assured that you will have a..err...final report for us to review Mlle. Wells?"

"Yes" she said.

He looked into his face, his eyes cold and unsmiling as the bonbon circled its way inside his mouth.

"So!" he said with a concluding sigh to Jacques. "I leave the details to you. A bientot!"

The housekeeper could be heard shutting the door in the Entrance lobby.

"Coffee?" he offered.

"Now look here Jacques. I don't know what the hell this is about, but I don't like the place I'm in..."she began.

"..the place?" he looked around. "But it's a beautiful place!"

He poured out a coffee from the Press, and moved to the silver tray or decanters. "Brandy?" he added, enjoying himself.

"it is better...don't you think ...than the *Accommodations* of the British Detention Center for people suspected of murder, non?'

"What?"

He waited.

" This is not known to Trevor?..."

"Trevor, my dear, has his hands full with an international case of political proportions..."

"what are you saying?"

"Yes. You are the chief suspect, being the last to leave the vault....before the boy was found dead"

"I don't like what you're implying Jacques..."

"Please" he said "take a seat!"

She stared at him, and sat down.

"Those men...who were here...They are not 'civility' people like me. They are hardened men of the antiquities trade. They want to know about those documents you had Trevor take from me! ..."

"*Take* from ...you?"

"In Paris" he put down his condiments.

"Where did those documents come from?" she asked, keeping her tone even.

He leaned forward "Are they not the diary of William Shakespeare?"

"God! *I don't know!*"

"Well. If they are, then I need them back. If they are not, then the insurance values are worthless. So you having nothing to fear. But either way, you are the one who was reading them!"

"Jacques. You don't think *I'm* responsible ...."

"You were the one talking about them all night in the café in Paris, Non?"

"Jacques...I was speaking to a friend...*You!* "

"Yes of course. Actually, I am here to protect you with all this... But the truth is, I can only give you time to produce them with a Report of Authenticity. These people are in the business of Acquisitions. At any cost! Understand? Your reputation...?"

 "What business is the Dutchman in?"

"The business of ...Criminology. Security. I'll agree to say, yes?"

"Whose...exactly?"

"Well that depends..."

"On auction prices for an authentic manuscript of say easily...25 million pounds?"

"But Amanda. You are not even close! Let me see now" he took a seat across from her "There are museums. Private collectors. Government repositories. Tourism trade. Historic Tows, Restaurants. Collateral equity against capital building loans. Non-profit grants and charters. Educational interests.   Commercial and Retail trade like books, movies, theater and ...and Insurance values..."

"Enough to murder for, is that what you are saying...?"

He looked at her soberly. "Enough to murder for"

Amanda shot up hotly. "And you dragged me into this mess...what? Purposefully? Because I'm a research historian?"

Jacques looked thoughtfully at the table between them, leaving much unspoken.

Then he smiled. "Amanda. Amanda" he said softly. "Relax. If they are forgeries, then the insurance companies and the collectors will disappear! They are worth little.... And you have nothing to worry about if your report says that they are no more than the fragmented Treatise of some seventeenth century miscreant. Perhaps worth a few thousand pounds at auction, and insured!"

"And if they are real?"

"Then their ownership will be a matter...of serious value...?"

"I see." Amanda wanted to bolt from the room. She looked up.

"Jacques. May I go home now?"

He regarded her for a moment, trying to read her thoughts. "But of course."

She looked into his eyes, for a man with such a dark complexion, he had remarkably blue eyes, and they revealed oceans of icy coldness. She caught her breath a little.

"Why not?" he added, as if that were an option. They drove back in silence.

Before letting her out he touched her hand and said "Amanda. Be careful. Say nothing. Not even to Trevor..."

He must have sensed the tiny gasp in her throat at the sound of Trevor's name.

"You will want to give him room just now. The boy that ...err... *quote-* murdered-*unquote*...oh, *allegedly* murdered...Edward was his name. His father had been related by a marriage somewhere in the history of the family. The boy was Trevor MacDonnell's godchild...."

There was no blunting the shock of his words. She should have stared, or ranted, or found some icy response, surely. But she went numb inside. Deep within her a ghostly sense of survival suddenly shrouded her emotions with a firm silence. She managed to exit the car and walk steadily to her apartment. Once inside her apartment, it was all she could do to keep from throwing up.

Jacques was right.

The last thing Amanda could do was approach Trevor until her name was cleared. Until then, as a suspect in the murder investigation against his relative, she was a liability to his reputation. Especially now, as a member of the House of Lords, during the trial.

Trevor was out of her life.

Jacques and his bloody henchmen didn't need to lock her up. Or silence her. She was trapped. And there was a police report on her.

**

Thirty Four

She wasn't sure how she got to the floor of her front room. But she was cold and stiff. Jack was licking her arm. It was the middle of the night.

 Emily had fed the cat. Emily had left some bacon, bread and a beer in the fridge. Add cheese and she'd have a Welsh rarebit. Enough to get human again. Together, she and Jack ate their food - he, at his bowl and she, at the table above him.

Jack walked off from his empty dish of moist-mush. Thank you. He found a place and stood licking himself clean. Then he just stared at her, waiting.

She cleared out the stale food from the fridge and swiped it with warm soapy cloth. She washed off dishes; scrubbed clean the small stove and sanitized her two kitchen surfaces. The tiny oak kitchen table got a quick scrub and somehow, she felt better. Finally she retired Jack's greatest source of malaise, the now-odorous kitchen trash left by Emily. And she freshened up his kitty litter tray.

They settled down together.

"Come here!" she had said, tapping her knees.

He thought about it, then acquiesced.

They must have sat there, stroking and purring for almost half an hour. Then she made coffee.

She couldn't even talk about Jacques. Her thoughts were gray.

Finally her cell phone rang.

Emily!

"Ok. So I won't ask where you've been. Because I'm not shit talking to you. But I wanted to know if Jack had someone there to feed him!"

"Yes!" began Amanda.

"Shit you!" Said Emily, and hung up.

A text followed. "Sorry"

Amanda looked up at the ceiling, a blank loss, and tossed the cell on the sofa.

She felt broken. *What the hell...* she wanted to shout.

Another text came in. She ignored it.

Jack went back to eat some dry cat-food crunchies, no mush.

She got up and paced her room. Distress giving place to anger.

You don't take a highly motivated individual working in top gear and...and...reduce them with hostage-taking threats and proffer threats.

Not to her!

No way!

No damned Frenchman, Dutchman or Henchman for that matter could do that to a working professional!

Then again, what passed for professional these days?

Jeannette Bevan? Student murderers? University

Deans dispensing patronage? Department Heads? Antiquarians meddling with history for personal plundering?

What happened to loyalty? Historical integrity? Protection by Administration? Police trust?

She moved around her room, anger increasing at what had happened.

She was pissed. *Who cared?*

The answer was simple. *Nobody.* Because nobody wants to make sacrifices. *Nobody* cared about teaching. About human dignity.

It stank of spreading decay, she decided. Greed. Gain and... Laziness!

One thing she was certain of. It was dangerous. One false move somewhere, and someone could get hurt.

Be careful, she decided.

* *

It was a while before she started to refocus. She noticed the things in the room.

Someone had been here. Emily of course, she knew. Not disordered, but just...different! The books on the shelf, the plants in their pot holders, watered...if barely alive. Those damned cigarettes in the ashtray, cat-hair on cushions. A tiny vomit from Jack, days old...

She got up. Opened the windows for some air, shook up a couple of cushions and beat on the sofa fabric, stale dander everywhere...

God how she hated disorder.

She picked up the ashtrays, vacuumed the rug and mopped the kitchen floor with disinfectant solutions.

By the time she straightened her bedroom, folded laundry and took a shower, she was both hungry again, and exhausted.

Two more calls had come in, she noticed. Neither from Emily.

"Come for dinner!" she texted Emily.

"tomorrow" came the reply. "No food"

Jack was waiting for her in the center of the room. If only she'd perfume herself with pretty sniffs and go out shopping...

"Okay!" she said, pushing back her wet hair, and returned into the bathroom for the hairdryer.

The measure of her mood had improved considerably. She was back in control of her life.

Two hours later, there was no mistaking the level of excitement that stirred the tiny apartment when Amanda returned with two armfuls of bagged groceries. For one thing, the place was aired out and cold by now.

French bread. Salami. Lamb chops. Ground beef. Soft cat food (Mackerel). Butter. Eggs. Spinach. And cheese. Swiss, parmegian, goat. ...Limes. Jam. Pasta. Fresh ground coffee.

Then out came the piece-de-resistance. She tossed it across the room and Jack pounced on it. The toy mouse was visible for only half a second then disappeared behind the desk.

Provisions stowed and coffee in hand, her day was on! Her thoughts were clear.

She had pushed reality to the edges of her existence. Resuming a normal life was the source of her resilience, in a way. She looked about the place. Old and decrepit this student housing was, there was something intriguing about the purpose of the structure. It had housed many an intellectual before her! The ability to immerse herself in intellectual thinking with calm, methodical, and careful annotations gave her soul fresh air as nourishment.

Jack streaked across the room in pursuit of his prey, and Amanda switched on soothing tunes and her desk lamp.

Amanda observed that the coins found on the sunken vessels were at the core of the issue. Provenance. Yet, whose *authority* did they represent? That would surely establish the question of ownership.

She looked first at numismatics. Prior to the English Civil War, all coins were hammered. The business of minting coins was dispensed by the royals to their favored Lords as license. License was like a patent. It gave exclusive rights, privileges and profits.

After the Civil War, coins were milled. Milled hand press coinage continued to be produced in England through the remainder of the period. But values depended on the availability of the metals. Mining was poor, supply even poorer... counterfeit coins in abundance.

Amanda noticed that suddenly during the reign of William III, coins which were once stamped by a salaried mint master, was now privatized to individuals. Contractors were to purchase rolled sheets of copper in the required thickness and then cut out blanks of the proper diameter.

However, as an economy measure the contractors did not produce blank planchets in the normal manner. Rather they were simply melted as copper ore then poured into molds producing cast blanks.

Only the Spanish and Dutch were able to provide reliable sources of metals for coin minting. So gold took on "super power" dominance. But trafficking was designed for the elite. That is, trade was abundant, but channeled ostensibly for Royals, but rather for Empire builders!

Traditional vehicles of law, religion, and Parliament to do so with edicts, laws, acts and taxations was recognized. But since most mobility was by sea, the Navigation Acts was central to all.

The challenge then, for bankers, was not so much the production of coinage, but the laws that channeled trade revenues into the hands of the select.

Next, Amanda turned to the dictates. Export taxes had to be lifted. Redistribution laws had to be opened up. These were matters less for domestic consumption as for centralized imperialism. So it was the matter of law and its authority, that could be described by sovereign iconography.

Interestingly, this monetization project had funded the colonial venturing of the new world just prior to the Civil War. She read the works of various scholars.

"Copper farthing minted about 1625 by the Duchess of Richmond under license from King Charles I was supposed to be used in England, Ireland and in the American colonies."

Then Amanda's attention turned to the players of the monetization of the ventures at sea. Specifically, the colonial trade ventures in the early part of the century. Here suddenly, was the man who sat on the Council of the Virginia Trade Company, Sir Henry Neville!

Clearly he was not only a highly connected politician, but through family ties and resources a man of major financial corporate capabilities. His pedigree brought him close to the Crown, perhaps a little too close.

Most significantly, he came from a tradition of metallurgy, learning, writing and debating. His family table was full of such discussion, clearly. Their commercial ties were enormous, legendary and inherited as Princes of land.

In Parliament, he sat New Windsor 1584-5 and 1593, Sussex 1588-9, Liskeard 1597-8, Kent 1601, Lewes 1603-4 and Berkshire 1604-11 and 1614.

Yet he operated as an Independent Entity.

Amanda's eyes moved around the desk, her thoughts settling.

How...How do you determine *truth*? She paused, looking around. Auth... The authenticity of the plays were to be found in revelations of a diary!

That's when it struck her. A sudden surprise that sent her to the kitchen for a glass of water. *Jacques was missing the originals!*

Where were they? He was fishing... God. How safe did that make her?

She did what she always did when she felt like she was sinking. Back to work. She looked for facts..

What is truth? What is history, she wondered. Do people manipulate it, for gain?

How much is fact, and how much is speculation, she wondered. How do you extrapolate from facts, exactly, with any degree of certainty?

Written testimony of some kind, and/ or the record must show evidence to support a theory. Then it can offer logical conclusions. But corroboration is essential, she concluded.

The bibliographic search of previous scholarship helps - and it saves reinventing the wheel, so to speak. But what if one piece of evidence led to some conclusions, some assumption that was in error. And what if the rest of the bibliographic compilations based on *that* finding remained incorrect?

It occurred to Amanda that dislodging the familiar idea that Shakespeare wrote his plays was tantamount to launching a modern day assault on a cultural stronghold!

Shakespeare did not write the plays? Shakespeare was an Actor. *Sir Henry Neville wrote the Shakespeare plays?*

Yes. She decided. She could be convinced if she thought about it...

Shakespeare *might not* have written those plays himself - perhaps being insufficiently informed to do so. His patron, Sir Henry Neville was of course educated, exposed and informed - "wired" - to produce those sophisticated plays!

Yet if he did, then why did he hide his identity. *Why?*

Several new historians were coming to this same questioning. They were amongst the bravest, thought Amanda. And they should all be allowed to arrive at their position without academic scorn, which of course they were receiving! After all, they were reversing much of the scholarship held for centuries about literature, if not human language itself!

But were they correct in their assertions?

Amanda got up. Some things were bothering her.

Why was it that Sir Henry Neville hid his identity as the author of the plays?

Neville, clearly, for a time, carried on the business of an iron-founder in Sussex. He had mining and foundry capabilities in many regions with various related commercial ventures, including ship building, ironworks, tin mining, making of cannon and minting of coins. It carried well throughout his family into his inheritance. In fact, beyond his life to create the century of change in Europe. Including America.

What had she read in Paris?

So, overtones of Protest with the establishment sufficient to start a new world and mint new coin for the new realm held... credence. Clearly, this did resonate within the plays themselves.

On the other hand, young playwright William Shakespeare of Stratford on Avon knew and studied the works of an influential bishop of Worcester, Edwin Sandy.

Edwin Sandy, who later became bishop of the great city of London when Queen Elizabeth I ascended to the throne of England, became Archbishop of York – his words and verse of protest the crucible of a divided England!

Punished in the famous Marian exile by the Catholic Queen Mary following his sermon, he was reinstated in England to translated the Bishop's Bible. In this divided Protestant world of Queen Elizabeth where Pope Pius V ordered all her Catholic subjects "not to obey her, or her munitions, mandates and laws" many saw plots of overthrow and counter-plot conspiracies in a quest for the love with the tools of cruelty.

For those seeking elsewhere to expand and live free of Catholic dominion, his second son, Sir Edwin Sandy became the colonial organizer and treasurer in London of the New World colony of Virginia.

From the moment that Queen Elizabeth's father, Henry VIII Reformed the Church of England to end Catholic control by the Popes of Europe, all religious orders had been dissolved; pilgrimage sites and Latin ritual overturned by English Protestant reformers.

William Shakespeare, Amanda felt, was possibly a closet Catholic like his mother Mary Arden who lived in a divided household where his father was a Protestant Stratford alderman.

Indeed, William Shakespeare's early years reflected conflicted passions, if not skepticism with authority.

Oh, no question, decided Amanda. Young Will Shakespeare knew his feelings of outrage and protest of a divided world, on a stage of an England struggling to assert itself as a Protestant state...

How to separate the class-ordered in society? How was it possible that a high-born gentleman like Neville might be the author of the plays, competing with the identity of a young man from Stratford on Avon, she wondered.

Shakespeare understood the order of society as he laced his plays around the human condition. And he understood, like no other writer in the history of playwriting, that a man was defined by what he did. If he fashioned feeling and thoughts, they were universally recognized.

But she knew that in his works there was a mysterious imagination that neither class nor distinction could define. In these elements, matters of the heart, the soul, the conscience and morality gave life meaning - as only he could freely write them. A gentleman, on the other hand, might feel socially constrained by uttering such things.

Certainly, a trade and craft marked the fortunes of a man. If found without license to trade, a vagrant then might be rounded up under the laws of the Vagabond Act of 1604, then "to commit his body to painful labor" as Shakespeare put it. So where exactly did he fit into the social order of his day? *How did you become a playwright when you came from Stratford, without university schooling?*

Amanda discerned that Shakespeare viewed himself as a player. He wrote for the theater not as a poet, but as a player. Yet, even if provincial in roots, he had a nimbleness of conservatism that uniquely found its voice in *Henry VI* trilogy.

True, Shakespeare competed with poets and scholars – university wits -   as companions. These were gentlemen poets supplying the touring playing companies with plays, men like Greene, Nashe and Peele. Possibly, Neville did write too, maybe for the very troupe of players and actors that Shakespeare wrote.

Amanda turned to her notes. Even testimony of a critic can cast shadows of identification.

She found the reference and refreshed the situation. Shakespeare did feel the lash of professional envy from those poets snobbish and superior - one amongst them Robert Greene who seeing Shakespeare's success warned his friends of actors that *"speak from our mouths...Yes, trust them not; for there is an upstart Crow, beautified with our feathers, ...supposes he is as well able to bombast out a blank verse as the best of you. [he]...is in his own conceit the only Shakescene in the country."*

No, she decided. It would not be easy to unseat William Shakespeare.

That is not to say that Neville was absent from these plays.
Queen Elizabeth I, after all, presided over the colonial ventures of the new world for her Gentlemen Adventurers and for England's expansionism.
Shakespeare was clearly on board with this.

But a new world would require money-making and minting capabilities. Money for the realm! *The new realm?*

Sir Henry Neville carried on the business of an iron-founder in Sussex. He had mining and foundry capabilities in many regions with various related commercial ventures, including ship building, ironworks, tin mining, making of cannon and minting of coins. It carried well throughout his family into his inheritance.   In fact, beyond his life to create the century of change in Europe. Including America.

What had she read in Paris?

His nephew, Thomas Gresham was the founder of the Royal Exchange, and one of the best known merchants in Elizabethan England. He it was that granted the Gresham College, at Holt with words that would ring long enough as being the first of all laws named Gresham's Law, that "Bad money drives out good" that would be to mean by it that money of gold could be hoarded by ordinary people even if the government introduced lesser metals...and thus the power of the poor to trade as ordinary men.

Amanda noticed something else. Was he a *Reformist*? Or seditious Parliamentarian?

His Lordly influence with the Stuarts, at the turn of the century after Queen Elizabeth, mapped the road from Monarchical Rule by Divine Right to responsible governance by the end of the century – Even if at the cost one Regicide; one civil war; one foreign monarch and multiple wars against the Holy Roman Empire.

Plus a bankrupt Treasury and an entire British fleet sinking off Gibraltar...

On the other hand, it ushered into society circulation the age of domestic trade, carrying trade, finance and individual representation for a modern Europe.

She was impressed by the prodigious talent and ability of one man, even before she looked at his writings. Did Shakespeare advance his cause?

How did he do this?

Just before Queen Elizabeth died, and before the new King James came to the throne, Neville was knighted and sent as Ambassador to France to the Court of Henri IV. It was, ostensibly, to reconcile a dispute between the unfaithfulness of the Royal couple of France, royal progeny being the vehicle for patronage and credit amongst early empires, still.

Yes. Yes. All this she knew.

While at Calais, on his way to Paris, he had a dispute with the Spanish Ambassador as to the royal precedence. It was a matter of law. Not God's divine right to rule. But law.

"Dispute with the Spanish Ambassador as to *precedence*"?

Amanda shuddered at what the consequence of that occasion might have been.

It was the basis upon which Justice stood! Law cases. Mosaic Laws. And Laws of the Land.

So...if he was meddling with laws of the land, and had probable cause for mal-contentment...was he plotting to establish the new world?

America?

But he was challenging sovereign authority!

She read on.

At Paris, he negotiated the Treaty of Boulogne, and was considered a Puritan.

He returned in 1600 on the heels of the Huguenot Massacre, and was imprisoned briefly in the Tower of London on his return. Attributed with great works of writing, he there wrote extensively and exhaustively.

She paused, thinking. How would his work braid with the words of Shakespeare. Who were his agents? His London Merchants? His ...money?

She read on.

"In the service of an angry James I, following Elizabeth, who could get no supply for a standing Army from Parliament, he inserted the first seed of separation of powers as the King called for a Parliament . In the first session of 1610, he advised the King to give way to the demands of the House of Commons. In 1612, he urged the calling of a parliament and drew up a paper on the subject, in which he recommended what James should be given supplies - if grievances were redressed.

Amanda looked up. He framed the governance that would start Early Modern Europe!

The night was well advanced.

Little but an occasional car drove by, the street lights flickering a small light show for falling snow.

Jack was warmly curled up and fast asleep. She, safe, cozy and lost in her world of early discoveries...

Normally, she would have started on her computer. But she knew that once she opened her passwords, there would be Trevor's feed. Something she must avoid.

Instead she turned to the pile of papers on her desk. Some she filed. Others she straightened - including student's exam papers to be graded - which she had spirited away from her inbox a couple of days ago in an effort to avoid Jeannette.

Hell. Jeannette! That was nothing....

Emily had brought in some of her mail too.

Then she stopped short.

It was a brown envelope. Addressed in hand on the front to her address. The back had been sealed.

Not just sealed. But wax sealed with an imprinted with a signet crest of a Royal harp, lamb and lion.

Lamb of Wales. Lion of England. Combined in three shields...

The seal was already opened. So, what was this package of stuff. Already opened.

Out came documents that were faxcimilies of old scripts.

Half the stuff Trevor gave her to read in Paris was here! *Who* gave her this? How did it arrive on her desk?

"....so it was that for his life, he did give his oath never to reveal the true identify of himself as author of all that was written by him. My Lord. My Master. Sir Henry Neville. For he is the man who wrote the plays, the poems, the histories and the words that would change the world. A new world, a new wealth and new industries and new commonwealth for the men of trade. For though savages were to overthrow, and tobacco to export beyond the license of the King, he was wrongly

accused, and greatly honored for his lineage...but to give his name no more.

"And it is in the family of his married cousin, trader and merchant from the plantation of Ireland, that I shall keep this testimony, true and secret, until I do die. And the world shall change. ..."

Amanda sat down. A dozen times she must have examined the calligraphy. There was no way to know for sure...But it looked awful real!

What puzzled Amanda most was a Post It attached to the pile that came out of the envelope.

I thought you should have these.

Emily. -

* *

Thirty Five

The next couple of days passed blindly without time.
Amanda went shopping in London. It took the whole
day. And yes. It felt good. She even went to the Theater.
To see a play. Any play.
Emily called back twice. It was a reply to a text message
that said "Explain papers"
When she got in, it was as if she had never left her desk.
And it was dark already.
Amana had fallen asleep on the sofa.
"Hello?" she said. It was three thirty in the morning.
"So, they were Edward's. He...gave them to me, and I
made a copy. I figured you'd want to see them"
"That's..." she cleared he sleepy voice "That's ...
generous of you!" She wanted to hang up. Go back to
sleep."
"So. What do you think?"
"Think...About what?"
"the papers" said Emily with an attitude.
Amanda was a very patient person. But something here
irked the hell out of her.

"The...? Wait. I've been kidnapped, pressed into labor, picked by New Scotland yard accusing me of murder; threatened by a bunch of Euro-thugs and you turn up fresh as a pansy offering me evidence that will turn the assumptions of literature upside down! Jesus Christ Emily! What do you think you're playing at?"

There. She said it all. And in her way. She was awake.
 Emily was giggling. "I fed your cat didn't I?" said Emily. Life was back to normal. "But its true. He said it was his family stuff..in the vault. I want you to have it"
"Gee thanks. It's not damned funny Emily. Someone could get hurt..."
There was no reply.
"Emily. You there?"
Emily became distant, and there was a sad hushness to it.
 "Someone *did* get hurt. Edward"
"Geez, I'm sorry Emily. I didn't mean..."
Emily was gone.
The next call she heard eating, an apple by the sound of the crunch
 "And you'd better be careful. The guy in the picture on Jeannette's desk. That was the guy on your cell phone when you were out on a date in Paris. That was him!"
"Jacques?"
"Cute. Except for the leather thing. He's the one that looks like he could be a mean dude."
"Not Jacques. He's a French lover, playing at being gangster."

"Ok. Whatever you say." Another slurping bite out of the apple "So. Tomorrow then. For dinner. You gonna cook?"

"You sound like you haven't had a decent meal since the last time you were here" As soon as the words were out of her mouth, Amanda knew she was right.

"Anyway" continued Emily "Those things were Edwards. Keep them!"

"Where are the originals?"

"Safe!"

"Emily. Wait. Emily...?"

Hearing her voice did wonders to recalibrate her thinking. It was like playing mother.

Only, there was something Emily said that struck a discord somewhere. What was it?

She felt more positive now. And there was one last time she wanted to view something. It was Trevor's Feed of the Proceedings. Her final access to his files of the case. Something he had asked her to monitor...

Something she would do just once more, before erasing the encryptions on her computer that gave her access. It helped, having the computer on in the dark room, alone with something familiar ....She looked up. It would soon be dawn.

Sleep did not come easily. Trevor would be in his white wig and gown, arguing for the defense of something that occurred three centuries ago. Talk about the honor of the realm!

She made coffee. It was morning.

And then those documents that Emily produced. She looked at them in the light of the desk lamp. Extraordinary. Real? Surely not!

A testimony to what? That Shakespeare was a fake? She sat in the dark. Thinking.

So. Who wrote those plays? What had Jacques implied, that she verify the identity of those documents as being without authenticity?...If so, why the veiled threats about a story to the police? Why the intervention ploy? Intimidation? And as for those damned documents! Now Emily had them on her desk. Originals. On parchment paper.

They were not even reported missing! Yet they were.

But then, she saw the picture on Jeannette's desk left by the Investigating Detective?

Who did she say? Or See in that image, rather?

* *

It lay there not because crustaceous covering exposed its shape, nor because the bottom was on an incline. But because the subsurface current moving through the Straights could have abrasive effects on everything, including the mountain sides of the rocky cliff underwater.

Karmosky was saying things again.

Somehow, it's own weight had wedged it between two smallish outcrops that acted like stops.

Karmoski had seen it coming, he later said. No. He sensed it. Not even on the screen, but through the robot's cameras. Not that it wouldn't become obvious later. But it had lodged itself in his imagination.

And suddenly. There is was. A ship's cannon.

Fortunately, the seas had held calm, and being a disciplined bunch, they had strayed little from their shipboard schedule. So, with flawless management of the robotic arm on the seafloor, the seventeenth century cannon was hoisted, and broke surface just at daybreak.

And not a second too soon. For with the water wash still glistening within cast iron pores and bacterium of the ship's cannon, it was less than 12 hours later when the salvage boat had to weigh anchor and leave those waters. And that included a four hour ascent by the robot which looked no worse for wear when nestled carefully into her cradle on the stern of the salvage ship.

But leave they were required to do...As instructed by email from their own company headquarters. Not that it took long for the maritime police to present themselves in a large cutter off their stern.

Very clearly they were informed to vacate the territorial waters of Spain. And at gunpoint.

Evidently, evidence had been produced that artifacts on board the salvage vessel once belonged to Spain. And that was that!

Such was the speed with which the documentation was dispatched by the authorities of the government.

Fortunately for the *Vienna* 's crew, there had not been time to scrape any of the crust off the cannon when the Spanish Investigators came aboard. It looked like waterlogged debris. Along with all the rest of the stuff, gear and useless metals retrieved off the bottom.   A glass bottle or two were inspected more closely. Other less onerous mangled metals were inspected as well. Anything seventeenth century was considered suspect and Spanish.

But for the most part, nothing was confiscated of any significance by the Spanish authorities.

Only later, well on the voyage home did Karmoski and his team pick away at the pitted metal and rusted coating mantle of the old ships cannon. He reached the part of the cannon that would show the stamp of the manufacture.

He imaged the inscription, scanned the copy to his computer, and sent it in on as a secure encrypted message. Someone would want to do some homework on it, he evidently had decided.

The image found its way into Trevor's case file as a piece of evidence within 12 hours. Just before Amanda was about to shut down the program and passwords.

It was almost lost when Amanda first saw the dark brown shape of the filed image. Sort of a digital finding aid on the program, it stood out, as a smaller icon. She clicked on it to enlarge the image.

Actually, she almost missed the area cleared away. But she gasped. The inscription on the cannon was familiar. Still on her desk in fact...

The Royal harp, lamb and lion of Ireland.

She sat down at her computer and started to research.
All bets are off Jacques!
By the time she switched off the lamp on her desk, most of the morning had gone.

* *

Amanda entered her Department at the College earlier than anyone else this morning.

She went to her Inbox, sorted through her mail, then settled at her desk where she found a blue stuffed Easter Bunny holding a small pencil and pad with the big Letter "A" on it. Inside was the name of a student. Happy Easter!

A *Post It* on her computer said that the large bouquet of flowers on the Front Office table of the Department came addressed to her from another adoring student - "which we all decided to share thank you!" And two baskets of Easter Egg chocolates had already made the rounds - (Also from the same source of suppliers...) "So keep 'em coming Commando!" signed Emily.

Amanda cleared away some space, and made a listing of items she wanted her research assistant to print up from the electronic databanks at the University Library.

Finally, she wrote the email.

"Proceeding with Sir Walter Raleigh...OK?"

Amanda turned to other email, hundreds, and answered several. Especially those to her students, and those requiring administrative responses. The rest were queries, dated issues, or spam

She had made coffee at the front desk, and poured herself a cup. The first.

 Emily may have been sloppy a housekeeper at home – more like a lovesick sentimentalist when it came to Edward's adored bits and pieces - but here in the office, it was part of her gothic- *persona* to be the best coffee maker in the town; something that invoked a measure of respect amongst the ranks.

It had been a couple of weeks since Amanda had been in. Officially "telecommuting" from offsite, as they liked to say at some Human Resources. Today she would actually sit through Jeanette's Office Staff Meeting just long enough to be seen, then slip out the rear.

Still early, Amanda looked around. Little had changed in the Department, even now that most of the students had gone for Easter Break. Scraps of paper and college Departmental debris has been cleared away by janitors. One area was being refurbished and closed off with drop cloths. But here was the aura of debate: Here echoed the words of Discussion. Deciding and Defining. It was what most good Universities should be, she thought. Not thought-police stations, as some would have it.

Satisfied that she had touched on all the basis, she was preparing to leave and wanted to clear her desk and load her car. She gathered her books, notes and briefcase - even her leftover Exhibits from a previous lecture. That is, before anyone with ideas of investigative license decided to show her the door, like Jeannette Bevan, for instance.

With her hands full she made for the main hallway. Then paused.

Jeannette's office door was open. Remarkably, it was wide open. Either left that way by wayward workmen, or purposefully ajar for a function.

She looked inside, and saw a desk cleared of the usual semester clutter that gathered on a Department Chair's Desk. Entirely possible that Jeannette had taken a week off, and had not been in at all for days? It was entirely possible that she had left already, given the semester break.

She noticed a fresh brown envelope folded neatly tied with string atop the desk. It was unopened. But not secure, nor private. It had little stitching across an odd sized corner that was familiar. The logo on it was the emblem of the United Kingdom. The same as that seen on everything in the offices of New Scotland Yard.

Since the case under investigation had involved her name and she worked here as Faculty, she felt perfectly entitled to inspect the file sitting on the Department Chair's desk. At the very least, it should be secured.

It was a copy of an official deposition.

The transcript stunned her.

NSC, Sergeant Simmons.

"How do you explain the cigarettes in the Vault Miss Evans?"

> Ms Evans: "Edward and I entered it again for the second time that evening"
>
> "Why?"
>
> "Because I persuaded Edward to take out the manuscripts from the vault here. I just had a bad feeling about the integrity of the vault...."
>
> NSC: " A bad feeling?"
>
> "I dunno"
>
> NCO . "So explain the sequence and timing of the second time you both came in...Why?"

"Edward and I entered. We searched for the manuscript. Edward was very upset not to find it. He said he was going home."
"Did anyone see you?"
"Yes! Mr. Robertson, the vault manger"
"Why did you not say this earlier, Miss Evans?"
"Ms. Bevan said that I could lose my grant if ..."
"In your economy with the truth, Ms. Evans, you are setting up another person to be a suspect, let alone committing perjury. So the question now is, Why? Because you knew that Ms. Wells was a visiting professor?"

* *

Thirty Six

Emily came through the door bundled up and holding a bottle of wine. Jack and she did their usual snuggles. She dropped a load of the research papers on Amanda's desk, and called out.

She found Amanda sitting in an almost dark room.

"Why?" she said simply, her face pale, a beer bottle still in her hand.

There was no masking the hurt.

Emily sat down, herself weary, it seemed, from carrying her burdens

"Why? ...The death of Edward...No. The *horrid* death of Edward changed everything....With him gone, and the manuscripts missing, I wanted time to find out what happened to the manuscript that cost him so .."

Her voice trailed

"leaving me to play   the default target of the investigation. Is that it?" said Amanda

 Emily looked up, her eyes full of tears and pain "I was going to get it all out...I couldn't betray you Amanda ....even if I go to jail!"

"Well that's nice!"

Emily stared at the rug. Jack managed to maneuver himself under her hand for a stroke.

"At this rate, we'll both be aging in jail!" Amanda took a swig of beer

Emily looked up, a dot of hope in her face.

"Oh hell. I've been through worse. Come on. Let's get cleaned up and eat!"

Emily seemed to thaw. Jack saw to that.

"And so... where's the wine? And it's pasta tonight!" yelled Amanda from the kitchen, her Dean and Delucca apron tied at the waist like a duty mantle. She was lifting the noodles out of the boiling water, and started to plate the sauce. But she stopped and came out of the kitchen holding the noodle claw. "There's one thing I can't figure out."

Emily followed her into the kitchen and pulled out the cutlery. "What?"

" In your deposition...Did you say that Robertson knew what happened?"

"Why?"

"He's dead."

"What?"

"Oh yeah. I found out thru Interpol or something. He met with a tragic traffic accident in Wales"

"I..uh. .didn't know that" said Emily, pausing at the table. She went to the bathroom.

At the dinner table they ate everything. Cheese. Garlic bread. Salad and pasta.

Finally the wine was finished. Coffee and something sweet followed.

"Come on. Pitch in!"

After washing up, they picked a movie to watch. Less than half way through it, Emily had crashed on the sofa. Amanda turned everything off, turned a cover over Emily, and went to bed, exhausted.

It was Sunday morning. They had a mug of coffee, then strolled outside across the park for a newspaper.

Church song filled the air with the slow wooden pipe echoes of a 17th century organ playing, and they sprinted up the granite step of the wide open Cathedral. At the rear, they ooched themselves into a standing congregation, and even joined in a few hymns. Above them a small rainbow appeared as the sun hit a beveled window and refracted through the gothic stained glass. They smiled, giggled rather at their spontaneous disposition. Nor did they stay long enough to hear any benediction. But singing somehow brought poetry back to their souls, and they skipped down the great steps again and proceeded across the park.

It was bright and crisp.

A small bistro lunch spot sat them outdoors in the warm sun of an early Spring. They were served salad and cheese. From their seats they could see the river and the rooftops of the University boathouse. Amanda followed Emily's eyes.

"You loved him, didn't you?" she said. Such admission would not come easily to a girl half way through her degree program and wearing vampire jewelry.

Emily looked up. "I did"

They didn't speak for a long time. But Amanda was glad she asked.

On the way back they shopped at the local fish market, bought French bread and pastries from the bakery next door and headed back, the wind now subduing the park with grey coloring and a cold chill.

They pulled up their collars, and quickened back to the apartment. A few chores followed, and Emily plugged herself into her iTunes and picked up a stack of fashion magazines, the TV Controller at the ready for duty.

Amanda retreated to her desk and switched on the work light. Within minutes, her eyeglasses on and a pencil weaved into her chignon, her mind was a thousand miles away. Two centuries passed through her notes, the soft desk light tenting her like an icon, and the clock advanced three hours, unnoticed.

Amanda announced they would have broiled salmon with dill sauce and a baked potatoes for dinner, followed by pastries and cappuccino for dessert.

"Great!" said Emily. "You're spoiling me with all this gourmet food..."

"Easy to make" said Amanda. "Susie and Fred called it their Sunday evening special..."

So with the potatoes in the oven, and the salmon prepared to bake, Amanda returned to the front room, and came over to Emily with a folder of papers.

"Now. Explain all of this, will you?"

Emily looked at the material in her hand, poured Jack off her lap, and picked up the remote control to the television. She switched the Off button.

Some minutes passed.

"...And then tell me all about Edward and the vault..." added Amanda.

"Those documents... are Edwards. He said they were the object of some investigation that might expose some facts 'detrimental' to the family."

"His family?"

"Yes."

"'If they were subpoenaed by the court, they would have to be examined, he said. He wanted them off the premises of his home, and in a safe place. 'Just for a few months' he said."

"A few months...!" wailed Amanda "Sorry!. Ok. Sorry. Sorry. Go on"

"The only place I thought of was the Vault. It was safe. *Nobody* went in there but us anyway. You're the only lecturer who gives a damn in that Department..."

"Ok. Ok." said Amanda, calming her. "Go on!"

"He knew I was working with you at the University that afternoon, for the evening class. He had posited them when he accompanied me into the vault...where I was getting your material ready... "

"without anyone knowing?"

"without anyone knowing. Yes"

"Then when he told me what he had done, I told him he was a stupid shit and should get them out of there! After you were done, I took him in with me on the pretext that I was wrapping up things for you. Once in the vault, we argued. Then we...Well, you know..."

"Was he smoking?

"Yes. His brand of cigarillos. As usual"

"When we went in, it was to *retrieve* the documents. I had persuaded him to take them back home! "

"Is that when Robinson saw you?"

"Yes. I even made copies of the damned things to show that I was working on your project...That's what you have. That's what I showed him. He looked at them, and told me to give them to you in case... "

"in case what?"

"in case anything happened to him, he said" Emily was getting distraught.

"So Robinson wouldn't suspect anything unusual in your presence, with your boyfriend hanging around, let alone the documents you were imaging – for me!"

"Right"

Amanda stood up, and walked about the room once, just holding her breath.

"I'm sorry. They would naturally accuse you!" Emily said.

"Wait. The original documents – not the ones you copied - what happened to them after you made copies? ..."

Emily shrugged, a little confused.

"What did you and Edward do with his stuff?"

"Well. We went outside. It was getting dark. That's when I showed him the copies I had made, and he made his rude remark. We argued. He told me he'd keep his materials, and that I was no help at all. That's the last time I saw him"

"Except for one detail. You see, Edward had made the switch himself! *He* left the originals with the copies, and kept only odd papers. He left you with the originals. You didn't see that?"

"No."

"Did anyone else see you?"

"No." said Emily

"Did anyone overhear you?"

"Obviously! Robinson, for one..."

"And...?"

"Nobody else was there. Except, maybe, this..."

Out came the folder Amanda had seen sitting on Jeanette's desk from New Scotland Yard.

"You *took* that?"

Emily look up, shrugged her shoulders. "She'll have it back on her desk by Monday..and never know the difference"

Only the page that Emily was pulling came out from the back of the folder. A large black and white photograph.

"A photograph taken by security cameras. Robinson identified them as being the two people outside the main gate when he was locking up!"

To Amanda, the image was nothing unusual. It was Jacques, always interested in antiquities and libraries, with the Interpol police officer introduced to her as the Dutchman. Given his interest, he'd naturally be in the investigation file.

"You recognized Jacques from my camera phone the night you called?" said Amanda incredulously.

"Sure"

Amanda looked down then and stopped talking. Emily's finger was pointing to the black leather jacket. Not Jacques. The man beside him. The Dutchman

"I'm certain he killed Edward and took the documents!"

"No. What are...you...saying...?" Amanda paced the room, ran her fingers through a mass of silky hair, and then sat down.

"Are you SURE?"

"But that's not who I was with...in the Paris shot..." said Amanda. " Hang on. Of course..."

The Dutchman was there too with them in Paris. He was in the shot! How could Emily possibly have known which figure was Jacques...or which was the Dutchman?

"What about him?" said Emily, her chin indicating Jacques "Who is he?"

"He's an antiquities dealer. I've known him since Beirut. He's honest, if colorful, but not a criminal!"

They ate dinner. Then returned to the police files purloined from Jeannette's desk by Emily.

"If... it was found that Edward did NOT have the Treatises on him by the killer, then they must have assumed that the manuscript was still in the vault, right?"

"Who was the last to leave the vault that night then?"

"Robinson!"

"So the killer would assume that Robinson had kept the Treatises and followed him....?"

Emily leaned back into the sofa and crossed her arms. "So. Your turn. What's with the documents?"

"Emily. The documents are a testimony of some sort. A seventeenth century testimonial about a revelation, that if true, could reverse four centuries of assumptions about literature, if not the most famous body of literature we hold as a culture. It's almost immoral to reverse all that sacred conviction about the authorship..."

"That's what Edward said"

"..to say nothing of the insurances; museums; university careers; publications and precepts of assumptions that follow and ....and stand on its foundations...."

"that's what Edward said.." repeated Emily. "So. What is it?"

Amanda got up and showed her the last and first pages. First the signatures. Then the seal.

"It's Shakespeare saying that the true sponsor of the plays is the same man as the owner of the seal."

"Let's see?"

"This!" She showed Emily the Harp. The Lion. The Lamb.

"Who....then?"

"That's the heraldic seal of the Neville Family. Sir Henry Neville, his patron"

"What are you saying?"

"Shakespeare is testifying that Sir Henry Neville was the author of the *ideas* in the plays, if not the author perhaps!"

Emily's hands went up to her face, unbelieving.

"Edward...wanted to hide these...in a safe place..." she muttered.

She looked at Amanda. "He said that it was a secret his family had kept a long time. That he had a responsibility as a legacy thing..."

They sat there, both absorbing the information.

"Oh My God..." said Emily finally.

"What?"

"Edward...he was a...*Neville!*"

Amanda looked at the Coat of Arms.

"A descendant?" said Emily

"That explains why his family vault... held such items as...sacred."

The ramifications then hit her. "He was murdered...for this?"

The truth was too awful to contemplate. And it was a long time before they spoke.

But Emily was the one who said it. "So ...if these murderers went after Edward for this...Then, won't they come after ....*you*?"

"God!"

"You'd better go to the police" said Emily.

Amanda's thoughts flew to Trevor.

The Dutchman: He said he was with Interpol. A lie!

That could mean that he was the killer who confronted Edward? Impossible!

But if, when finding no Treatises on Edward, he would hunt for another means, surely, of acquiring the manuscript?

Except for Robinson. He might have seen all this. He was a liability, having both noticed the articles in the vault of interest to Edward, plus, spotted men that Edward might have encountered outside - even if on a security camera screen?

Amanda's thoughts were a jumble.

"Come to think of it," said Amanda. "How was he *informed* of Robinson's 'road accident'...?"

"Because he had him killed..." finished Emily.

"In Wales...? Who knew he lived in Wales?"

"You did!" said Emily.

"How...?"

"Your phone was tapped. You were a suspect, remember? New Scotland Yard has license to pursue possible leads...right?"

Amanda turned brusquely and eyed her desk strewn with all her research. "That means...that means that everything, I mean *everything* here is...is..."

"Compromised!" said Emily.

Amanda went into the tiny kitchen to wash up. There was much she was concealing: What evidence had Trevor received from Amanda that was intercepted and being leaked out...?

How much money was at stake if his case failed to pass the argument that British bullion belonged not to the Catholic Spanish, but to the sovereign of England. As in, what costs in damages, reparations, penalties and public funds...

A King's ransom!

Amanda returned to Emily, and eyed her gravely. "Look. Even if is, all of it...There is nothing that we have done wrongfully! Even if we have to answer for every concluding piece of evidence and finding! We are opening the past, perhaps, to reveal a foundational truth...But don't worry. We are doing what we are supposed to be doing! Got it?"

Emily nodded.

"Now it's time you went home, and got some rest. Ok?" said Amanda. "Until this blows over, can you stay somewhere, with family...?"

Outside the building, they crossed the street to where Emily was parked.

"Thanks for the research!" said Amanda in parting.
 "Thanks for weekend!"
"And...Not finished..." waved Emily, roaring her Mini into Reverse. Two more short pitches and she was out of her tight parking spot and onto the road. The little brake lights of the Mini twinkled down the road and disappeared at the next junction.

Amanda was standing on the sidewalk, watching her go, a tender worry still on her face. The wind brought on a chill, and, closing her sweater, she folded both arms to her chest for warmth. The park across the street had darkened.

It was only as she ascended the steps to reenter the building that Amanda noticed the car.

Barely a movement, it was a small shiny flash of a movement within a car that had been parked across the street. Not that she and Emily would have noticed, but since parking meters were checked regularly and parking violation tickets proffered by roaming police officers, they had periodically looked out the window to check on the Mini. This car had been there for 24 hours. In fact, since Emily arrived. And definitely, someone was in it.

Amanda did little to show her concern. Instead, she turned calmly, climbed the dozen granite steps flanked by iron rail, and walked back into the building, a magnificent architectural Beaux Arts block of red stone that could have been once a grand Hotel, now serving as apartments for visiting Faculty.

The entrance, an oak-framed door laced with decorative wrought iron over paned cut glass, begged to be bolted from the inside. Rarely was it left unbolted. For a *Special Occasion* party, perhaps – with hosts and guests in motion. Or someone moving- into, or moving out of one of the four apartments, the cargo truck ramp perched at the steps.

She walked across the Foyer, still visible still to the outside, and passed the four mail boxes of polished brass plates. She stepped up the grand stairway with balustrade of brass to Mezzo Level balcony.

The elevator worked. She called it down, punching the button with clear gestures, then just as the doors closed, in split second timing, Amanda popped out and vanished from view. She ducked up the stair well to the third floor, entered her apartment and locked the door behind her. Quietly, Amanda sealed the windows for the night. At the last window, she noticed the car had gone. Downstairs, she heard the elevator doors open and a half dozen students and faculty spill into the Foyer, all of them lingering, chatting.

She scanned much of what Emily had given her, saved them as a Word Files, labeling them carefully. And uploaded them on an electronic memory stick which she unsheathed, and then re-sheathed once extracted from the computer. Included were materials related to the wealth of coin and sovereignty, underlying issues of authority and ownership – the treasure of England! It revealed how and where it arrived in the coffers, and which armed wars it would finance.

The wealth of Sir Francis Drake alone had astonished her. But more importantly the connections and players of the ventures behind the wealth.

She would read it all, later. For now, Emily was safely out of harm's way.

She should however, take precautions.

Drawing the curtains she gathered a few essentials and placed them in plastic sealed wrapping. She tucked them deeply into the hydra sealed compartments of her backpack.

In the bedroom, she pulled on a microfilament shirt, sweater, and deactivated her cellphone, which she also sealed, with keys, in another hermetically sealed plastic bag.

She had turned off her lights, and sat at the desk, the laptop her only torch.

Sounds outside were neighbors coming back from the weekend. They joined the crowd.

Amanda worked quietly. She found stamps, addressed an envelope, and placed some of the material on her desk in that envelope. They too were placed in the back-pack.

If there was one thing she had learned as a US Athlete on College Sailing teams, it was to be always in readiness; packed, planned and weather-tight at all times. It had served her well.

Now she could hope for the best, but plan for the worst. With this load, anything was possible.

She started to read her notes on a file she kept on her laptop. The screen lit up on some older material, general knowledge. Should she upload all this lot to Trevor's Research Site?

Drake plundered a Spanish warship at the Port of Callo.

Actually, Amanda knew that Drake's real mission was information on the heading of a Spanish galleon the *Nuestra Senora de la Conception* - popularly named by the Spanish sailors as *Cacafuego*.

She was a 120-ton merchant vessel, sailing from Peru to Panama, where her treasure and passengers would cross the Isthmus on her way to Spain.

Pirates had been raiding the West Indies for decades, Drake himself had been the first to pass from the Atlantic to the Pacific coast of South America.

Since the Spaniards did not expect to encounter marauders, most ships went unarmed.

Only Drake knew the amount of booty on board with his takings, and he obeyed the Queen's order never to reveal the secret.

Spanish merchants in Seville claimed that the *Cacafuego* carried 400,000 pesos in illegal cargo in addition to registered treasure worth £360,000. If this estimate was accurate, Drake took some £266,000 in gold and silver. And he also seized jewels and other valuables concealed in the passengers luggage.

Drake's loot was remarkable.

Among the families Drake may have met through the Champernownes, none was more prestigious than the Blounts who were connected, by the marriage of Catherine Blount, sister of Mountjoy, to John Champernowne.

John's sister Catherine Champernowne was the mother of Sir Walter Raleigh, married to the Gilberts who were sent to colonize Ireland, and plunder.

Sir Henry Neville was their financial backer!

This she should pass on to uploaded files.

Amanda paused. She was beginning to wonder at herself. Was there cause for alarm? Should she cover her track of research? Would she be buying time and privacy from anyone prying?

Surely not! She felt like she was in a state of flight: She was getting doubtful, and glanced at her gear.

The room was darkened. Perhaps her fears were groundless, after all.

Still, she would shut down her computer. She would check on Jack and turn in for the night.

Then she froze.

The floor shadows that crossed the base of her front door told her someone was outside. She felt cold, but not fear.

OK.

So Trevor's web site was not coming up! She copied everything and uploaded the rest on her own website as Attachment.

The knob was being softly tested.

She wanted to panic, but she stayed with her mission. It was critical to commit her files to cyberspace memory.

 She started to send an email to Trevor, options closing. She knew, just knew, someone was coming in...

She went back to her portal, and changed the password. Then closed all the uplinks.

She sent herself an email instead. Adding the documents as Attachments.

There were large documents with images, too large to load. She saved them at a lesser resolution and was shutting down her programs and passwords when the power went out.

The place was all black.

She abandoned the desk, picked up her gear, and went into her bedroom, locking the door.

She knew there was an intruder in the house.

She opened the window, picked up Jack who was fast asleep, the bed a huddled mass of bed coverings.

Amanda had stepped out the window onto the fire ladder when she heard the bedroom door open and Jack let out a growl. Two thuds followed, as if a pillow might deliver its feathers in protest.

They were definitely gun shots. She knew.

Furthermore, she knew Jack would find his way about.

He was a cat.

* *

Thirty Seven

Instead of climbing down, she had climbed up, moved up and down a few fire ladders along the adjacent buildings without touching the street level.

Almost a block away, she hit the alley and entered the Church premises, slide into a side garden gate and into the Vestry porch where a door let in early choristers arriving before the first communion service, and into the Cathedral.

She paused, catching her breath in the shadows of the Rectory Porch. Slowly she kneeled, and pulled out the envelope carefully addressed. She slid it into the letterbox. There, it would be picked up by her neighbor Lucy, who worked at the Rector's Office as Secretary. Instructions within, were to re-mail it out the next day. Lucy would comply, she knew.

And the original documents given to her by Emily would be safer out of her apartment! For a few days, at least. Later, they would be committed to a bank vault.

 With little traffic outside, she moved behind the Main Alter, and slipped into the choir cloister that led to the bell pulls. Flush against the paneling was the door leading up to the belfry. She pulled the knob, which squealed like a banshee and proceeded up the wooden stairways, wrapping up around the organ, and through into the structure.

Easily at one hundred and fifty feet she stepped into the bell tower.

It's not that she saw anyone, or even heard anything. But the pigeons and bats that flew off at her disturbance, and settled back into their perches, flushed out again, suggesting another disturbance.

She was panting, the backpack getting heavy. Stepped outside the bell tower housing, crouched like a gargoyle.

Then a familiar sound made her look back down the street. There on the roof of her own building was Jack, howling like a fire siren. He had attempted to follow her out the window.

She muttered a few obscenities, even as she felt gratified that he was unharmed. Only now she felt much like a cat herself, padding along the rooftops of medieval churches.

She teetered gently along the gabled ridgelines and towers of the Cathedral's main buttress vaulting, then shimmied down to the crenellated wall than banded the high slopes; jumping down to several telescoped roof elevations, one by one, until she reached the roof of the Vicar's residence. From there she managed a 20ft drop to the lawn. It was grassy. At the soft banks of the canal, her hands bleeding from meeting occasionally with the iron anchors that cradled slate tiling, she left the green and crossed the road.

And that's when she got a fright. The car that had been parked outside her building was suddenly there. The headlights went on. Two stepped out. She must have been spotted from across the park when she crossed the road.

"Over there!" said one voice.

She dodged behind two parked cars, then across a lawn to reach a cobbled canal street pathway that she knew would lead to the river. The car passed cruised along canal street. They would soon be back she knew.

Some lay assumptions in this environment were predictable. She picked her spot to slip into the water, holding a bough of tree. Keeping her backpack up by her head, barely, with the tree bough, she started walking out into the water. When the bottom fell away, she forced herself to float, softly, gently on the surface, like a piece of river debris, across to the other embankment. It took forever, so slow in fact, that she seemed motionless in the slow moving water. But she resisted the temptation to push.

She waited, soaked, the cold seeping through her bones. She thought of the lovely Ophelia floating down the River...

Then she felt the bottom rise on the other side. Amanda scrambled up the bank and made for the University boathouse, safe or no. It was all she could do, frost lingering on the night ground from a cold Spring dampness.

She found a boat on blocks secured by a tarp. She lay inside it, knowing enough to peel off her wet clothes.

Before dawn she had found her way inside the boathouse; suited up into a midsized wetsuit, and just as daybreak came, Amanda was on the water in a skull, rowing down the river with others in training for the school Crew team, her backpack stowed in the bow with two bungee cords.

Two miles down the river, the sun was burning the morning haze off the water, and the next township came into view.

* *

How she managed to get herself to Kensington was a blur. Fatigue and dehydration had started to take it's toll on her body. Watching her steps, backtracking, and assuring herself that she was not followed, consumed most of her energy and time.

 Were it not for the wallet, keys and few personal items in her trusty backpack Amanda would not have made it out of harm's way and into the mainstream of London. Nowhere was she noticed particularly. Having a destination however, helped her nerves hold steady enough.

It was a good two hours of hanging around to spot any pursuers in the vicinity of Druce House.

Of course her father still had it locked up. But she had her ways of entering. Even on a cold Spring night, the shelter of a place familiar was more than sufficient encouragement. And unless the whole episode was a hoax, or worse, a misunderstanding on her part that sent her roof prowling and then up the Thames to evade an imaginary assailant, she was most relieved to be in surroundings she could trust. Here she was safe. Still, she checked the windows.

She approached the housing unit of the power box inside the basement alcove, unthreaded a neck key, and unlocked the panel padlock. Inside, she opened the face to a digital touchpad and entered twelve numbers straight, followed by a pound sign. The light turned green, and the house alarm system, she knew, was deactivated.

The kitchen of Druce House was good enough. The flagstone floors nicely maintained, the oak wooden table well scrubbed by Fred and Susie when they were still here, and the pantry closed, and all dry goods sealed told her it was clear.

Inside, two cases of bottled spring water were stowed. She drank a couple.

She found a package of ready mix muffin flour, added dry powder milk, oil, water and placed it in a baking dish. She turned on the oven, its little oven light her only lamp. Careful to stay away from any windows, she moved to the fridge and opened a jar of pickled herring. And a can of red beans. She ate.

The bathroom downstairs served her well enough, and she padded upstairs to haul down some bedding which she spread out on a mat on the floor of the kitchen, not far from the warm oven. There she could spend the night, the house still dark and locked.

Exhausted, sleep came quickly.

* *

By the light of the window, Amanda put in a full day at the desk.

Fortunately, with only minimal power on to support the security systems, she had disabled the alarms and used the kitchen, careful not to offer any sign that the house was inhabited. She behaved herself like an intruder.

From the bottom drawer of her father's desk, she retrieved his personal cell phone and recharged it. It was his London number, fully subscribed, but used only when he was in the UK. Otherwise, it was disabled. His business calls, she knew, were redirected to his answering agent.

She sheltered well away from windows, including the computer, and there hunkered down for her research online.

 She accessed all her data bases without leaving trace of her signature. Her e-mail she left unanswered.

..."a list of all the ships taken by Sir Francis Drake and his cousin Sir Walter Raleigh" Emily, she saw, had sent her more.

 What she ended up with was a bibliographic field of findings that showed the movements of necessary transactions in the 17th century at the time of the sinking of the Sussex.

In searching the sources of all those players she started to establish a pattern of financial underwriters. And therefore those who might have a claim on those interests, and the laws of the land that prevailed.

It was long list. "Follow the money honey" was the advice her father had given her when she first announced she would pursue the study of history. Good advice, she decided.

Firstly, why were the Spanish claiming that the money was *theirs*?

In the case of Sir Francis Drake. One of the early West-Country gentlemen seeking new words, new wealth, and new reform, it was clear that his wealth actually came from the Spanish.

Drake had planned an attack on the Panama Isthmus, known to the Spanish as Tierra Firma and the English as the Spanish Main. TGoohis was the point at which the silver and gold treasure of Peru had to be landed, and then sent overland by mule train to the Caribbean Sea, where galleons from Spain would load it up at the town of *Nombre de Dios*. There might have been a back-story here, an unresolved dispute of legacy land, or even a longstanding feud amongst rival nations competing for colonial trade...

Drake went on for more venturing!

May 24, 1572, he left Portsmouth with a crew of 73 men in two small vessels, the *Pasha* (70 tons) and the *Swan* (25 tons), to capture *Nombre de Dios*.

1573. With Guillaume Le Testu the 20 tons of silver and gold –

By August 9, 1573, he was back in Plymouth.

Drake's prize ship *Nuestra Señora de la Concepción*, had a cargo whose tally was 36 kg of gold, including a large golden crucifix, jewels, 13 chests full of royal plate and 26 tons of silver...

No wonder the Spanish were ticked, she thought.

Spanish Armada. 1587 Drake intercepted Spanish supply lines, including 1600–1700 tons of barrel staves, enough "to make 25,000 to 30,000 barrels (4,800 m³) for containing provisions for the soldiers" she read from the public account.

Finally, there was his capture of the Spanish galleon *Rosario*, along with Admiral Pedro de Valdés and all his crew. The Spanish ship was known to be carrying substantial funds to pay the Spanish Army in the Low Countries.

Ample room for bad blood between the nations. Especially when Elizabeth was under constant threat of invasion by the Spanish Armada.

Amanda read on.

Drake's kinsman was Sir Walter Raleigh. A continuation of sorts, followed.

Raleigh's "City of Gold" (El Dorado) came to him early. Like his uncle, Drake, he had a plantation in Ireland, reward as land to defend England against the Spanish. Now in favor with the Queen of England, Elizabeth knighted Sir Walter Raleigh as a Royal Lord 1585.

He became deeply involved in the early English colonization of the new world. He planted the first English colony in America on Roanoke Island. But it was a Virginia Company Venture, funded by London Merchants, with Sir Henry Neville as it Governor that prevailed.

The venture in Roanoke failed, and he never returned to that coast, leaving instead a romantic legend later called *"The Lost Colony"*.

Raleigh was imprisoned in the Tower for his secret marriage to Elizabeth Throckmorton, she knew. But he was released from prison to divide the spoils from the captured Spanish ship *Madre de Dios...*"

There's that *Tower* again. What was it exactly? A prison? A manufacturing place of precious commodities? A safe house? A secret place kept from Spanish spies? Or a repository of gold being guarded by a watch of the crown? What did that mean in terms of legal sovereign ownership?

After Elizabeth died, Raleigh was incarcerated in the Tower a *second* time for the allegation of involvement with a plot against her successor, King James I of England, IV of Scotland.

Clearly, a political change.

A negotiated settlement, perhaps between the now friendly Court of James to the Spanish, was offered in 1616, and Raleigh was released in order to conduct a second expedition in search of El Dorado. This was unsuccessful and men under his command ransacked a Spanish settlement.

 Why?

Raleigh did return to England, a hero of sorts. But in a diplomatic move to appease the Spanish, he was executed in 1618. Even as he taught the King's son Edward, navigation technologies to make conquest of the new world and beyond...

Strange idea of diplomacy thought Amanda.

She paused. There was something familiar in this thread. She looked closely at his family. So, his half brothers were John Gilbert, Humphrey Gilbert, Adrian Gilbert, and full brother Carew Raleigh ...all of them well-known explorers, ship men, and colonial trade ventures...

Something else?

Suddenly, the place was silent and dark. She felt so lonely.

She got up to check on the lighting quotient of each room. The kitchen. The Bathroom. The Front Room. Without power, things looked dull.

She went upstairs again. Oh how show cherished those children's books! The Potter... There was Daffy the Duck. Septimus Beam's Flying Machine, her favorite. Milk and Cookies. Grandma's Elephants. Elmer Fudd. Alice in Wonderland. The Hat in the Cat...Bicycle Bears...

Her stomach growled.

Food was not lavish. But she had been resourceful.

What was it that lingered... in all this? She tucked herself in and was determined to get some sleep. Then she sat upright in the dark.

Dark. Like the Tower of London. What was the Tower of London. An armory? A prison? A Treasury? *A Scriptorium...?*

No! Just months previously something had occurred ...what had she read?

Then in came as clear as light to her.

If ... Sir Neville was in France as an Ambassador trying to repair a Palatine entitled marriage between Marguerite de Valois and Henry IV of France, and...at the wedding feast of his new wife, Marie deMedici, a massacre occurred that killed all the guests who were Huguenots...

...then clearly, the argument follows that the rights of sovereign title *was* the issue. The Huguenots were Palatine Princes of Crusader traditions.

It was not their gold that threatened France, it was their land title claims!

So, who were these Palatine Princes?

They were not only owners of territories, but had Princely Proprietary rights of their Palatinate kingdoms! Territories that could own the resources of their own land; raise standing Armies and hold sovereign rights of territorial proprietary claim – *outside* the dominion of the Holy Roman Catholic Authority!

In a world where the Divinely Anointed King owned all his subjects lands, rights, hearts, minds and labor. Then others, *outside* the Holy Roman Catholic Empire, held their own sovereign title to land in Europe as well. More. If territorial rights of ownership, then territorial rights of expansionism!

Such then, were the aims and ambitions of William III making off with the British Fleet and Treasure - almost 100 years later, on a *Palatinate* venture?

All she had to do now was to find out what that venture was. And to show title of claimant upon *that* venture.

She would call up Trevor. From a paying phone-booth! "I've got the answer" she said on his answering machine. "I'll call you later!"

All she had to do now, was prove it.

So, William III, almost ninety-four years later, was a *product* of all those outstanding issues when, as King of England, he sent the English Fleet to the Mediterranean to outfit. On the Sussex was treasure for his *cousin,* the Duke of Savoy

They were Protestant Palatine Princes with Proprietary Rights of Title.

She was very proud of herself. She found the linkages. The *why* behind the case. And once you have the motive, you have the means...

* *

The pounding at the front door made her jump like a cat. She picked up the brass pestle from the mortar bowl and edged forward, obscured from view, toward the front of the house.

The clattering was still going on.

It was the postman, clumsily feeding mail through the slot of the entrance. He had dropped his heavy gear against the foot- plate of the front door, and left the slot cover slamming behind him, evidently assured that the house was unattended. Two letters got jammed and never made it through.

She left them, suspended like doves in flight.

She picked up the cell phone, and made a call to her office on the desk phone.

"This is the Secretary for Mr. Aaron Wells leaving a message for Amanda, his daughter. Please to call back. Thank you!"

Amanda knew that Emily would hear it. With any luck, she would take note of the cell phone number.

It was almost an hour before she returned to the computer. There were only so many more hours of natural daylight and she needed to read her notes and provide citations. Even if the computer monitor had its own light source.

She knew she was close to an explanation. But she needed to prove the connections with land claims in descending order in order to describe the titles of ownership.

The case in Westminster Palace was tenuous at best. Too many uncertain claims. Too many claimants! And too much assumption lost to history, perhaps.

If Trevor wasn't careful, he could lose his reputation and the Bank of England could lose its shirt. Or the other way around. She sent in a report from her father's computer.

"So, when the young prince from the Netherlands grew up and later became King William III of England - reigning alongside with Mary, granddaughter of Charles – he evidently considered himself *entitled* to retrieve his money!

"Once Mary died, he *commandeered* the English treasure, and put it on a Royal Navy fleet to give to the Duke of Savoy, his cousin in the great Palatinate dynasty.

"Hence, the money on the Sussex was indeed originally Spanish... But acquired as prize by the English en-route to a designated grantee ...

"For arguments sake, having belonged to the English where it stayed in the Tower, and was guarded by one of its own - Sir Walter Raleigh - as a maritime prize, it's title is by right English under Maritime Law of the Sea.

"Further, its uses were for the *defense* of England against the Spanish Armada invasion. Thus by English law...It holds sovereign immunity as being in the commission of war for the defense of the Realm."

She wrote. "We do know that less than year later, Savoy allied with the French, even though William had promised him more money – as you know. Anyway, Savoy held a title, King of Jerusalem, Sardinia, Cyprus ..." These were palatine claims to title.

"Facts about the Crusaders earlier centuries come largely from hearsay. But one can assume that they were garnering knowledge, connections, trade routes with the East, and all their attending wealth..."

"The French and Spanish were Catholic Empires. But the Dutch Republic, home of William III and the English were both Protestants.

"By the middle of the 17th century they dominated the North Atlantic trade. They owned 75% of all trading ships.

"1692 the Dutch Navy was placed under the command of the Royal Navy's admirals (though not incorporated into it) by order of William III.

"Two years later, William III sends his Royal Navy to the Mediterranean. Not only was he engaged in the Thirty Years War, but responsible for shipping supply and outfitting for the carry trades that paid for it all."

She uploaded her report to the Case File on Trevor's Website. Jacques be damned.

She finished off with "I hope you find this useful is establishing the linkages. It does trace the legacy of the money, and shows probable cause as a result.It also establishes ownership issues. "

And she told him. Over the phone. She left a convoluted message rather. He wasn't answering. And she invited him to dinner at Druce House!

"Tonight" she said, flinging open the drapes and picking up the mail...

It wasn't until she flung open the fridge door that she drooped. What *was* she thinking?

So she thawed sausage, found a jar or spaghetti sauce, and a dry white wine from her father's cellar. The noodles would have to be Fettuccini. She lay the table, in simple fashion. One white lace centerpiece, and two white damask table napkins, pub style.

* *

Thirty Eight

Trevor left off reading his materials. He visited the website posting placed by Amanda, and was amazed at the level of detail and distinctions that he could use in his legal arguments.

He turned next to the ship itself, material furnished by his team. Their reports were revealing as to the action of the event.

Roger had written to him about The Royal Ship Sussex was an 80-gun ship of the line. She was lost on 1 March 1694 off Gibraltar with a some 10 tons of gold coins. Today, perhaps worth $500 billion, including the bullion and antiquity values, making it one of the most valuable wrecks ever for modern salvage.

She was launched in 1693. Under Admiral Sir Francis Wheeler, she sailed from Portsmouth on 27 December as Flagship with an escort fleet of 48 warships and 166 merchant ships..

Her orders were sealed, and in cloth bound as follows.

'Nov. 22. Kensington. Instructions for Sir Francis Wheeler, knight, commander-in-chief of a squadron fitted out for the Straits were as follows. "*As soon as you join the Spanish armada, pursuant to the instructions of the Lords of the Admiralty, you shall act as most advisable for the annoying of the French, and shall give the Duke of Savoy notice of your arrival in the Mediterranean; and in case he desire your co-operation in any design against the French, you shall use your best endeavors to bring the same to a happy issue. During your stay in the Mediterranean you are to correspond as frequently as you can with Viscount Galway, our envoy extraordinary to the Duke of Savoy; and, as far as may be consistent with the service you are employed in, to act according to the advices you shall receive from him.*'

She stopped at Cadiz, then the fleet entered the Mediterranean. On 27 February a violent storm hit the Strait of Gibraltar and on day three she sank. All but but two "Turks" of the 500 crew onboard perished. Admiral Wheeler's body, it is told, was discovered in his night-shirt.

Some say the ships were unstable. An overloading of armaments...

Trevor turned to another account, more political in nature. Research says that Wheeler was on a secret mission; to pay a large sum of money to the Duke of Savoy, an ally of Britain in the War of the League of Augsburg.

Perhaps a bargain to ally with the English against France. Parliament resented the matter greatly in a great debate. Ostensibly, the case was closed. But there was more, he had to know. Or rather, some missing

link that must prove British sovereignty even though Parliament complains of its intent and mission...
Tough to prove, he thought.

* *

What came out of the oven was even more of a surprise to Trevor than his initial entry into Druce House.
"A candlelight dinner" she said, " in her father's house...spontaneous! With wine, chocolates, and brandy for dessert..."
"And in the kitchen!" she added.
They ate. Amanda fluttering nervously through the meager meal, Trevor cleaning his plate with a ravenous appetite.
When he asked why the house was so dark, she said he had a migraine and needed dimness.
"Dimness my ass..." he said hitting his shin against the wooden stool by the hearth. "I can't see a damned thing!"
Dessert was on the table, candles flickering. Her provisions and silver had been stowed away for so long that she had had to polish a few for the dinner.
Trevor had parked the car outside, and with *Courvoisier* nicely seeping into her consciousness, she began to wonder about the reality of her stealth... Maybe it was all in her imagination?
She had outlined the escapade to Trevor, braiding the tale nicely with humor and self deprecation to such effect that he was roaring with laughter and she, bordering on disbelief.

Still, she advanced to the front room and closed the drapes tightly to prevent any light from the house escaping into the night.

And that's when she saw it. Outside. The dark green Ford. Oh yes. The same as had parked outside her apartment in the University Park found her here! Waiting.

Amanda flew to the Kitchen and asked Trevor to drive his car around back for an Emergency. He was nibbling on food, chocolate at his lips, which he dabbed with his table napkin.

"Emerge.... ?"

"Yes. Damn it. I'll explain. Make it fast. Please!"

She sent him out the front door in open unobstructed fashion, hoping to buy a few moments without alerting the enemy. She even kissed him overtly. Clearly he would soon be gone, and she alone ...an easy prey in the house.

She grabbed the cell phone, her notes, and killed the screen in the library. Just before leaving she ran forward and peeped through the curtain. The car was gone.

She met Trevor outside the kitchen pathway through the garden. No one had fooled anyone.

The car was glistening in the dark misty night like a large Kafka beetle.

"Step on it!" she screamed.

Trevor was what she called a docile soul. But he and Amanda had been through enough together in the Middle East for him to recognize alarm when he heard it.

He drove like a fiend.

Were it not for a few propitious traffic lights and late night perambulating strollers crossing the street from the local pubs, he would never have evaded the stalker through the streets of London.

The matter suddenly gained deadly credibility.

"Where to now?" he asked.

How did everything relate...she wondered, his voice miles away.

"Wales" she said demurely.

"*Wales*?"

She sat there like a stubborn grandmother in the front seat.

"What? Why?"

"Go!" she admonished, pointing. "We will retrace the steps of Robinson!"

"What?...Why?"

"Because he was the last to see the manuscript before he...died. And I believe he had a brother up here...he told me".

She was winging it. What she didn't want to confess was her dreaded suspicion of a killer on her tail. Someone who might well have killed Robinson.

For what, exactly?

The coast of England presented itself like a craggy ribbon of storytelling. A rock hill here, a pebble beach there. The road going west was solitary and outlined by railway tracks. Below it a cove that once moored deep water ships, rugged and steep. Beyond it five miles, a cliff could conceal a competitor's fleet!

Villages, unhampered, had embedded themselves in the solid slopes of England that was, first and always, an island reached only by sea.

Onward they weaved, mostly in silence, tracing the tracks of modern industry, ancient castles and endless ocean.

Here the Romans reached, there the Normans. Clearly peoples had come, mainly to settle, but mostly to die, leaving legacies and loves and legends... living everywhere as evidence. England was England. That was the story of the coastline.

To leave these shores was to be silenced forever, Amanda decided.

Yet from this coast the West Country, Gentlemen had gone to sea in search of new worlds, plunder, trade, war and wealth. To say nothing of exporting culture, religion and sovereignty as an Empire that ruled five continents.

"Hungry?" interrupted Trevor from the driver's wheel. She looked up at him. His cheekbones and brow flushed with tussled hair, rain streaks and pale. He was on an endurance track, he'd been at the wheel for four hours of night driving.

"Absolutely!" she said eagerly. "I really appreciate your cooperation".

" Hardly the sequiter to a dinner invitation I'd expected. But hey!" he grinned at her.

She conceded a tight smile.

"What's up ahead?"

"Not sure yet. But we need gas. And this highway doesn't look too populated"

"Right". She rooted around for a car map. Peering under a couple of mohair travelling rugs, she found a first-aid box; a Traveler's supply of Swipe-its; Thermawear ponchos; sealed peanuts and bottles of drinking water. She tried a small flashlight that worked. And a night halogen reading bandana. "For joggers, campers and moving bicyclists" he explained with a boy scout grin.

"Ok. We're past Cardiff. That's Glamorganshire. So its Swansea and St. David's next on the map. We're....here!" she announced like a navigator on a car rally.

The lights to the Minimarket were unmistakable. Even in the middle of the night, the pumps were open and the advertising lights flashing. The roads were black.

 Trevor went inside to re-provision, and left her at the pumps. It started drizzling.

Trevor returned with his arms full of goodies, and his spirits were in good shape considering the tenuous nature of the dash out of London.

 He had just re-entered the car when she spotted the car, and she froze. The dark Ford. Not in pursuit. And not threatening. And she spotted the profile to the driver's right.

The Dutchman.

"How in the hell have they been able to pursue us all this distance without headlights on...that we would have noticed?" she said, shuddering.

"I dunno. But let's see here..." he said as he pulled out of the gas station.

They were well down the road and almost breathing normally when a car pulled out. Its headlights now brightly on.

"Oh God" said Amanda, shrinking into her seat. "Did you buy a map?"

"Yes. If you can read Welsh!"

"Oh God"

"How did they know....?"

"Your cell phone ...?" she began. "Oh God. What have I done!"

"Please. Melodrama suits you *not*..." said Trevor. He looked into the

rearview mirror. The car was approaching steadily. "So...ok. So..err.."

It was now raining in full.

"I have a plan" he said

"We'll cut through the mountains" he said, his head bumping off the ceiling as they veered off the road .

"This is coal-country" she said, a pitch of alarm in her voice "We could never evade them up there ..."

"We just did" he said as they gushed past in the rain.

"Pull out the map. We'll kill the lights. You're navigating. We'll drive this four wheel drive up a mountainside where no luxury car can follow..." he grinned. He reversed his Rover with dead-stick brutality up a side bend that appeared harmless.

"Wait. What ...How do you know...?" she began

"I hope to be three miles ahead before they stop and try to follow..."

"Without seeing in the dark?"

"You will light the way!" he said, bumping up a rocky dirt road

"*What?*"

He pulled up the slope with a force she couldn't imagine a Land Rover could accomplish. Then he stopped abruptly, jumped out and dug out some gear. He smashed the rear brake lights with a tire jack.

"The front lights I can leave off. But the brake lights are tied to the break action"

"This is ...dangerous..." she began.

He reached into the back seat, unpacked his Mini-Market bag and pulled out a good sized flashlight.

"Here! Shine it on the road...*That* they will NOT see if we kill the light on the straight stretches. It'll throw them. And if we're far enough ahead, they won't hear us either"

"That's crazy!" she said "How do you know it'll work?"

"I read about it once. It was done to evade the Germans in WWII..."

"In the Alps?"

"The desert" he said, jarring and slewing the car over rough road surface caked with black rain and fine mud. "We might drive ourselves off a mountain ledge too..." gritted Amanda

"We might...So pay attention!"

"Oh God..."

They stopped occasionally to survey the road behind them. There was no car in pursuit. Only once did they spot a headlight behind them. But no more.

Trevor was almost certain he had lost them, and Amanda was getting tired holding the flash light.

Then suddenly the headlight reappeared several bends below them.

They had caught on.

"The Map" said Trevor. "We need a diversion. A crossroads"

"They must have figured we'd be going Robinson's way!"

"So let's backtrack. Let's go back? That they won't anticipate…"

"OK" he said. "Search the map for a good spot…"

But there was none. They passed an abandoned stone barn house perilously close to a precipice. On the map was a marked monument site.

"What we have, they have… Only on GPS"

Trevor pulled off the road and bounced across a steep mountainside farmstead.

"What are you doing?"

"Spending the night" he said "Where there is a barn. There is a manger"

"Jesus!" said Amanda

"Exactly" said Trevor. "We'll just disappear… inside the stone shelter"

Trevor stopped the car. The stone shelter was a shrine memorial to a coalmining disaster.

Trevor walked to the precipice and could outline a gorge below him. He took the flash light, switched it on, then with the horn blown, flung it out down the gorge. It landed deep into the mountainside, barely discernable, if at all.

"They'll think we pitched over the side."

She looked at him. He was just assuring her.

He re-entered the Rover."Cozy up" he said tucking himself under the travelling rug. "We'll stay for daybreak" he said, and shut his eyes like a schoolboy.

"And all this time, I thought Jacques had his eye on you!" he mused naively.

She looked up at him demurely. "Jacques had no idea. He is still considering valuations of a manuscript at auction!"

"Umm" he said. "Goodnight!"

"Goodnight?" she asked. "But we're out in the middle of nowhere...How can you?"

"Oh don't be frightened" he said in his Scottish brogue. "We do this all the time in the Lochs of Inverness."

He was too ridiculous to laugh at thought Amanda angrily. Him and his bloody Lochs of Inver....

"Should I look out for Monsters then?" she said with as much sarcasm as she could muster, her patience running thin.

"No" he said. "Dragons. Is what the Welsh have..."

She lay back, sleepless, trying to find comfort under a mohair blanket in a car...Her mind was a restless mess. She...he...She couldn't reorient her bearings, let alone find rest.

"God" she muttered. "I'm going back to Boston!"

"No you're not" he said drawing her closer.

"Do I have a choice?" she asked.

"Of course. I could go sleep in the barn with the mules"

"You do that!" she said "And rightfully so!"

"Um?" his eyes firmly closed, but not really.

"...And then come back. To slay your dragons!"

His arm went up around her, and she snuggled up.

* *

It wasn't until pre-dawn that she found it. Unawares, at first, then in the gathering light, as the sun - having traversed the sky to reach England - unfolded a landscape before her.

The great and craggy coast of Wales, edged with white surf where mountains plunged into the North Atlantic sea, resembled the footstool on earth of God himself. But she turned suddenly.

It came slowly, really. The rumble of the great industrial beast that lumbered along the highway. A steel bucket, the size of an earth removal excavator dangled off its front-end like a proboscis looking for coal to dig.

At first the thing was shrouded in fog and morning mists. Yellow in color, but clearly having seen duty with rust. And it was close enough to evoke alarm, lumbering as it was.

Suddenly it disappeared off the road below them. She walked to the edge.

Then it reappeared. It had turned the bend, and was ascending. She hesitated. Then realized that it was making its way up the incline where they had parked, atop the hill.

Here, mudslides must be common. Nothing could offer traction. Unless it was industrial in nature and built for earth- moving.

"Trevor" she called out from where she stood. She backed away, and ran for the Rover.

He was already inside the car pressing on the ignition. The engine turned on, but the wheels had sunk into the mud somewhat and started skidding. It rocked, then moved ten feet. Then spun in place on slick mud, digging trenches beneath them.

The backhoe continued its ascend. Before it, nothing was unassailable, they both knew. And it approached with menacing disregard for all it crushed.

"Get in" he barked, the door now wide open.

"Put on all the padding you can. This safety vest. Strap in..." he said. "Roll up the windows, and don't panic. It has come for us. ..Use the car for shelter. It's our only chance....got it?"

Prepared as they were, it came as a terrifying jolt. Then another. The edge of the ravine was not far beyond them.

But they were not prepared for what happened next.

An explosion from the open mine shaft above them sent a mountain blast of debris from the upper ledges across into the gorge, almost over them.

It shook the side of the mountain, and the noise of breaking timber and rock fiercely an angry lightning bolt.   The damage was obscured by a cloud accumulating in cumulous mushrooms that remained grey and thick.

It tapered, the disturbance. But not for long.

 The impact had affected the side of the mountain as it started to cascade. It had been raining for over twelve hours, and the topsoil was moist, layered with fresh rubble, and without traction.

It happened slowly at first, almost as the fine dust was subsiding. Then from beneath the stacked dust storm, a mountain mudflow emerged, almost indiscernible, but gathering speed. A large boulder spun out, sheering rock face as it pushed the mud flow to an accelerated speed.

Trevor revved his engines. There was no outrunning this. Even if he had the wheel traction to do so. But of one thing he was certain. He was *not* about to get buried under a mudslide.

It advanced with menacing power, sheering off timber, rocks, ledges and stone in its path. As it approached, Trevor aimed his wheels for the gorge below them, and reached for an emergency kit in the glove compartment. Barely had he clipped it on to his safety vest that the vehicle was in motion, picked up off its wheel purchase and moving along like a toy.

"Hang On" shouted Trevor. "Don't panic. We're going over the side. Staying in the vehicle is our only chance!"

Amanda screamed.

The vehicle tumbled. The safety bags immediately popped open and they were engulfed. They were tumbled down the side of the mountain, bouncing and snagging on trees, once upside down... without stopping. The tumbling brutal, unceasing.

She heard one tire pop. Then another. The roof buckled and they were coated in grey shale, dirt and cloud dust.

You... alright?"

"Yes!" she said.

"Don't panic..." he said again. "Just hang on!"

The mountain side was endless. The windows were crunching and the steel body buckling. Suddenly the driver's door broke clear off the vehicle, and spun like a shield down to the gorge.

 Finally the car came to rest 100 feet from the bottom of the gorge. It had taken a final beating with loose rocks spinning laterally from the path of the mudslide. And it threatened to lose its integrity altogether.

"Wait. Wait" he said, boulders still settling around them.

"OK." said Trevor "Let's hoof it..." He pushed down the bags, and aimed his heels at the a loose bracket hanging at the door frame. They got out.

"Quickly. Get up there!" he yelled. Pointing across the stream he said "Over there, on the other side. Start climbing quickly!"

"Wait!" he said. "Where's the Scotch?"

"Trevor!" admonished Amanda. He put his hands to his mouth for silence. She obeyed.

"Move over there, down by the bushes, and wait. We follow the stream!"

She scrambled down the hillside as he poured the scotch all over the interior.

He lit a match, tossed it in, and flung himself forward for a long jump down to her level for a wretched landing on his shoulder.

The hollow boom that blew out as the blast ignited the vehicle sent them both down another twenty feet.

Smoke and fire rose into the air, sending a signal up the mountain that would not fail to impress their assailant. Or so Amanda thought. But as she looked back, she saw the mudslide splintering and advancing with a relentlessness that would only bury the vehicle entirely.

Any ideas of wading upstream were naive. Trevor had her climbing up sheer rock face with such ferocity that she was torn, scratched, bleeding and muddy within 100 ft. of the bottom.

She looked behind her. Everything had stopped. It looked calm, the brook now reduced to a trickle of muddy water.

"Keep climbing!" he said

"Please!"   she begged. "I can't...I need to catch my breath.."

"Move. Move. Move! " he screamed.

Another thirty five feet. She looked back. And that's when she saw the real danger.

The mudslide had created a dam that blocked the small river. The gorge was so steep that once the first 100 ft of rock were topped by timber and scrub.

Within minutes the damn burst with an explosion that shattered the entire canyon and flushed free a flood river, carrying with it fresh fallen timber splintered like a thousand javelins moving at great velocity.

It rose to within 35 feet of where they were perched.

* *

Thirty Nine

New York

Marguerite Shutters didn't like the call. Not only was the case in Britain going badly, but some banking interests in Europe were setting up objections. It was a matter of shifting ledgers, accounts that claims, sealed and deceased ownership of title, private equity and sovereign rights of secrecy were in jeopardy.

Worse. The case in the United States was citing insurance claims' fraud, issuing Injunctions and other road blocks - even surveillance, private investigation and political pressure.

So far, they had entered into no criminal activities. Their representation came from New York. Igoravich, Cahn and Smythe.

She had listened politely, then asked for the details to be mailed to her. They would doubtless receive an official reply, she told them.

Next, she picked up the phone and called London.

Forget profit and greed. This was a potential scandal.

* *

The case against Amanda was dropped.

"Proof of the cannon at the bottom of the sea corroborate the Neville claim to the fortune *stolen* by William and used for his unauthorized venture with ships and cannon of the Neville family...."

She looked at it.

"So" said Amanda "if the cannon proved that it was Neville whose ships provided the fleet. Then it was Neville who also wrote his plays...Reformed the world, created the framework of finance, backed the Darien plan with money to the Bank of Scotland and the Bank of England. All evidence held in the family vault for his descendants to safeguard!"

Hence the challenge, by the Dutchman, to the plays.

"... challenging the claims of sovereign immunity for missions underwritten by private individuals..." added Trevor, "with a full accounting of monies given by the London Merchants for the Ventures to the New world."

The killer, as New Scotland Yard explained, was the Dutchman. *After* he got the manuscript from Robertson. But because of Edward's switch in the vault, they turnout out to be copies only. Hardly worth a few million at an Auction!

The Americans provided the case, they said. The man walking besides Jacques, when the police inspected the photograph, was wrongly identified...

The originals turned up where Amanda had sent them, through her neighbor's diligence. A precaution well taken since her apartment had been ransacked to within a hair of Jack's fur. Something she could only imagine since she found him sitting outside her front door where she scooped him up for a long cuddle.

The Insurance company was willing to pay reparation and repatriation of the treasurer if its name remained in good standing, and it even offered to sponsor a museum exhibit once the treasure was extracted. But since they would also have to repay the government for lost shipping, it declined, and slipped off the radar.

The Foreign claimants had failed to file proper claims of loss for centuries. And that made their case moot.

So there was only one thing that mattered now.

* *

"How say you?" began the proceedings.

"My Lords" said Trevor MacDonnell in full regalia as Representative from Scotland. "It is therefore the findings of this court, with all due process, that these remains and deposits have been proven beyond any doubt as to belong to the State in full and without restitution needed to parties of the claimants..."

"Here Here!"

"And finally, I stand before you to declare that the real treasure of that day is not to be argued here in the details of this case. But rather, from those difficult times events of greater moment. For those Gentlemen of the sea found the colonies of America...And it can surely be said, that if there is any treasure here, it is that happy occasion of settling the colonies of the new world. A treasure to better enrich the world for centuries thereafter!"

Fluff, he knew. But enough to bring the damned hearings to a close.

The proceedings concluded with some fanfare and several interviews for the media on the steps of Westminster Palace.

Trevor was marching down the hallway to his offices, his gowns flowing where he could take his call from his mother.

Amanda met him outside his office, and got up. "I have good news" she said

He scowled at her and moved into his chambers. He threw off his wig, cap, gown and garters and went behind the screen where he put on his regular suit and tie.

"Susie?" he called out to his secretary.

"Yes Sir"

"Has Lady Marchant called back yet?"

"Not yet. I told her you would call the minute you were free..." she picked up his vestments from behind the screen and set them in the front office for delivery to the House staff for stowing and conservation.

"Trevor?" began Amanda, approaching softly.

"Just a sec..." he said. "I've got to call my mother. I've got to tell her that I'm getting nowhere with the lad's legacy estate instatement now that it remains vacant without an inheritor!"

Amanda smiled. She dug into her bag and pulled out her cell phone and held it up.

"Trevor..."she said again, softly.

He was dialing, a dark frown across his face.

"Trevor!" she called.

He looked up.

"Emily" she said, pointing to the cell phone "She's pregnant! She's going to have Edward's baby. .."

The words took a second to sink in.

Then he put down the phone "Let's have a drink!" he grinned. "I'll call her later...with better news for the locals up there!"

* *

He put his arm around her shoulder on the way into the pub "Any chance you and I can...err..you know?"

"What?"

"Well. Do what Edward and Emily did?"

"Oh that" she said, linking into him "Umm...We'll see..."

"You don't know" he whispered into her ear "...how much I wanted to ravish you on those Mountains of Wales!"

"Really?"

"Umm" he said, looking down at her.

London was waiting.

"Do you think Emily will like the hills of Scotland?" he asked, his arm around her shoulder.

"Emily will *move* the hills of Scotland if she has to!" laughed Amanda.

"Good. She can be claimed as his wife then!"

"So" he asked. "What are you doing?"

"Oh. I'm not sure yet. Bill has offered me a post at the Archives. I'm thinking about it. I thought I'd talk to my Dad, he's coming soon..."

"No. I mean tonight?"

She looked at him.

"Nothing?... Good! The night then, is ours!" He put on his bowler hat and offered her his arm.

* *

END